The Gift

The Gift

A Season of Trial

Stephen Pain

iUniverse, Inc.
New York   Bloomington

The Gift
A Season of Trial

This is a work of fiction. All of the characters, names, incidents, organizations, and dialogue in this novel are either the products of the author's imagination or are used fictitiously. iUniverse books may be ordered through booksellers or by contacting:

iUniverse
1663 Liberty Drive
Bloomington, IN 47403
www.iuniverse.com
1-800-Authors (1-800-288-4677)

ISBN: 978-0-595-52334-4 (pbk)
ISBN: 978-0-595-51106-8 (cloth)
ISBN: 978-0-595-62390-7 (ebk)

Printed in the United States of America

iUniverse Rev. 10/21/08

Dedicated to families everywhere who refuse to acknowledge defeat and remain strong and faithful irregardless of the obstacle. It has been my blessing to be a part of one.

Yesterday is not ours to recover, but tomorrow is ours to win or to lose.

—Lyndon B. Johnson

Prologue

The first light of Christmas morning filtered through the overcast sky of the Northern plains. George Edwards had been up since midnight and the freshness of the morning revitalized him as he breathed a deep breath of the crisp air. He hated this time of the year when darkness prevailed over the landscape for much of the day. *Winter – bah humbug*, he thought to himself. He trod silently towards the house along the beaten pathway of darkened snow. His wife June met him at the doorway.

"I'll be right out." She offered George a quick kiss. "I let the girls sleep. Okay?"

"Chores are finished, honey." George smiled at her. "I couldn't sleep and thought that I might as well spare you one morning of chores, being Christmas and all." He smiled at her.

"Thanks dear! What a wonderful gift! The girls will be thrilled. Christmas is definitely in the air!"

June closed the door behind her husband and gave him a mighty hug. The two of them looked deeply into each others eyes and stood there silently just staring at each other. George studied his woman's blue eyes, seemingly content to just hold onto his wife of twenty years for awhile. She examined his dark eyes and lean facial features while lightly brushing her hands through his fine, black hair. Their lips met and he caressed her softly with a warm kiss. The voices of the twins sounded from within the house. They were obviously opening their stockings and comparing their Santa gifts. Christmas had arrived.

"You go wash up while I get breakfast on, George," she said softly.

"Love you honey." But he did not let go, unwilling to break the spell of the moment.

"Love you too." She laughed and pushed him away. "Now go and get cleaned up." June headed upstairs into the kitchen. "Mary and Susan, let's get ready for breakfast. Your Dad has the chores all finished!"

George walked downstairs into the cloak room and removed his heavy work coat. He methodically placed his work boots on the boot rack and sat his work mitts on top of them. Upstairs he could hear the excited chatter of the girls as they helped their mother set the table for breakfast. He stepped into the shower and sighed as the warm water hit his skin. The steam was soon rising from the cabinet. He dried himself and put clean clothes on. Christmas music was filling the house. June yelled down, "Breakfast is served."

"I'll be right up, June."

George stopped abruptly and starred briefly at Jim's room. He slowly walked towards it and opened the door. The space was dark and cold. He glanced at the hockey trophy sitting on the shelf and studied the forbidding image of the painting illuminated by the hallways light. He quietly entered the room. His knees became numb and tears began to fill his tired eyes as he carefully sat down on the empty bed. He closed his eyes. His powerful hands began to shake as he remembered the events of the past fall. He weakly slipped to his knees as the events replayed themselves in his mind. He openly wept on the bed.

"Hey you, breakfast is getting cold!"

The words quickly brought George back to reality. He picked himself up and headed upstairs. The girls were waiting by the breakfast table with their stockings. June had prepared hot cereal and the steaming bowls filled the small kitchen with a wonderful odor. George looked at his two daughters, "Merry Christmas, I thought that you were too old for Santa?"

"No way Dad; never! See what we got."

"Later girls; let's eat now before your Mom's oatmeal is cold."

Mary and Susan gave their Dad a big hug and promptly sat down at the table. "Merry Christmas, Dad. Thanks for doing the chores. Can we open our gifts right after breakfast?"

"I may have a little work to do first, we'll have to see." George looked at his little twin girls. They would soon be twelve. They were growing up on him. The frown on the girl's faces did not belong on Christmas Day. "I think that Mom and I want to open those gifts as much as you do. The work can wait until later. Now let's have Mom give the blessing."

"God bless this meal before us and receive our thanks for his many gifts. Amen."

"Amen!"

If a smile was worth a million words then the beam from their faces was worth two. George looked at the content expression on June's face and attacked his oatmeal. The cereal was hot and satisfying. He glanced at his family through the corner of his eyes and for the moment felt a peace within himself. The work at hand was to devour that cereal and enjoy.

June broke the silence. "The Heiners will be here by ten. Do you want to open the gifts when they arrive? That will give us time to clean up and let Dad have a little rest before they arrive."

"Will they bring gifts too?"

"Oh, you two are terrible this morning. You probably will get something."

"We can wait and Dad can have a little rest then."

"Works for me, guys. A little catnap will go just right about now." Morning naps were certainly not normal routine for George but the prospect of a little rest on the sofa before Allan and his family arrived would be welcome. He moved silently to the old sofa and got himself comfortable. The girls were starting to wash dishes and the chatter flowed incessantly from the kitchen.

George glanced around the room. He briefly studied the Christmas tree and its contents, the gifts, the sparkling lights and the tinsel. His eyes came to rest on the family portrait that rested by the mantle next to the tree. His moment of bliss started to crack as the realization of this Christmas and the year past returned to haunt him. Once again his emotions could not be contained and his eyes filled with tears as he focused on his son's face. However, his early morning start combined with the warmth of breakfast and the comfort of the old sofa began to take their toll. He instantly fell into a deep sleep.

1

The Gift

It was September; harvest time on the northern plains. The area was being blessed with unusually warm, dry weather this year and the crops had matured quickly. The Lord had provided well and a bountiful harvest laid waiting. George sat comfortably in the cab of the combine as it consumed the golden swaths stretching in its path. Soon the kids would be home and his son Jim could take over the helm allowing him to start the grain dryer. The girls could help Mom with yard chores and supper. He glanced at his watch just as the trail of dust from the south road announced the arrival of the school bus. He nodded his head in approval. It was right on schedule.

George studied the western horizon. The blue sky and red sun suggested more beautiful weather to come. The warm, westerly winds carried a string of dust from the combine across the entire field. His ears tuned into the radio broadcast in the background. *"Looks good for the balance of this week but a major low could establish itself by the weekend bringing unsettled weather and significant amounts of rainfall."* The radio forecast jarred George back to the reality of the job facing him.

George fretted as he pondered over the weather forecast. It was so satisfying to watch the prospects of a good harvest start to flow into the bins. He knew the risks. Activity on the modest family farm was always busy but the demands of fall weather could bring work levels to an extreme. He knew how hard his family worked to make their farm unit viable. He was so proud of his family and their consistent contribution. The full bin level alarm sounded and George steered the machine towards the grain truck.

He pulled up beside the truck and began to unload the threshed wheat. As the plump kernels filled up the grain box, he noticed the school bus heading down the east road. He could pick up Jim on the return trip. He finished unloading and slowed the combine motor back to an idle. He was just about to climb out of the cab to get into the truck when he noticed the pickup entering the field. His lean cheeks grinned with approval at how quickly his son had moved after getting off the bus. But as the pickup pulled up beside the machine he noticed that it was not Jim driving. June jumped out of the cab. The gusting, westerly wind gave her dark hair a quick toss as she ran hastily towards the combine.

"I have to run into Royston and pick up Jim. He missed the school bus," June yelled out still catching her breath from her quick dash. She looked up at the tall figure in the combine cab.

"Damn it, June. What gets into that boy's head? He knows that it's harvest!" George hollered back. He held the door ajar with one leg while remaining seated in the cab of the machine.

"Girls are doing the night chores and I have stew in the crock pot, George. I will be as quick as I can. I know Jim will have a good reason. You know he's a good kid."

"Where's he meeting you?"

"He's with some school friends at Dobeys. You know the place across from the school. All the kids go there, George."

"It's them lazy yahoo's that mess with his mind. Well I better keep going." George gritted his teeth and clenched his fist on the steering wheel. "I will talk to Jim later, June. There is a time and a place for everything but now is definitely not the time for missing damn school buses."

"Just keep it calm, Hon. You love your son and he loves you. He's growing up, George. We couldn't ask for a more responsible young person if we tried. I am sure he didn't mean to miss the bus." June looked directly into her husband's tired eyes. "Do you want me to send him out when we get home?"

"Whatever. See how late you are? I know he's changing, growing up and all, but he has commitments at home too. Just because those other useless buggers have nothing else better to do than drink soda doesn't mean that he can too. Anyways, have a safe trip. Love you."

"Love you too. Please take it easy."

"Yes, I know. When the damn sun shines in our God forsaken fall you've got to be takin' advantage of it. We don't have extra help this year and the last thing we need is needless delays in getting the stuff off the field. Christ, it could start rainin' this weekend and stay all month. You know how we have struggled with harvests. You leave the stuff through the winter and take off chaff in the spring. Banker doesn't give a shit about my excuses. I'm sorry but we don't need to make it any harder than what it is. Anyways, I'm holdin' you up. Sorry!"

"It's okay, hon. Just remember that despite all of our struggles to get what the Lord has provided we always have managed to make it. It's still very early.

We have time on our side and the kids will do their part. They always have. Jim will settle down. Just be fair with him for me, please. Must run. Bye."

"Take care," George replied as he watched his wife run back towards the pickup. He thought about jumping out of the machine and giving her a quick kiss. But as usual he simply managed a blank stare before turning back to the job at hand. He watched as the pickup disappeared across the field. The dust from the dry ground and freshly threshed straw filled the air. George shrugged his brawny shoulders and shut down the combine. He jumped to the ground and ran to the awaiting truck. At forty he was still athletic and strong and his biceps filled his shirt sleeve as he reached up with his long, sinewy arms and pulled himself into the dusty truck cab. The Cat sprang to life with the turn of the key. George edged the truck into gear and slowly let out the clutch. Black smoke poured out of the stack as the motor groaned under the weight of the heavy load of wheat.

"Damn it anyways," he muttered to himself. Still fuming over Jim's delinquency George poured the coal to the truck's engine and headed towards home.

2

Jim flipped through the weekly school newspaper. His eyes came to rest on the notice for football try-outs and he eagerly read the article. He was eligible to try out for senior football. His last growth spurt had seen him equal his Dad's height and he could run like a deer. He had never been involved in many extra-circular school activities and he wished deep down that he could try out for football. *It just seemed that they were always busy on the farm and that the business of farming came first and foremost.*

"What's yah reading, Jim?" asked the attractive, brown eyed girl sitting at their table. "You've spent more time on that page than you're food."

"Just lookin' at the article on school football for the fall," said Jim. He rolled up his shirt sleeve and flexed his powerful, right bicep. "What do you think?"

"Are you going to tryout? I could picture you in a football jersey. You're so strong and all. With your stamina you'd blow them away, Jimmy," replied the second girl at the table. A widening grin quickly spread across her face.

"You really should go to the tryouts, Jim. I know that you would enjoy it," added Austaire. "I'd come and watch you play."

"Yah, but the timing is terrible. We are so busy at home this time of the year. We don't have hired help this fall and we didn't get a rural exchange student this summer so it makes it tougher."

"Whatever Jimmy, you'd be great."

The girls focused back to their fries and their own chatter. A true farm boy Jim mused as he listened to the girl's conversation giggling in the background. His Mom often commented on how she had raised such a fine looking son. The girls seemed to agree. He starred at Austaire and Megan. They seemed to not have a care in the world. He knew that his Dad would be upset but the girls company was worth it. He quickly brushed his short, blonde hair with his hand. His blue eyes focused on the youngest girl.

"Finish your cheese burger, Jim," Austaire giggled.

"You need to keep your strength up, Jimmy." Megan smiled directly at him and the subtle message of her words sunk in. Jim blushed and sheepishly smiled back.

"I'm more concerned about what my father is going to say."

"Fuck your old man, Jimmy," shrugged the oldest girl, Megan. "He doesn't own you. Hell, you say you want to play football. You say that you can't because of him. You've got to live your life too. It's 1994. Sometimes you'd think that your folks are still living back in the sixties or something."

"Parents are an over rated commodity." Austaire tossed her head. "I can hardly wait until I'm on my own. You and I can have it all, Jim. Look at Megan. Been on her own for a couple of years now and has never looked back. She's just livin' large and livin' well."

"It's just that it is harvest time and Dad depends on me to help get the crop in. It is a family thing. A lot of our income comes from harvest. I actually enjoy the machine work. I can get pretty stoked running the Deere."

"Harvest, smarvest," Austaire laughed. "Eat your burger. It's getting cold."

"Your old man should get his own help," Megan smirked. "You work too hard on that damn farm."

"Its how we make a living girls; the farm pays the bills. I know that sounds lame but it is the truth. It's not easy but it's sort of fun sometimes. I've always helped at home. Someday it'll change but for now I'm needed out there. It's mostly all good."

"You listen to your father too much. He just uses you. He asks way too much from you. There is a whole world out there just waiting for you, Jimmy Boy." Megan stared directly into Jim's eyes. She slowly moved her tongue across her lips and then blew a light kiss in Jim's direction.

Austaire picked up her coke; seemingly oblivious to Megan's actions. She too looked directly into Jim's eyes. "We need our own space. As if my folks actually care about me. They don't even know me. My folks just get in the way. You know how I despise them. Our parents can't run our lives anymore, Jim."

Jim looked across at Austaire. She was simply gorgeous. Jim loved to spend time with her. He had fallen head over heels for her when they had first met over the summer holidays shortly after her family had moved into town from the city of Ollen. She had turned eighteen in August and she was his girl. His eyes then wandered towards Megan. Megan was probably twenty. Her piercing eyes were dark and mysterious. Austaire had known her prior to coming to Royston. Megan was fun and experienced. Megan combined wicked and awesome into one perfect package. Jim straightened in his seat as the blue Ford turned into the parking lot.

"I've got to run. My Mom's here. See you tomorrow."

Austaire jumped up and planted a wet kiss securely on Jim's lips. "See yah."

Megan smiled at him with suggestive eyes. "You paying for this or are we?"

Jim slipped a bill from his wallet and placed it firmly on the table. "See you in school, Austaire." He darted out into the parking lot where his mom was waiting. He dumped his books on the seat and slid in beside her. She looked concerned. "Sorry Mom," he shrugged. "I just forgot the time."

"Don't tell your Dad that, Jim. You know how important it is to take advantage of this nice weather. You know how he worries about the crop and our fall payments."

"I have my own life too, Mom. We will get the crop off. We always do." Jim shrugged his broad shoulders and slowly fastened his seatbelt. He slumped against the truck door.

June put the truck into gear and exited the parking lot. "Is everything okay, son? George and I love you so much. I know that it is not easy sometimes but you know how your Dad says that as a family we must remain strong. The Lord has always seen us through."

"Don't start preaching to me, Mom." Jim stared out the window towards Dobeys. He could still see the outline of the girls through the front window. "I am sure that Dad will do enough of that. I know how important religion is to you but don't expect me to just follow suit. I am not a kid anymore. I'll be eighteen next year and it's time that I start making up my own mind about some things. In a couple of years I'll be on my own."

Tears started to flow from his Mom's eyes. She gripped the steering wheel of the pickup and gritted her teeth. She quietly muttered a prayer for her son.

"Don't cry, Mom. I'm sorry. I didn't mean to upset you. I just know that I must make up my own mind on some things as I get older. It's tough sometimes. It seems like the kids here in town just do whatever. I'm not really complaining or anything but sometimes I'd just like to do what I want to; that's all. Here's some tissue. I didn't mean to make you cry."

June accepted the tissue and slowly wiped her eyes. She glanced quickly at her son and then refocused on the road again. Jim stared back at his Mom with the full realization that she was upset and alarmed by his words. She said nothing more and concentrated on getting home as quickly as possible. Jim glanced up towards the approaching intersection. In a split second he yelled, "Watch out! Hit the brakes!"

The screeching brakes sent the pickup into a quick slide and brought it to an abrupt halt. The driver of the other vehicle continued slowly through the intersection apparently oblivious to the incident.

"Wow Mom, that was pretty close. Didn't you see him? You know we have to stop there."

"I guess I just wasn't thinking. Thank God for looking after us."

"Like whatever. It's a good thing I saw him." His Mom's face was as white as snow. Her hands were glued to the steering wheel of the pickup. Remnants of tear drops still clung to her cheeks. Jim looked sincerely at his mother and quietly asked her, "You okay? I can drive if you wish."

"No, I'm fine. Sorry about that. Just wasn't concentrating. Let's get home, son."

The pickup slowly crossed the intersection and headed towards the main highway. The remainder of the trip was silent. All along the road they could see harvest machines busily engaged in threshing and hauling grain. Jim sat back in the seat and closed his eyes allowing his mind to wander back to Dobeys and the girls. *He really enjoyed their company and he was missing them already. They were really fun to be around. Their lives were so different than his. Not that he complained about his roots. In many ways he was proud to come from a farm but sometimes it just seemed too much work and too little play.* The jarring noise of gravel, as the pickup turned up County Road 22, brought him back to reality and he wisely used the remaining time to concentrate on creating what he hoped was a good excuse to tell his father.

3

The sun was starting to settle into the west as they drove into the yard. The throb of combines groaning under the approaching dew filled the evening air. Patches of grey dust rising from the machines filled the horizon. Harvest was literally in the air.

"You had best get to your homework, Jim." June slammed the door of the pickup closed. "Your Dad will probably be trying for another load before he shuts down. I will go out and check on him if he's not up after I see how the girls made out."

Jim shrugged his shoulders and nervously looked at his mother. "Homework can wait. I haven't much of anything anyways, Mom. Should I go out now or wait in the yard? I know that he is going to be mad. It was pretty dumb of me."

June cut her son's words short. "Just go out, Jim. Your Dad is a fair man. You know that. Just be honest and don't get him riled." She gave Jim a quick hug and headed towards the house.

"Take the old truck, Jim. I've got some things in the pickup."

"Okay. See you in a bit."

Jim darted for the old Chev and started her up. He was soon bouncing out the lane. The dust was still rising behind him but the evening air was cooling quickly. It would soon be dark.

George looked directly ahead of the machine into the awaiting swath. The groans from the machine were getting louder and he knew that the day was almost finished. *"More great weather headed our way for tomorrow and probably through this week. But we may have our weekend plans changed with increasing chances of showers or perhaps periods of rain coming our way."* George turned the radio off. He had heard that forecast about a dozen times now. It could easily be wrong.

The lights from the old Chev veered into the far end of the quarter. *They must be home George thought.* He also thought of the grain waiting to be dried at home. A loud thud had him jabbing the clutch quickly to the floor. The halt in forward movement was enough to allow the diesel to digest the damp swath and send it through the machine. He turned on the light switch and an abundance of light instantly illuminated the swath lying before him. He would nurse her to the grain truck and call it a day.

Jim stood by the truck at the end of the field. He watched as his Dad skillfully maneuvered the groaning combine towards him. The dew was quickly setting now and the bark from the diesel cut through the night air. The cloud of dust that had risen into the air when Jim and his Mom had got home was gone. The lights cast great grotesque shadows on either side of the machine as it ever so slowly got closer and closer. Cold sweat gathered on his forehead. He felt clammy and cold. *His father was a hard working, honest man who unfortunately was easily angered. He had experienced that wrath many times throughout his childhood and Jim still feared it.*

George could see the tandem clearly now. He could also see the Chev parked beside it. He saw the outline of his son standing by the truck. One last bit of swath headed through the machine as he lifted the header and swung the unloading auger out towards the box of the tandem. The clatter of metal vibrating against metal soon softened and faded as the auger filled with the golden kernels of wheat and sent them showering into the truck box.

Jim just stood there and watched as the grain piled into the box. George sat in the machine slowly moving the auger and topping off the load in the truck. Finally the auger began to clatter again and George shut it down and swung it back onto the combine. He let the diesel idle for a moment and pulled the fuel stop out. He shut off the lights, opened the cab door and stepped out into the cool, night air. Jim watched as his Dad stepped down off the machine and walked towards him.

"Hi Dad, I'm sorry about the bus. I kinda' forgot the time." His hands were ice cold and shaking.

"Hi Jim, you forget your watch today? What happened?" George was obviously fighting his emotions.

"No, I had a burger with some friends and just missed the bus. No excuse really. We were talking about trying out for football."

George interrupted his son. "You were having a burger with some friends. We talked about this before, Jim. We agreed that you would have more time for your friends this year. But not at harvest! We get one shot at this, Jim." The pitch of his voice was increasing.

"Dad, it was a mistake. It won't happen again. I promise. It was just one night. We just got talkin' and time went by."

"Damn it, Jim!" shouted George. "That's not good enough. Your Mom had to drive in and pick you up. She's tired as it is. The girls did all the chores by themselves. What about your homework? Did you do that in town too?"

"No, I have next to nothing. I can do it later. It's all good there. We didn't mean any harm. It won't happen again." Jim's words remained resilient. Two pairs of eyes locked as their formidable figures stood entrenched in the darkening field.

"Don't you glare at me, Jim?"

"I'm not glaring. I made a mistake. I'm sorry and it will not happen again. I know how tired Mom is. Shit, she almost hit a car on the way home. It was a good thing that I saw it in time."

"What the hell happened?"

"She almost missed the stop coming out of town. It was not her fault. We were just talking and she got upset. Anyway, we got stopped in time."

"Your foolishness almost cost us a truck. You guys could have been badly hurt. That would have done wonders to the harvest cause. Son of a bitch, son!"

"You don't have to swear at me. I did wrong. The girls said that you wouldn't understand. I just wanted to maybe try out for football. I told them that it would interfere with harvest. I just screwed up. Listen Dad, it will not happen again," yelled Jim. "You were young once, too."

The words seemed to hang in the coolness of the night air. The two combatants stepped back from each other as if to gather stamina for round two. George looked earnestly at his son.

"Okay, okay! Enough! I'm getting tired. I've got grain to dry after chores in the morning now. You've got some homework and tomorrow will bring a new opportunity."

Tears began to gather in Jim's eyes. "I'm truly sorry, Dad. I won't let you down again. I know how important getting' the grain off is."

"Damn it. Come here." George clutched his son and the two exchanged robust hugs. "Let's get up to the house. I'll take the tandem and you take the old girl back. The combine can sit in the field. Did you say that you ate? That burger won't amount to much. Girls had stew on earlier."

Jim started to walk towards the Chev. He was about to open the driver's door when his father's voice broke the silence.

"You know that I wish we could help you play. Maybe if we get the most of the crop off you could still have some playing time. If that exchange student hadn't of decided to not come we would have been fine."

"I know, Dad. It's not your fault. It's not anybody's fault. Don't worry about it. Harvest is where it's at. I know!"

"See you in the morning, Jim."

"You too, Dad, I'll make it right."

"I know you will. Now get that ole pig back into the yard."

Jim turned towards his Dad who was hardly visible now in the darkness of the night. "Thanks for understanding, Dad. You know for not getting too mad. I thought that you were going to clobber me."

George gave a small grin and let out with a chuckle, "Count your blessings son, count your blessings. I know you're damn near as big as me now but don't test me too far. Now get some damn sleep."

Jim slammed the door of the Chev and started her up. He rolled down the window. His Dad was rolling out the tarp on the box of the tandem. "Night Dad," he said and then he left for the yard.

"Goodnight son," answered George as he watched the tail lights of the Chev disappear from the field. He crawled down from the box and slid into the cab of the tandem. At the turn of the key the diesel came to life and George headed towards home. His son was growing up and many challenges lay ahead. Growing up was never easy. The yard lights cast a welcome haze over the yard as George walked across the wet grass towards the house. He looked up at the clear, night sky loaded with bright stars. How beautiful was that?

June was waiting in the kitchen when George walked in.

"So, how did it go with Jim?" she asked.

"Okay, I guess. He's growing up," replied George. "You okay, Hon? Jim tells me you had a scare in town."

"I'm fine. You look concerned, George."

"Just tired. It's his friends in town. We know nothin' about them. I hope they don't mess with him. Damn kids anyway. Feed him full of crap and then what?"

"Jim's strong, George. He'll be fine. He knows right from wrong. Now dump those dirty clothes. I've got tea ready."

"Sounds good, Hon. Be right up." His words faded as George wearily descended the steps into the basement. *Life was always a question and in a way everyday was a gift. Another day had come and gone. He should be thankful for what they had accomplished. So Jim had messed up this once. He would come around and perform just like always. What on earth would they do without him? He was a truly an attribute to this farm and indeed a gift to this family.*

4

The remainder of the week had gone well for the Edwards. The weather had co-operated to it's fullest with warm and windy fall weather that was a farmer's dream. Jim more than fulfilled his promise to his father by pulling his share of the harvest load like the true trooper that he was. He was more than just a good-looking, clean-cut farm boy. Jim was a responsible and dedicated young adult. Friday night had seen the family work together as a team happily engaged in their chosen livelihood.

George awoke to the pitter-patter of raindrops on the bedroom window early Saturday morning. He quietly arose and carefully sat down on the side of the bed attempting not to awaken June. His tired eyes were fixed on those solemn splashes of water that now ran down the darkened panes of glass. He peered through the rain drops and watched the mist from the descending moisture wash across the yellow beam of the yard light.

"What time is it?" questioned a very drowsy June, "Did I miss the alarm, Hon?"

"No alarm; just some rain. It woke me up. Hopefully it won't amount to much."

"I guess the Good Lord thought we needed a little rest, eh?" June snuggled up to George. She slowly rubbed his muscular back. "Well there, George Edwards. You've got me awake now."

George quickly turned to face his wife. He spoke softly, "You keep that up and I may just keep you awake. Just when I was going to let you sleep in. You are right about the damn rain. We probably could use a little break."

"Well George, what's your next move?" whispered June as she mischievously moved closer to her husband. "Hey, that's a good start. Not bad for a farm boy."

The moment was abruptly broken by the sound of gentle knocking on their bedroom door. It was Susan.

"Are you guys awake in there? Did you hear the rain? Mary won't let me have any covers. Is it time to get up yet? Can we have pancakes for breakfast, Mom?"

"Hey, slow down there girl." George laughed. "Your Mom is barely awake and I do mean barely." He glanced over at the alarm clock. It was five thirty. "I better get going, June. Catch up to you later?"

June smiled back as she watched her husband get dressed. "Yep, okay. Susan, get your sister up. We might as well get breakfast. Pancakes it is."

"Do you want me to knock on Jim's door too?" asked Mary, who had now joined her sister by the door.

"Might as well. He may already be up with all this activity going on up here," June chuckled.

Jim had awoken about five and had been content to lie in the comfort of his basement bedroom and listen to the chatter from above. He listened to the sounds of the footsteps as his two younger, twin sisters ran down the cellar steps.

"Hey sleepy head it's time to rise and shine," the girls chorused. "Pancakes for breakfast!"

"Yah, Yah. Be right there. Did you characters say pancakes? Just so long as you guys aren't making them." Jim lay back on his pillow and smiled to himself as the girls left. He loved his Mom's pancakes. That was incentive to leave this comfort zone.

"Oh, by the way, it's raining out," shouted Mary as the girls disappeared up the stairs. *Rain, now that opened up some doors thought Jim. Best tread softly as Dad will definitely not be in good mood.*

The rain was now cascading from the sky as the darkness of early morning still prevailed. The family sat around the kitchen table in relative quiet downing those famous pancakes. The radio added background noise to the clatter of rain hitting the window panes. *Rain should stop this afternoon with good possibilities for the unsettled conditions to last into early next week as another low pressure system enters the region on Sunday. Strong westerly flow should clear these systems by the middle of next week bringing clear conditions with a touch of frost possible.*

Jim broke the silence. "It sounds like it won't last long."

"No, it looks like your Mom is just getting that break that she figures we all deserved," George smiled directly at June. "Good pancakes, Hon."

"Can we have some more, Mom?" the twins chorused.

"Yes," Jim quickly added, "I'll have another couple."

"Whoa there guys. Let your Mom eat," said George.

June glanced up at her family. Her face lit up at all the sudden appreciation. "There is still lots of batter in the kitchen, girls. You know what to do."

"Does that mean Jim has to eat our cooking, Mom?" Susan giggled.

"Just go get them made." June smiled. "I believe that Jim can handle a couple of your creations."

"Just don't burn them," added Jim. "You know how they taste if they're burnt." He turned to his father. "So Dad, seeing as it is raining out, do you think that I can go into town later with Glen? He had asked me to call him."

George interrupted his son. "What do you think, Jim?"

June gave her husband and her son both a stern look. "No haggling now guys. Jim more than made up for his little blunder, George."

"Taking sides are we now, June? No, you are right. Did you mean Glen Rollins, Jim? I haven't heard you mention him in awhile. Heard that his father might be pullin' up stakes and goin' to town."

"Yep, Glen's Dad and Mom are separating and he and his Dad are probably movin' to Royston," replied Jim. "We still hang out lots."

"That's a bitch about his folks. I heard that too. Damn rumors. How is Glen, anyway? You used to bring him over lots?"

"Good Dad, he's pretty sharp in school. Always was."

"Yes, maybe a little will rub off on you." A big smile swept across George's face. "I'll tell you what. Help me finish up chores and do a couple of little repairs out there and you can let that Glen character know that you can go into Royston with him." George watched as June gave him her nod of approval. "Just do not be late, Jim. We've got church tomorrow. Chores start early."

"Great, thanks Dad. Can I give Glen a call?"

"It's pretty early but if you want to wake him up be my guest," replied his Dad. George had little time to focus his sober eyes on his son as almost instantly Jim jumped from his chair and ran downstairs to his bedroom. George quickly wiped his broad forehead and returned to finishing his meal. *Trust always danced on a fine line.*

"Hey what about your pancakes?" asked Mary.

"Be right back. Serve them up," replied Jim on the run. He closed his bedroom door and rang Glen's number. It rang and rang. "Come on answer the damn phone, Glen." A half awake someone answered on the other end. "Hello."

"Hey there, Glen. It's me, Jim Edwards. How you doing? Do you think that you could do me a big a favor?"

"Jim? Do you know what time it is? What kind of favor you lookin' for? Can't this wait until later? I know how you guys are up with the rooster and all."

"I need a ride into town this afternoon," interrupted Jim. "Dad said it was okay and I kinda' suggested that you had asked me to come with you."

There was silence on the other end of the line. Finally, a groggy Glen replied. "You still seeing those girls, aren't you? Do you think that you could fix me up too?"

"Sure thing, Glen. There is this big party tonight. I'm pretty much stoked about it and they'll be lots of girls there. Just don't mention it to my folks. They won't understand. So can you pick me up or not?"

"What time?" Glen sounded as if he was still shaking cow webs from his head. "I told my Dad that I would help him for a bit this morning."

"That's all good. Let's say two. See you then. Thanks bud," replied an eager Jim. Jim quietly danced a little victory jig on his bedroom floor. His smile was enough to burst his cheeks.

"Yah, see you around two. You owe me guy. I don't like foolin' around with your folks. Gotta' go, I hear my Dad."

Jim excitedly hung up the phone and ran upstairs. His chest was pounding as he sat down to finish the fresh pancakes sitting on his plate.

"Everything fine there, Jim? You took awhile." His mother raised her eyebrows.

"Just took a bit to wake Glen." Jim blurted out a quick reply. "That's all. He said that he would pick me up around two."

"I knew you would wake him up," George grumbled. "You could have easily called him later. Anyways that works fine here. Just remember to be home in decent time tonight."

"He was kinda' wondering if I could stay over. Glen said it was okay with his Dad and all. I'd be home first thing in the morning. His place is on the way here." Jim hesitated, "He'd drive me over early, promise."

George looked at Jim and then at June. She was looking directly into her son's eyes. George scratched his head. Light perspiration covered the expanding baldness on his forehead. Outside the rain was pouring down. George gazed up at the shadows on the white tile ceiling and then looked sternly at Jim. "Okay, but you must promise to be home early. No goofing around here young man. I still remember Monday's bullshit so you can consider yourself more than fortunate. You know how your Mom feels about church and she was thinking about having Heiners back after for the afternoon since it is wet and all."

"Please be back early," added his Mom. "I think that you deserve a break too. Just abide by our guidelines."

"So when do we get our break?" asked Mary.

"Yes, we helped even when Jim screwed up," added her sister.

George spoke first before Jim could reply to Susan. "Okay, enough is enough. You girls are right though. Perhaps your Mom can take you shopping this afternoon; if we ever get breakfast over and the chores done. That's if it's fine with your mother?"

Eager eyes turned quickly on their mother in anticipation of her approval. "Can we, Mom?"

June simply nodded her head, "Yes, but like your Dad says we had better get things done or the day will be over before we start."

Jim quickly finished his breakfast and pushed his chair away from the table. "Just getting my chore clothes and I will get started out there. Thanks again, I really appreciate this." With that he grabbed his plate and deposited it in the kitchen before disappearing down the basement stairway.

"Boy, there is some action," June smiled, looking up at George. "Praise the Lord."

"Just hope that the Lord knows enough to shut off that moisture out there." George stared out the window as the early light illuminated a yard of growing puddles of standing water.

"It'll be just fine, George. We always make it through."

"Now you are starting to sound like your son." George allowed a small smile. "Well girls, let's move before your brother has everything done out there."

Jim had quickly dressed and darted to the barns splashing through the puddles. He was almost breathless when he opened the door into the utility room. He ratcheted the phone from the receiver, listened for the dial tone and sped through the numbers. He let the phone ring on the other end until he was greeted with a recording. *This is Megan. I'm not around at the moment but leave me some info and I'll know you called. Bye.* "Hey, it's Jim. I'll be there tonight. Tell Austaire. Bye." Jim slammed the phone back on the receiver and left to attend to his chores.

A drowsy Megan was half listening to the message on the other end. She smiled and uttered softly to herself, "We will party tonight."

The house phone rang shortly after Jim had left his message for Megan. June answered in her usual professional way. "Hello, the Edwards farm. How may I help you?"

"You talk pretty convincingly," replied Allan Heiner. "Is that workaholic husband of yours still there or has he started chores?"

"No Allan, he was just leaving. We are getting off to a slow start this morning with the rain and all. Oh, I was goin to give Irene a call later and ask you guys out after church tomorrow. Just a minute now." June hollered down to George. "Hey pick up the phone in Jim's room. It's Allan Heiner."

"Thanks Hon, I'll be right there." George picked up the phone. "Yes Allan. What are you doin' up this early in the morning?" His sarcasm brought an easy smile to his face.

"Yah, okay. Thought that maybe I would have to call at this God forsaken hour to reach you. When are you folks goin' to join the rest of civilized man anyways?"

"Someone has to feed the world," George chuckled.

"Yes, I know all about it. Anyways June tells me we are invited to lunch tomorrow so I can talk with you then. Irene just gave me the nod of approval. It's nothin' that can't wait until tomorrow. It'll be better than talkin' on the phone anyways."

"You sound serious guy. Is everything okay, Allan? Is there something I can do?" George frowned.

"No, it will be better to chat after a good lunch. Well I had better run too. I'd hate to be guilty of keeping you good folks from feeding the world and all." Allan laughed. The sarcasm was now at his end of the phone.

"Okay then, Allan. Look forward to seeing you then. Jim is already out doing chores so I'd better run or I'll be getting fired."

"Jim doin' good?" inquired Allan.

"Oh yah, he missed the bus once this week but hell it happens. Jim is Jim. He's growing up quickly. Anything in particular?"

"No, no, George," a seemingly distant Allan inquired. "Anyways we will see you tomorrow. Don't work too hard guy."

"You too, Allan. Catch you later." George put the phone down and walked up the stairs. June noticed his puzzled look.

"Everything okay with Allan, George?" she asked.

"I guess so. It seemed like he had something to talk about but would rather talk in person tomorrow. It's kinda' weird for Allan. You know he never seems to have a lack of things to talk about or any hesitation in talkin' about them. Anyways, sounds like it can wait until tomorrow. I gotta run. Girls and Jim will think that I got lost or something."

"Got a quick kiss?" asked June. "Hey, don't worry about it. You know Allan. I just hope that everything is fine at home with his family and all. I guess you will find out tomorrow. He has a way of making a mountain out of a mole hill."

"Isn't that the truth, now? Love yah."

"Love you too, farm boy."

Their smiles met and they quickly exchanged a warm hug and a kiss. George closed the beaten and weathered porch door and slowly walked to the barns still puzzled by the words and early morning phone call from his best friend. He cast a glance across the wet farmyard.

The white board fence surrounding the perimeter was paled by the low-lying and grey overcast skies. Water was rushing off the eaves of the buildings as the torrent fell from above. The row of grain bins that were situated towards the road was barely visible as a light mist rose in the distance. The machinery that had worked so hard yesterday now sat in a somber row. George pulled his hat down tighter over his head and shrugged his shoulders. *It was September and it was still early in the season. He had work to do.*

5

Jim cast an anxious glance out the lane just as the Glen Rollins turned off the main road. He watched for a moment as the pickup splashed through puddles that lay in abundance on the roadway. The rain had stopped but the overcast sky remained filled with threatening, grey clouds.

"Glen's here! Catch you later, Mom." Jim hastily put on his school jacket and tied his shoes. The drone of the vacuum cleaner filled the house as the girls finished up their chores. Jim ran downstairs to the laundry room. "Glen's here, Mom. See you tomorrow." Jim walked towards her and extended a hug.

June returned the welcome hug from her son. "Have fun and take care, Jim. We will see you early in the morning. The Heiners are coming back after church. Be safe on those wet roads."

"You bet, Mom. Well, Glen is waiting. Thanks again."

"Thank your Dad, Jim. Just remember to be back in good time."

"No problem." Jim darted up the stairs and opened the porch door on the run. He was soon sitting in the pickup.

"Hi there, Glen! You're right on time. Like, let's get out of here man before they find another chore for me."

"Done deal, this party must be something special. You are some hype." Glen grinned as he put the truck in drive and they quickly navigated the distance onto the main road. "So are we meeting the girls at Dobeys?"

"Austaire is going to meet us there but the party is at Megans. She has her own place on the south side. I've been there before. She definitely knows how to entertain, if you know what I mean?"

"Sounds wicked; you must really like this Austaire? I see you guys at school lots. Can't say that I have seen much of you since last spring but everyone knows that you guys have a thing going."

"She's awesome, Glen. Sorry about not callin' you much. Life gets congested at times. I owe you one for this ride and all though. I would never have gotten away on my own."

"What? Your folks won't let you drive into town?"

"No, no, its nothin' like that but I know that they would never understand me staying over at Megans. I've been keeping that under the covers. Their ideas are pretty lame when it comes to dating and such. You and I are going to party tonight, Glen. Those girls know how to really chill out."

"Sounds like you're the man, Jim. I'm just not one to outright lie to my folks and I don't think that you are either. Not a biggie but always liked your folks."

"Don't even go there, Glen. As long as you get me home early tomorrow there will be no harm done. No one is the wiser and we have a great time. It's not everyday that you get to party like we will party tonight. You'll see!"

"Sounds good, Jim. Like, lead the way. Your chauffeur is at your command."

The cab of the pickup erupted into spontaneous laughter. Jim turned the volume up on the radio and let the music fill the cab. He slowly stretched back into the seat and shut his eyes. He blanked out his mind and envisioned making out with the girls. The journey into town could not go quick enough.

Austaire was seated in their booth at Dobeys. She had ordered a coke and was slowly sipping at the drink when the boys arrived. She noticed them entering the main door and walked over towards Jim. She promptly gave him a huge hug and planted a kiss on his cheek. "It's about time that you got here. Who's your friend?"

"Glen, meet Austaire," Jim smiled. "Glen is an old buddy who was kind enough to invite me out for the night and will take me home tomorrow morning."

"Well Glen, it's a pleasure to meet you." Austaire acknowledged Glen's presence and then fixed her blue eyes on Jim. She slowly brushed her right hand through her blonde hair and then held Jim's outstretched hand. The grip was warm and inviting. "When Megan said that you were coming to the party Jim she did not tell me that you were staying over. Now I'm like totally ecstatic!" Her eyes remained transfixed on Jim's. They both blushed. "Megan said that we could come over anytime. Crowd won't be there until later, but hey it's never too early for a party."

"Well Glen, do we have room for this pretty lady?" Jim grinned at his friend. "A party is waiting."

"Lead the way. Your ride awaits people," said Glen.

Jim quickly paid for the coke and the three party goers exited Dobeys. Under Austaire's' direction they proceeded to a row of older townhouses in a secluded block on the south end of Royston. Megan's unit was at the very end of the complex. Her old, red Honda was parked in front. They left the pickup across the street in a vacant lot and walked up the pathway. Austaire knocked three times and then waited before knocking three more times. The single upstairs window facing the street opened slowly.

"You're early," shouted Megan to the threesome below her. "Who's the cute guy with you two?"

"A good bud of Jim's, Meg," said Austaire. "Glen brought Jim into town and will take him home tomorrow morning."

"Oh Jimmy Boy, you have come to party now, haven't you. Welcome Glen, any friend of Jimmies is a friend of ours. Well don't just stand there, Austaire. Show our early guests in and make yourselves comfortable. I'll be down in minute."

Jim opened the door and the three entered Megan's townhouse. The main doorway opened into a dimly lit but large living room sparsely furnished with two older sofas, a large recliner, a coffee table and a couple of end tables. A narrow stairway on the right headed upstairs and a door underneath the stairway led downstairs. The room had an intoxicating but pleasant aroma that tickled ones nostrils. Jim and Austaire headed directly for the kitchen which was located at the rear of the unit while Glen seated himself on a sofa and waited for Megan to come down.

"You got anything to eat here?" Austaire shouted up to Megan. "The cupboards look bare."

"I thought that we could order in pizza. The numbers should be by the phone. Perhaps the boys want to pick them up and give us time to finish preparing. There's lots of ice in the freezer and there's beer in the fridge. Hard stuff is on the counter."

"Sounds good, Megan," said Jim. "You guys call Dobeys and Glen and I will pick up the pizza." He cast a wandering smile at Glen who was still busy studying the room he sat in. "Ready there, bud. I'm starved."

"Sure thing, let's get those pizzas."

Jim and Austaire shared a long kiss and then the two boys left the townhouse to perform their errand. Jim walked quickly to the pickup and waited for Glen by the truck. "Come on there old man, we have pizzas to deliver."

"Right on there, Jim. Is that smell in there what I think it is? I mean I'm not sure but I think that someone has been smokin' in there and it definitely isn't tobacco."

"You've never tried pot, Glen?" Jim laughed and looked at his friend sitting across from him in the pickup. "It's cool man. Just relaxes you, that's all. I can't believe that you haven't used it. I can see where you are going to have to like major chill tonight. Makes the girls horny and makes me hungry just thinking about it. Come on now. Those pizzas will be cold. I told you it was going to be some party, didn't I?"

"You're the boss, Jim. Pizza is waiting." Glen started the pickup and they left down the street. Inside the townhouse Megan and Austaire were deep in conversation; both of them ecstatic that Jim was there for the night.

6

The afternoon was drawing to a close by the time the boys returned with the pizzas. The mist that been present when the boys left was now turning into a light rain and the air felt damp and cool. The vacant lot across from Megan's townhouse was quickly filling up with vehicles.

"I hope that we brought enough of these," Jim laughed as he reached for the warm boxes. "I'm starved."

"Yes, a dozen extra large Dobeys specials coming up," said Glen. "I haven't eaten since this morning either."

Jim knocked three times on the door and then waited before knocking three more times. Megan opened the door.

"Bout' time that you two arrived with those things. Hmm, they smell good. Let me grab a couple and take a load off you. I'm Megan, Glen. You can make your own acquaintances. Hey everyone; its pizza time." A chorus of appreciation filled the room.

"Pleasure, Megan. Lead the way." Glen nodded his head and followed her into the kitchen while Jim passed his boxes out to eager hands. Austaire grabbed a pepperoni/cheese and handed Jim a can of beer in return.

"Thought you might be thirsty. I've got more over here for us." She smiled at Jim. Her eyes sparkled as her free hand clasped around Jim's arm. "You look good in that denim and you feel real good. I've been waiting for this evening for awhile."

Jim just nodded his head as he took a large gulp of the cold beer and silently followed his girl towards a large pillow in one corner of the living room. He returned smiles from others in the room as he and Austaire walked. The couple quickly made themselves comfortable on the pillow. He finished his beer and reached for another.

"You are definitely thirsty," said Austaire laughing as she watched Jim wolf down the cold beer.

"Got to wash this pizza down some how. God, I'm hungry. I haven't had much since Mom's pancakes before chores this morning. This is like totally awesome."

"There's lots more here, babe, lots more."

Most of the pizza was consumed before more partygoers arrived. The familiar three knocks on the door was barely audible over the chatter of conversation and the rousing beat of the Ace of Base coming from the basement dance floor. Megan opened the door and several more party goers entered. Jim raised his beer can in response to various greetings coming from the newcomers. He recognized most of the kids from school but a few he had never seen before. Their age suggested that they must be friends of Megan. Megan approached Austaire and Jim with one in tow.

"Hey guys, meet Jason." Megan giggled as she let him fondle her. "Jason is our candy man for tonight and I will be taking donations into the candy fund." Megan looked bewitchingly at Jim as he dug into his pocket and passed her some bills. "Thanks Jimmy, you take care of my boy for me now, Austaire." Megan passed her a joint and a lighter. "Now the party begins. See you later, Sunshine."

The room began filling with the aroma of freshly lit joints as the party goers indulged in the offerings from Megan and Jason. Jim and Austaire became engulfed in a haze of blue, arid smoke. The couple was soon giggling and chatting with others absorbed in the relaxed atmosphere of Megan's living room. *Pizza, beer and pot in abundance Jim thought to himself. He felt a twinge of guilt as he briefly wandered what his parents would think of such a spectacle but it quickly faded.* He looked across the room and noticed that Glen was occupied with a new friend. Jim briefly glanced at his wristwatch. It was eight o'clock. He brought his undivided attention back to Austaire and inhaled hard on the joint that she was offering him.

"Enjoy, my Jimmy!" she laughed as he coughed after inhaling. "You'll get on to it. It's all good now." Austaire slowly rose up and gave Jim a gentle tug on his arm. "How be we head upstairs for awhile? Megan said to use her room."

Jim looked intently into her blue eyes. He softly whispered into her ear, "Lead the way, girl, lead the way."

As the night advanced the effects of the alcohol and the pot became quite evident. The music and dancing faded into the darkness of the evening. Most of the participants were totally stoned, passed out or consumed in some form of mutual enjoyment. Time had seemingly slowed to a crawl. Jim and Austaire were no exception. They had returned from upstairs to party and then eventually dozed off snuggled on their pillow. Jim was abruptly awoken by Megan's kiss at about three in the morning. He managed to open his eyelids and peer at her through stoned eyes.

"So, how you doin', Jimmy? Meg's here to party now. How be we venture upstairs?"

"Oh yah, right now." Jim managed in a slurred voice. "Lead the way." He giggled as he attempted to get up.

"Perhaps I should stay here with Austaire, Meg?" Jim looked down at his girlfriend who remained engulfed in sleep.

"It's okay with Austaire, Jimmy. We've been though this before. Instead of a threesome it'll just be you and I tonight. Besides she completely wasted."

"I'm feelin' pretty thrashed myself, Meg." Jim had finally managed to stand upright but felt weak and giddy. "Austaire is really out of it, isn't she?"

"She sure is. Now take this and you'll get your strength back." Megan offered Jim a capsule and encouraged him to wash it down with a portion of alcohol. "It's all good. You'll see. Trust me."

Jim hesitated briefly and then accepted the offering and swallowed the small capsule. *He had no idea what it was or what it would do. He really did not care as sanity was not an issue at this moment in time. Enjoyment was only footsteps away.* He cast a blank smile at Megan and silently followed her upstairs. He turned once to glance towards Austaire. She remained in a deep slumber. He gradually felt himself awakening from within and with it came a growing eagerness for whatever Megan had in store. They entered her room and Jim leaned back against the door to close it. His eyes remained spell bound as he watched her menacingly disrobe by the bed. She was definitely a fox and he was in her den.

7

Glen carefully opened the bedroom door and stared into the room. The partially open window was allowing a cool breeze to enter the room. The street light was casting faint shadows from the blowing window curtains across the room. He recognized Jim and quietly walked over to the bed. Jim was stirred to attention by his steady shaking.

"Hey, we got to get, Jim. You've got to wake up."

"Hey there, bud. Like chill out; we aren't in any big hurry."

"It's six o'clock in the morning guy. You got chores to go to. Remember, I'm supposed to be taking you home from my house."

"Oh yah, what time is it? Did you say six? Shit, it's still early."

"Have it your way, Jim. It's your funeral, not mine."

"Yah, whatever, just give me a moment. I've got to find some clothes here. Damn it's cold in here."

"I'm going out to the truck, Jim. Don't be too long. You were sure right about one thing. It was one hell of a party. I'm out of here before your partner awakes."

Jim watched as Glen left the room. He thought about closing the window but figured that it would only awake Megan. She remained fast asleep despite Glen's action to wake him up. He struggled into his clothes and left the room. The living room was very dark and very quiet. He managed to shift around bodies to the corner where Austaire still lay snuggled into the pillow. He reached down and whispered, "Sleep tight, girl," and promptly left the townhouse. Glen was waiting in his pickup in front of Megan's townhouse. Jim slid into the passenger side and Glen put the truck in gear.

"You awake there now, Jim?"

"Kind of, thanks. Question? How did you manage to get up so early?"

"Not sure. Had to take a leak bad and happened to look at my watch. Whatever? When I did not see you downstairs I kinda' thought you might be upstairs. Like, you sure get around. I'm envious."

"Yah, I'll share my secrets with you sometime." Jim smiled at the thought and then rubbed his head. "Damn it, my head hurts. How's yours?"

"Not bad. Drank a lot of beer but didn't smoke much. I didn't have to. That room was plastered. You only had to breathe the stuff and get stoned. Quite a party, Jim."

"Megan knows how to look after you." Jim glanced at Glen and they both burst into laughter. "Damn it, don't make me laugh. My head is just splitting apart here."

"What time is it getting to be anyway? I think that I left my watch in Megan's room. Not sure."

"You were so busy. It is no wonder. It's about six thirty Jim. Should have you home for seven? You can say we slept in or something."

"Always better late than never! Dad will still not be impressed but it should not be too bad. It's still pretty early and I will make church. Damn my head hurts."

"Okay, nurse your head there buddy and let me get you home."

"Yah, I just need a little catnap. Wake me up in the morning." Jim smiled at Glen and then stretched back on the seat and closed his eyes. He promptly dozed off. Glen drove home in silence.

A light mist had started to envelope the countryside when Glen turned onto County Road 22. The early morning light was shrouded by grey skies that threatened to generate more moisture later in the morning. The puddles covering the road were stark evidence that there had been more rain during the night. Glen approached the Edward's drive way and yelled across to Jim.

"Hey there Jim, wake up, we're just about to your place." Glen let out a chuckle as Jim aroused from his slumber. "It's time to rise and shine."

Jim slowly turned his head towards Glen and struggled to get upright in his seat. "That went fast. Damn my head hurts. How's our time, anyhow?"

"It's just about seven. Not too bad, considering."

"Yes, I probably would have slept till noon. I owe you again my friend. Thanks for the ride. Boy, she is wet out. Dad is not going to be impressed."

Jim glanced at the soaked harvesting equipment sitting in the yard. This rain was definitely not what the doctor had ordered. His senses were slowly returning to reality as Glen pulled the truck to a stop. Jim stepped out into the morning mist and turned to his old friend.

"Thanks again, Glen. We'll be in touch."

"Yep, you bet. Just don't forget about your old bud, eh? I had a good time too. It was quite a night if I may say so." Glen's conversation was cut short by the voice of Jim's Dad coming from the layer barn.

"Hey, Jim! You don't need to be standing out there gallivanting around. Your chores are waiting. Let's get a move on, now."

"Be right there, Dad," Jim yelled back. "I'd better run, Glen. Dad is definitely not in a good mood. Talk to you and thanks again."

"You bet, Jim. Catch you later. Perhaps you and I can hang out again if you're free sometime."

"You bet. Sometimes Austaire goes with Meg to the city on the weekend. See you later and thanks again."

Jim slammed the door shut and hurriedly ran towards the house. He opened the porch door on the run, leaving his wet shoes there before slipping down the stairs to the change room. His aching head would not interfere with the job at hand. In a moment he was heading out of the house towards the layer barn ready for work. In his haste he slipped on the wet walkway and fell head first onto the soaked ground. He uttered a quiet "shit" to himself and then slowly got up and continued towards the barn. The dull, thudding pain in his head continued with a vengeance. He glanced up at the grey sky before opening the barn door. The sky was reminiscent of how he felt at the moment. It was shaping up to be a very long day.

8

The sun was making brief attempts to break through the generally overcast sky when the Edwards family returned home from church services. A light wind was now blowing from the south-east and the surface of the gravel lane was beginning to dry leaving only scattered puddles in the depressions of the roadway. George brought the pickup to a stop in the farm yard.

"Everyone out, we've got visitors on our tail," he said.

"Yes, Allan and Sheila will be along shortly," replied June. "Girls, you can set the table for me." June and the girls left the pickup and headed towards the house. Jim and George had just shut their doors when his Dad spoke.

"So, how'd your night go, Jim? By the way I appreciate you boys getting home in decent time this morning. You did well. You look tired though. Have a late night?"

"Thanks Dad. Gee, I thought that we had slept in and was worried that you might be upset. Yah, Glen and I had a good time. We were just hanging out with some others. Nothin' special." Jim looked out the lane and noticed the green car turning into the laneway. "Looks like the Heiners are here. I'd best get in and see if Mom needs anything."

"I'm sure that she'd appreciate that, Jim," said George as he watched Allan Heiner slowly navigate the long laneway. He turned momentarily to continue the conversation but Jim was already walking around the house. Allan pulled the Dodge up beside him and his family exited the car. George spoke first.

"Welcome folks. It looks like the weather is starting to turn for the better again. June and the girls will have lunch set out shortly."

"No rush, George," replied Allan's wife Sheila. "Come along girls and let's see if we can help June out."

"We'll be right along, Sheila. Just enjoying this sunshine for a minute," said Allan. The two men stood bathing in the warmth of the sun as it broke through the cloud cover. Allan turned to George, "Good service, eh? Good to see you out. The Lord must be attended to as well."

"Don't you start preaching to me too? Yes, it was a good service. That young preacher speaks well. Damn that sun feels nice."

"Yes, it sure does. How are you making out with the harvest?"

"We're just nicely into it. Yields are good and quality seems okay. Hopefully we will not have too much of a break here." George looked directly into his best friends face. "So what was it that you had to tell me that you couldn't say on the phone? You sounded pretty serious there. You had me worried. Is everything okay with you folks? Work okay?"

Allan looked directly back at his friend. "No, no, everything is fine. Just wandered how Jim was making out with school and home and all. He has a pretty full plate for his age. He has always been your right arm, George. I know how much you depend on him. Not sure if that is right or wrong and I'm not here to preach to you. Just curious how things were and how his new friends were working out. Anyways, you and I can chat after lunch. Right now I'm starved."

"Jim is fine, Allan. Not sure where you are leading with this but you don't have to worry about him. What's the deal about his friends? I know I worry about that sometimes. Do you know something that we should?"

The conversation was interrupted by June's voice. "You two can talk later. Lunch is served."

"Be right there, Hon." George looked back at Allan. "We will continue this after lunch. You've got my attention. Now let's get in before the girls disown us or something."

Lunch was typical of the spread that June routinely set out for her Sunday lunches. Homemade soup and warm biscuits were followed by fresh salad with cheese and salami side dishes. June had made the cheese cake as well and served it with a special homemade, strawberry topping. The warm sunshine cascading through the dining room window gave the luncheon a festive flair.

"Excellent lunch, June," said Sheila. "You and the girls continue to excel."

A beaming June politely interrupted, "Thanks Sheila. It's always nice to have a compliment. Kids all helped though. Even Jim got home early to help with chores outside."

"So they let you out for the weekend, Jim?" asked Allan.

"Just out with Glen Rollins and some friends. I stayed overnight there. Mom and Dad let me off early yesterday with the rain and all." His face began to smile. "Even farm boys need some R & R. And with that if you guys would excuse me I've got some homework to do."

"Yes, get that homework done. With all this sun we might get busy sooner than later. Get some rest too. Your eyes tell me you had a long night."

"Yah, right Dad. See you, Allan."

"You bet, Jim. We'll have to get together and go canoeing or something. Take care."

"Sounds good, Allan. We haven't done that in a long time." Jim got up from the table and slowly walked downstairs towards his room. Sweat was forming on his forehead and he quickly detoured into the basement washroom. He shut the door and buried his head into the toilet where he promptly threw up his lunch. His forehead was burning as he wiped a cool, wet washcloth over his face. He walked back to his room and silently closed the door. The room was dark and cool. He crawled into his bed and instantly fell fast asleep.

The women were in the process of cleaning off the table now. The girls were in the front room setting up the Monopoly game. Allan and George were sitting back in their chairs seemingly oblivious to the world. No one had heard Jim being sick downstairs.

"Shall we venture out onto the deck with our coffee, Allan? We have a conversation to finish."

"That sounds fine. Thanks once again for the lunch, June. Lead the way, sir."

The two men exited through the front room casting glances at the girls who were now deep into their board game. In no time both men were comfortably seated outside on the deck. George was the first to speak.

"So what do you know that you think we don't?"

"George, I've seen Jim hanging out with some kids in town that perhaps he shouldn't be. Roy Warrack keeps warning me about some individuals that they watch. My girls are getting close to heading into Royston too…"

"Roy Warrack?" George interrupted.

"He's a good friend in town. Roy is a constable. It's a small town and they have a pretty good idea of what goes on. We're talkin' drugs here, George. Pot and cocaine and who knows what else? Anyways they suspect a few individuals that work with the kids and get them onto this stuff."

"Oh, Jim would not get into anything like that. He may forget the time once in a while and miss the bus but I can't see him getting mixed up with that stuff. I appreciate you giving me the heads up but Jim would never get involved with kids like that. He has friends like Glen Rollins and the like."

"Okay George, but perhaps you should talk with him sometime about this stuff. I've always liked Jim. He's definitely smarter than his Dad." Both men took time to share a laugh and then Allan continued. "I just think that you owe it to the both of you to warn him of the dangers that exist out there. Don't get in with the wrong crowd. Keep the lines of communication goin'? He is just at the age where kids like to experiment."

"Appreciate this talk, Allan. I really do and I know that there are kids in Royston that we definitely don't want Jim to associate with. I'll chat with him. Thanks."

The conversation dropped a few tiers and the usual amounts of political and economical chatter continued into the afternoon. The women eventually joined the men outside on the deck enjoying the fall sunshine while the girls remained glued to their Monopoly game. It was close to five when the Heiner family left.

"I'll just get Jim and finish up the night chores, June. Let you finish up in here. Be back in to catch the evening news and weather. God that sky looks good again."

"Sure Hon, haven't heard a peep from him all afternoon. Some fresh air will do him good."

George changed his clothes and knocked on Jim's door. He waited a moment before entering. In the darkness he could see his son sleeping on the bed. He silently exited the room and walked upstairs.

"He's fast asleep. I can manage. Maybe get the girls to come out and give me a hand with the eggs."

"Okay. He did look mighty tired this morning. They were probably up till the wee hours playing games or something. I'll send the girls out to help."

"Good. I'll check in on him when I come in. He'll get hungry and wake up. Hope that he got his homework done."

George left the house and headed directly for the grower barn. He finished the night feeding but was delayed by some maintenance on a couple of drinking fountains. By the time he was finished it was turning nightfall. The girls had finished collecting the eggs in the layer barn. They met and walked back together into the house. The western horizon looked bright and promising. *George thought how things would start to really dry up tomorrow. He was eager to resume harvest.*

"You girls had best get your supper now. I'm just going to check in on your brother." George slowly opened the door and looked inside the room. Jim was sitting on the side of his bed in the darkness. George turned on the light. Jim's eyes squinted as they adjusted to the light.

"Hi Dad, I kinda' crashed there. I'll be right there. It must be chore time."

"They're done, girls helped me out. Your Mom has supper ready. Did you get your homework done?"

"No, I'll get to that now. Sorry, I just didn't realize how tired I was. Tell Mom not to worry about me for supper. I've got to get my studies finished."

"Are you feeling okay? You still look kinda' white. You haven't picked up something, have you?

"No, no, I just didn't get enough sleep last night. We stayed up pretty late."

"What did you do last night anyways?"

Jim hesitated for a moment and then said, "Nothin' much, hung out at Dobeys and played some videos later. We were just hanging out with some others mostly. Why?"

"Can I sit down for a second? Allan mentioned seeing you with some kids that may not be up to any good and he was concerned about you."

Jim immediately sat up defensively and angrily broke into the conversation. "Allan has been spying on me? Damn, I thought that he was my friend. Like what else did he feed you?"

George sat for a moment and just looked at his son. "Don't get upset, Jim. I didn't come in here to question you. Allan just had concerns and wanted me to talk to you. You know how Allan is. Besides he has a constable friend in town."

"I'm not doing anything wrong and neither are my friends and they are none of anybodies business," Jim shouted. "Bloody adults! Maybe Megan is right."

"Megan. One of your new friends, Jim? Is she why you missed the bus? Is she feeding you full of useless crap?"

"She's not feeding me anything. Is this all over me missing the bus last week or is it last night now? Am I not allowed to have some time to myself? I do everything that you ask me to."

"Whoa, whoa, there now, young man. Enough is enough. I came down here to have a simple conversation." George glared at his son. "You jump on my case because we are concerned about your future and your well being. Best you just cool down for a while, Jim. We're just asking you to be careful. I'm going to go upstairs and forget this conversation happened. In the meantime you get your damn homework done. One more outbreak like this and you will be grounded. We love you son and care about you. I did not come in here to pick a fight."

Their eyes were locked in combat now. Seconds of silence went by before Jim continued in a much softer tone of voice. "Sorry, I just didn't feel like I needed another lecture on how bad teens are and how much trouble they are and how they are up to no good. You know where I'm coming from, Dad. I appreciate your caring but believe me I can look after myself. I know better and I know my friends. Okay?"

George stood up and walked towards the door. His hand felt hot as he reached for the door knob. He was struggling to regain some composure. "Okay son, just be careful. Mom and I and our friends all appreciate and completely trust you. I didn't mean to get you upset. Now get your homework done. If you want some supper it's up there. See you in the morning."

"Thanks, but I'm just not that hungry right now. Good night, Dad."

"Good night, Jim."

George gently shut the door and slowly walked up the steps to the kitchen. June was standing in the doorway.

"Is everything okay? What's going on now?"

"Nothin' Hon, just something that Allan had mentioned and when I talked with Jim he took the wrong way. I'll tell you later when the girls are in bed. Jim just woke up and he said that he didn't need supper right now. He wants to get his studies done first."

"Okay, but you've got to level with me, George Edwards. I'm part of this family too. It didn't sound like it was nothing from up here."

George reached out and gave his wife a warm hug. The two of them stood there embraced until Susan yelled from the dinner table. "Can Mary and I eat now? Supper is getting cold."

George responded, "You bet. Mom and I will be there in a second. Go ahead and say grace for all of us."

The couple moved into the dining room and sat down in the midst of Mary saying the blessing. George and June sat down with their family which temporarily was minus one member. George looked at the empty chair and a cold chill passed through his body. *He told himself that everything was fine. Kids grow up and families mature. Crops ripen and are harvested. Bills get paid and people eat. He joined into the family meal but remained deep in thought.*

9

A cool east wind greeted the Edwards family as they returned from early chores on Monday morning. The sky that had looked so promising the night before now appeared as a haze of red with scattered low lying stratus clouds stretching westward from the eastern horizon. George had remained in the grower barn finishing feeding while the kids had breakfast and got ready for school. He left the barn in time to watch them entering the bus at the end of the lane. He headed for the house still contemplating the discussion that he had with Jim the night before. June had bacon and eggs sizzling on the stove when he sat down at the kitchen table.

"Breakfast is just about there, George."

"No hurry, Hon. Have you had the radio on? That sky looks like crap again this morning. Damn east wind, too."

"No, I haven't. I know the tube was still calling for gradual clearing with a slight chance of a shower when we watched the evening news last night." June served George his breakfast and turned the radio on. "There we can catch the eight o'clock news."

"Thanks. About last night, June." George was devouring his eggs as he spoke. "Jim just seemed really jumpy. I just asked about his friends like Allan had suggested. He mentioned a Megan. Didn't catch much after that. Do you think that he has a girlfriend? It would not surprise me. He seemed pretty defensive. I remember how I felt when my folks started asking about my girlfriends."

"Hate to interrupt your ramblings, George, but the weather will be on shortly. I know what you are saying. Knowing Jim, he probably didn't appreciate you telling him about Allan watching him in town. He has never mentioned a Megan to me but who knows. I sure wouldn't be surprised if he has acquired a girlfriend. He is turning into quite a fine-looking, young man. If he has, I'm sure that he will let us know all about her once he feels comfortable about it. Anyhow, he seemed fine this morning."

George had finished his bacon and was sipping his morning coffee when the radio announcer commenced with the morning weather update. *The clearing that we saw yesterday will be short lived as another low pressure system settles into the area by late today. It will bring generally unsettled weather with light rain possible by mid-week. Look for lows near freezing by late week and clearing into the weekend...* George reached over and shut the radio off.

"I've heard enough of that. Damn it, another week shot. Hopefully those fools are wrong." George finished his cup of coffee and looked up at June. "Sorry about that, Hon. By the way did you order that chicken truck? Those broilers are basically there."

"The truck is coming Friday night. I called last Wednesday as you had asked. Driver said he would call first but expected to be here to load those birds around eight o'clock."

"That sounds good. Friday works well. It's not a school night and it would be good to get the barn emptied before the weather changes again. Something has to work right around here."

"Don't even go there, George." June slipped another cup of coffee into her husband's hand. "The Lord will see that it all gets done. For all we know it may not even rain at all and we will have to stop harvest to load those broilers." She held her husbands hand for a moment and looked directly at him. "Just take it easy and have some faith. It will all work out with a little help from above."

"I know, I know. Well June Edwards perhaps I can swallow this coffee and get finished up out there." He glanced through the dining room window and noticed the fuel truck coming up the lane. "Looks like another bill coming into the yard to me. Damn fuel never stops. One thing about it; they have a vested interest in us finishing harvest too." George hastily swallowed the hot liquid and left the kitchen, stopping only to pull on his rubber boots before exiting the house. He looked up into the grey sky. The air was cool and humid. Scattered raindrops were already hitting the beaten walkway.

10

Jim stood by the curb at Royston High School and looked up into the grey sky. He noticed a brief interlude of blue sky breaking through the cloud cover. It had been a horrid week of seemingly constant showers and definitely cool temperatures. He could hardly wait for the weather to change. A week of this stuff was enough for everyone. Austaire was standing beside him.

"Still watching that sky, eh Jim? Hey, are we taking in the football game tomorrow afternoon? Maybe we could hang out afterwards or something?"

"Shit, I forgot about that game tomorrow. Yes, we get out early for that. What do you want to do tomorrow night anyhow? Is Megan around? You said that you haven't seen her around all week."

"She'll be around by the weekend. Maybe we can visit her later tomorrow night or something. You look like you are deep in thought there, Jim."

Jim was scratching his head. "Oh, I just remembered we are loading birds tomorrow so I can't get in tomorrow night. But we can go to the game until bus time. How about Saturday night? Perhaps I can get the pickup for then?"

"What time are you loading the birds? Perhaps you can get the pickup for tomorrow and then you can leave once the game is finished. Why do you have to load birds, anyhow?"

Jim broke into laughter. "I guess because they won't load themselves." He continued to laugh aloud for awhile. "Sorry about that. They're broilers. You know, eating birds ready for market. Like we sneak into the barn in the dark and grab them and put them all into the liner. Its part of what we do to make a living."

Austaire looked longingly at her boyfriend. "Bout' time that you laughed there. You've been mighty serious this week. Anyways, perhaps you can bring the pickup to school and we can see the whole game and you can take me out Saturday night too."

"I'll see what Dad says. He isn't too humored this week with the weather being what it is. It should be okay, though. I'll call you later if I can. Bus is coming, girl."

The couple exchanged a healthy kiss and embraced each other until Monty's bus drove up the street beside the school. "See yah later, Austaire." Jim walked towards the group waiting for Monty's bus and boarded as soon as the bus was stopped in the parking lot. The public school kids were already onboard and he greeted his sisters with a nod of his head as he walked past them. Jim found a seat towards the rear of the bus next to a window. He glanced outside and watched Austaire walking towards Main Street. He continued his observation until the bus pulled out of the parking lot.

A light rain shower had dampened the Edwards' farm yard by the time the kids arrived home. The chores had been quick and silent as they went about their duties attempting to remain cheerful and upbeat despite the sickening weather. June had prepared a wonderful roast beef dinner in an attempt to lighten the family's spirits. Nevertheless the supper conversation remained constrained until Jim broke the relative silence.

"We've got a football game tomorrow afternoon at school so we all get out early to attend. It should be a good game as we are playin' Groen High School. Hopefully the weather is decent. The field is pretty wet but it's on irregardless."

"Wish we could come to your game, Jim," said Mary.

"Yes, some of the kids in town go over to the High School after classes are finished at three," said Susan.

"You two just have to wait another couple of years and you'll be standing there cheering for Royston High too. In the meantime, it's too bad for you." Jim laughed at the girls and they in turn gave him respective dirty looks. Jim turned to his Dad.

"Anyways Dad, I was wandering if I could take the Ford to school tomorrow so that I could watch the whole game? It'll be over by six and that'll still leave me lots of time to get home to load those birds."

George looked at June, "Great supper, Hon. What time did that trucker say he was coming here?"

June cleared her mouth of food and sipped on her cup of tea. "He wasn't right sure but he figured somewhere around eight. Just after dark is what he said."

George sat back in his chair and looked out the window. The western horizon remained bright despite the prevailing darkness that was setting in. "Sky looks a bit better to the west. Maybe we are starting to run out of this crap. Tell you what, Jim. You can take the Ford in the morning with one stipulation. You slip over to the girl's school at three and pick them up and take them back to watch the game. You guys can drive home together."

The twins looked ecstatic. Susan was quick to respond, "Yes, Jim you can pick us up and take us to the game." The two girls issued a chorus, "Please?"

Jim sneered at the girls and then looked at his parents. His face was serious. "Dad, they'll just be bored watching an old football game. There are hardly any younger kids watching those games. How be I just come home on the bus and perhaps I can take the truck into town Saturday night?"

"Not this weekend son. We will have to get that broiler barn cleaned out this weekend. New chicks arrive in a week's time and that barn has to have some time to air out before they arrive. Sorry, but it's the best that I can offer this weekend."

Jim thought quickly to himself and then spoke directly to the twins. "Looks like you guys are goin' to a football game. I'll pick you up at your school in the afternoon. Just wait out front for me there." He swallowed the last of his vanilla pudding and turned to his parents. "Good supper, Mom. Thanks for the use of the Ford, Dad. I've got homework to do so if you'll excuse me I best be getting her done."

Jim slowly rose from the table and headed downstairs. He tried to hide his anger but could not refrain from cursing to himself when he bumped his toe into one of steps while heading downstairs. He shut the door to his room and picked up his telephone. He dialed Austaire's number and waited. Her familiar voice answered, "Hello."

"Hi Austaire, its Jim. I just wanted you to know that I will bring the pickup in tomorrow morning."

Austaire was quick to respond, "Great, Jim. Are we going out tomorrow night too?"

"Not quite. Actually, I've got to pick up my sisters and take them over to the game. It was the only option Dad gave me."

"So, do you have to go home after, Jim?"

"Yes, I'll have to take the girls home. I told you that we had to load broilers tomorrow night. I was thinking that maybe we could skip school in the morning instead. I'm pretty light for classes tomorrow. So how about you?"

"Yep, we can certainly do that. School is lame anyways. I like that idea big time, Jim. We will make a day out of it somehow. Bring your ride and we will run. Maybe Megan will be back and we can get together or something. I'm excited already."

"Anyways I've gotta' run now, Austaire. See yah in the morning. Bye."

"Kisses, Jim. Night."

Jim carefully put the phone down and sat looking around his room. *Taking one day off school was not going to hurt anything. Besides they had wheels so they had to take advantage of that. He would deliver his Dad's wishes and still enjoy the day. There was more than one way to skin a cat. His Dad had always preached that necessity was the mother of invention. Missing a day of school here and there wasn't the end of the world. He would catch up his homework on the weekend. It would all work out just fine.* Jim spread his homework over the bedspread and studied the items. The math and the English essay could wait. He grabbed his paint easel and installed a fresh canvas before carefully opening some paint and selecting an appropriate brush. He inserted an Enigma tape into his player and contently commenced applying color to the blank canvas.

Upstairs the family had retreated to the living room for the evening. June and the twins were sprawled on the floor enjoying playing a game of Hearts. George sat quietly in his lounge chair reading the Farm Weekly paper. Outside a light but steady, westerly breeze had developed. It rattled the frosted ivy vines surrounding the living room window promising a better tomorrow.

11

The westerly wind continued to blow on Friday morning. The clouds that had prevailed through most of the week were giving way to bursts of sunshine. Jim had offered to give the twins a ride into school. He brought the Ford to a stop in front of their school about eight thirty.

"There you go girls. I will see you two about three. Just wait out front here so that I can see you. Don't keep me waiting."

"Okay there, Jim," said Susan. "We will be ready for you."

"Thanks for the ride," added Mary. "See you then."

Jim watched as the twins entered the school and then he quickly exited the parking lot. He drove quickly to Royston High. Austaire was waiting for him in the rear parking lot. He brought the Ford to an abrupt halt beside her and turned to her as she jumped into the cab. "Good morning."

"Good morning, Jim. Let's get out of here before the buses arrive."

"Okay girl, so where to?"

"I talked with Megan last night. She got in late but said for us to drop by if we wanted. She has some fresh stuff for us to try."

"Oh, I don't know if I want anything at this time of the day, but hey if it pleases you girl why not?"

"Thanks Jim, we don't have to go there. We can just hang out for a while. My parents will be both gone by noon. I just thought that maybe we could visit with Meg for a while since she was gone all week." She looked across at Jim. "You sure shine in denim."

"Thanks, but not half as good as you do." Jim blushed. "So consider it done. Let's leave before some teacher recognizes us."

Jim put the Ford into gear and hit the gas pedal. The rear tires squealed and the back of the truck slid quickly to the left. Jim corrected the swaying motion of the pickup and they hurriedly exited the parking lot just prior to his school bus entering into the unloading zone. Jim looked back in his mirror wondering if the driver, Monty, had recognized the truck. Small towns kept no secrets. Perhaps it was best if they did hang out at Megans.

"Nice day, Jim. Looks like that sunshine your Dad has been looking for is happening."

"Let's hope that it holds for while. I hate it when he gets so upset about things. It's a wonder that he let me take the truck in today. If I hadn't agreed to take the girls to that damn football game it would not have happened. He can be pretty obnoxious at times."

"All parents can be, Jim. Megan keeps telling me that it was the best day of her life when she left home. Sometimes I could just pickup and leave but then where do you go? Megan seems to do well on her own, but she is older too."

"What does Megan do anyhow? She doesn't seem to be hurting for anything?"

"Megan has her goods. She's always talking about her clients in the city too. Whenever I go with her we just chill out somewhere. Like whatever works I guess? Not my business really. Just know that she is awesome and is a best friend, just like you."

"It's about time that we got back to talkin' about ourselves. Did I mention how great you look today?"

"Like only a minute ago. Flattery will get you everywhere, Jim."

"I know. Oh, how I know."

The couple laughed together as Jim pulled into the familiar street where Megan's townhouse was located. A blue Yukon with dark tint windows was pulling out onto the street. It was being followed by a yellow Mustang. Jim recognized the driver. It was Jason, the chap who had delivered the pot last Saturday night. Jim turned to Austaire as he brought the Ford to a halt adjacent Megan's townhouse.

"It looks like Meg was busy this morning."

"Yah, lots of company. Well, let's go see what she's up to. I really feel like a morning fix."

They were just about to hit the doorbell when Megan opened the door. She wore a red housecoat that was loosely tied around her waist with a white cord. She had a white towel rapped around her head. "You're early. I saw you come up the street from upstairs. Come in guys." She grabbed Jim by the waist as he entered the doorway and revealingly swayed her body against him. "You're lookin' good there, Jimmy. They should make denim ads with you."

Austaire headed directly for the kitchen. She was a girl on a mission. After a little commotion she re-entered the living room contently drawing back on a fresh joint. She let a huge draft of the enticing smoke drift across the room as she contentedly sat down on the sofa. "Pay the good lady there Jim and come and join me. It's party time."

Megan stepped aside from Jim. "You heard the girl, Jimmy. Just leave it on the table and chill out. It's time to get it on. Fresh from the kitchen cupboard." She laughed and headed back upstairs turning briefly to look at Jim. "Damn it, you do look good there Jimmy, real good! Have fun."

Jim smiled. He stood still for a second and watched as Megan slowly walked up the stairs. He turned and walked across the room to Austaire holding back his temptation to follow Megan upstairs. Austaire sat on the sofa engulfed in her joint. *He really wished that she didn't trip so much. It's not that he didn't enjoy trippin' with her but just not all the time. It seemed like Austaire never wanted to stop.*

"Sit down Jim and join in. I'm totally stoked over this stuff."

The morning soon slipped into afternoon. Time seemingly stood still as the threesome chilled out in the townhouse. The darkness of the living room was comforting and private. There was no rush, no hurry, just the excitement of the moment. There was nothing to care about and there were no worries to be had. Life was a peaceful and enjoyable string of events that carried no relationship to the outside world.

Outside the day had become ablaze with sunshine. The warm wind brushed leaves quickly up the street. The curtains of Megan's bedroom bellowed out into the room. Jim awoke from his sleep and slowly focused his eyes on the mantle clock. It read three-thirty. *He thought to himself that this time should mean something but brushed it aside.* He turned his attention to the two warm bodies lying on either side of him. He looked again at the clock. It was the game. He had to pick up his sisters for the damn game.

He carefully crawled off the end of the bed attempting not to disturb the other occupants. Austaire briefly turned over but continued with her sleep. Megan lifted up her head and drowsily nodded to Jim. "Goin' somewhere, Sunshine?"

Jim whispered, "Gotta' pick up my sisters for the football game." He let out a soft chuckle. "It appears like I'm a little late. They will be waiting for me at their school. I promised Dad that I would pick them up in exchange for using the pickup. Damn, I hope that they don't call home lookin' for me."

Jim dressed as quickly as was possible. His mind was telling him that he was late but his head was still pretty foggy. "Thanks again, Meg. I won't wake, Austaire. Do you think that you can take her home? She knows that I have to go."

"No problem there, Jimmy. Come give me a kiss for her."

Jim walked over to the bed and softly kissed Megan. Her lips were inviting him back into the bed. She looked longingly into his eyes. "Sure you have to leave?"

"Oh, I wish that I did not have to but duty calls. Damn you are hot, Meg."

"I know, Jimmy. I know. If you ever run into a problem you know that both you and Austaire are welcome here, anytime. I'm always here on the weekends and you can always leave me a message on the machine."

"Thanks. Catch you later, Meg."

Jim turned and left the room. He was still struggling with his belt. It seemed to be stuck or something. *He mused at how funny it was for the buckle to suddenly not work properly.* He entered the bathroom and dampened a facecloth. The wet facecloth felt good against his skin. He found his watch that he had misplaced from the prior weekend and strapped it onto his wrist. It said four o'clock. He giggled about finding his watch oblivious to the fact that he was so late. He walked downstairs and grabbed his jacket glancing at the currency that he had placed on the coffee table earlier. *Money well invested he thought to himself.* The late afternoon sunshine hit him as he left the townhouse. Lord, was it nice out.

The girls were still waiting in front of the school when Jim pulled up front. He was thankful that they had waited for him. He watched them as they climbed into the cab of the Ford. Susan was the first to speak.

"Nice timing there, Jim. Mary and I were beginning to think that you had forgotten about us. Is the game still on?"

"Yes, it's about half time. Sorry about that girls. We got out early and some of us went over to Dobeys. Just forgot the time."

"We were just about ready to call home," said Mary.

"You haven't called home then? That's great. I would have been in shit. Thanks girls. Are you two hungry?"

"Sure Jim," said Mary, "But I thought that you said that you had just came from Dobeys?"

"Just had a Coke. Anyways I'm starved. It's my treat. We can catch a burger and then finish up the game. Or I can drop you two off at school and come back?"

"No way, Jim," said Susan. "We are not letting you out of our sight. Besides you owe us."

Mary burst in, "Again brother."

"Okay girls, the treats are on me. Just remember that it was a great first half of football that you saw."

The twins laughed contently as Jim navigated out of the parking area and headed towards Dobeys. He felt a strong urge to wipe his brow. He grabbed a Kleenex from the dispenser and wiped the sweat from his forehead. He fought to concentrate on the road and the driving.

"You okay?" asked Mary. "You don't look so good."

"I'm fine, just nerves or something. Sure did turn out to be a nice day."

"Yes, Dad should be in a better humor when we get home," said Susan. "I know that he worries about the weather and the crops this time of the year."

"Dad worries about everything, all of the time," said Mary. "I'm used to it just so long as he doesn't blow up."

"Dad is Dad," replied Susan. "His temper is bad but he's okay. Not like Mom though. I just hope that this weather stays so that you guys can get back to the harvest. Are you feelin' better, Jim?"

"Yes, just a chill or something. What's with you and your concern for your dear brother all of a sudden?" Jim let out a loud laugh as he turned the Ford off Twelfth Street into Dobeys parking area. "Well, we're here."

Mary looked at her brother. "Awesome. Hey Jim, I don't know what you were doing before you picked us up but you stink. Next time Susan can sit beside you. Have you been smoking? Dad will kill you if you are."

"Thanks a lot sis'. I'll remember that the next time you land in the chicken shit. No, I am not smoking but lots of my friends do. It's not the end of the world. Anyways, let's get in. I can smell those burgers from here."

The kids left the Ford and walked hastily towards Dobeys. The bright sunshine and brisk wind continued to bathe them with fall warmth. *Jim thought how fortunate everything had worked out. His mind was slowly clearing and he was able to focus more clearly now.* He opened the door for the girls and eagerly followed them in. He was so hungry. The wind blew into the doorway as they entered and he dragged his hands through his hair once inside. Did he really smell? He let out a quiet chuckle and sat down in a booth with his two sisters. Damn those burgers smelt good.

Glen Rollins entered the burger joint shortly after the kids were seated. He spied them sitting together and walked directly towards their booth. "Mine if I sit with you?"

"No problem there, Glen. We were just ordering some burgers. Are you hungry too?"

"No, I'm just looking for a coke. It's half-time at the game." Glen looked at the twins, "Are you girls looking after your big brother today?"

"Someone has to," Mary laughed, "Our brother has his moments."

The waitress arrived with their order and quickly dispersed it around the table. Glen picked up his coke and returned to the booth and sat down. "So I didn't see you around today?"

Jim leaned over to Glen and whispered into his ear, "Not in front of the twins." He then sat back in his seat and took a large bite from his burger. "I must have just missed you. I was pretty occupied." He smiled at Glen. "So how's the game going?"

"We're ahead by seven points at half time. It's an okay game so far as football goes. The day sure turned out nice for it."

"The girls and I were going over after so perhaps we can go together if you want?"

"Sure. Perhaps you can give me a ride home then? It would save me calling my Dad later."

"No problem." Jim finished the last of his fries and swallowed the soda. "Damn that was good. Well girls, how be we go and take in the balance of that game? It's good to have you with us, Glen." He glanced over at his friend before getting up to leave, "Like, really good!"

12

George Edwards sat on the edge of the bed struggling to get his mind in gear. The alarm had gone off promptly at five o'clock that morning but the work from the previous night had taken its toll on everyone in the family. The kids had been late arriving home after their football game but fortunately the trucker had not arrived until almost nine o'clock. It had made for a very late evening as they had not finished loading the birds until nearly eleven. June came back in from the bathroom.

"Hey there, farm boy. It's not like you to be slow off the start." She sat down beside George. "Those birds poop you out last night?"

"Very funny there misses. I'm running. It sounds quiet out there. That wind must have stopped overnight. That sunset sure looked promising last night. Another couple of days of this and we will be running again."

"Yes, the weather looks promising. You and Jim are cleaning out the broiler barn today?"

"Yes, we had better get it done. Give it a chance to air out before those chicks arrive next Saturday. It was Saturday?"

"Yep, they will be here around nine or so. Just like always. Well I had better see if there is any life out there."

"Yes, they worked hard last night. I shouldn't have blown up at them for being a bit late. There was no harm done."

"You have to start giving them a bit of leeway, George. They try so hard to please you."

"Yes and if you don't keep them in line they will eventually run all over you. Young Jim there is getting pretty independent."

"Just like his father? You raise them to leave you. That's what you've always said." June planted a light kiss on her husband's forehead and looked out the window. The first glimpse of morning light was beginning to shine through the window. "Looks like another nice one."

"Yep and with that Mrs. Edwards I had better get rollin'." George finished pulling on his trousers and tucked in his shirt. "I'm just going to take a quick look at some swaths and make sure that manure field is dry enough. I can get Jim hauling right after breakfast." He returned a kiss on June's cheek and headed out of the bedroom. "Catch you in bit. Love Yah."

"Love you too, George. I'll get those kids rolling."

George hopped into the old Chev and headed down the lane. The sun was rising on the eastern horizon and it cast shadows into the cab. The air was still and he rolled the window down to let some morning freshness hit his face. It felt good. Soon they would be back on track putting that harvested grain into storage.

He stopped at a field they had already harvested and stepped out of the truck. The black soil still stuck lightly on his boots as he walked but it would carry the tractor and spreader. He was amazed that the soil was still that damp. Back to the Chev he trod and drove down the road another mile bringing the pickup to a halt beside a field of swathed barley. He slowly ventured out into the field carefully avoiding stepping on the swaths. He methodically lifted the grain in his hands and felt the moisture that remained at the base of the straw. It was still damp. *Definitely not dry enough yet but give it two days he thought.* Satisfied with his findings he jumped back into the Chev and headed home.

The warm sunshine provided a perfect backdrop for the day's activities. Jim was kept busy hauling as George and the girls performed clean up duties in the broiler barn. By late afternoon they had finished the cleaning and Jim had headed to the field with the last load. From the open door of the empty barn George watched his son drive out the lane. All of a sudden the tractor veered to the left and George watched as the unit bounced off the roadway into the ditch and then back onto the roadway. He ran to the Chev and headed out the lane. He caught up to his son in the field and ran to the tractor shouting.

"What the hell was that back there? Is everything okay?"

"Sorry about that, Dad. My mind must have wandered for a minute there. Everything is fine. It's all good. Nothing hurt."

"Damn it all, you could have wrecked the spreader or flipped the tractor. Sometimes I wonder if you keep your brains in your damn feet."

"I'm just a little tired, that's all. We were pretty late last night."

"Don't you go interrupting me there young man. If you are getting tired then let me finish here. Just don't go breaking the damn machine."

"I'm okay, Dad. It was just some loose gravel. I'm fine. Just because harvest is going slowly you don't have to take it out on me."

"This has nothing to do with the damn harvest and you know it. Anyways I'd best be getting back. Just smarten up and if you can't manage let me know. You kids sometimes just get too cocky and don't watch what you're doing."

"This has nothing to do with kids, Dad. I just goofed off for a moment. Megan says that adults blame us for everything even when nothing happens."

"And who the hell is Megan, anyways? You mentioned her before. Got yourself a girlfriend in town and she is fillin' your head with foolishness?" George glared at his son and Jim contently returned the glare back.

"No, she is not my girlfriend and I will make up my own mind on things. I'm old enough to make my own decisions. Besides this has nothing to do with anything. I slipped up. It will not happen again. Damn it anyways. I've been driving damn tractors since I was seven."

"Well just learn to be more careful." George stamped the soil on his boots and turned to walk back to the Chev. "Just be careful. We are not made of money and I don't need you or anyone else getting hurt from stinking foolishness. I know that you are a good operator. Just keep your mind on what the hell you are doing."

George walked back to the pickup and headed onto the roadway. He looked back into the mirror and glanced at the spreader in the field. Jim was unloading his load. George shook his head and drove home.

It was five o'clock by the time everyone had washed up for supper. June had prepared a virtual feast for her family. The table was adorned with platters full of pork chops, mashed potatoes, green beans and gravy. The family members were quick to sit themselves around the table and commenced eating immediately after June had said the blessing. The sun was well into the west but it still cast warm rays across the table as the family ate. The room was quiet as the hungry participants eagerly devoured their meal. June looked across the table at her crew. "Wow, I've got a hungry bunch here. Best save a little room for dessert though. Any takers for warm, apple pie and ice cream?"

"You sure know how to quench an appetite Mom," said Jim. "This is great."

George, content with finishing off his pork chop was quick to add. "Yes, super meal, June. Makes a days effort seem worthwhile."

"I watched you guys working so hard so I thought you'd be hungry."

"Aren't we always, June?" George said and then let out a little laugh. "Young Jim here is always hungry."

"Thanks a lot, Dad. With food like this it is pretty easy to be hungry."

The twins nodded their heads in agreement. June proceeded to serve the dessert to her complimentary family. The room clang with the sounds of forks sliding into the pieces of warm pie. George looked up at the clock and turned to Mary.

"Turn the news on, Mary. It's almost six. Time to come see what all is wrong with the world today. Best catch the weather too."

"Sure Dad."

George finished up his desert and wiped his mouth with a napkin. The television was on now and he decided to make his way into the living room and listen to the broadcast. He carried his cup of tea and made himself comfortable. He was soon absorbed in the broadcast. Jim tugged at his shirt sleeve.

"Can I talk to you for a minute, Dad?"

"What's up son?"

"I was just wondering if I could run into Royston for awhile seeing' as we finished early and all. I thought that maybe I'd see if Glen was around."

"This is coming from the same young man that could not keep his eyes open earlier. I think that you had better stay put tonight and get some rest. We could have a game of crib if you feel like it?"

"I wouldn't be late. I'm wide awake now."

"Not tonight son. You did a big days work. We all did. We need to get our rest. Hopefully, we've got a busy week coming next week."

"Please Dad, I'd back by midnight. We don't have much for chores tomorrow with the broiler barn sitting empty. It doesn't take us long to do the layers."

"Jim, read my lips. The answer is no. I just think that it would be better if you get your rest tonight."

"Okay, you're probably right." Jim shrugged his shoulders and turned and left the room. "I guess that I'll go downstairs and start some homework."

"My cribbage invitation still stands if you feel up to it."

"Maybe later, Dad. I'll see in a bit."

George briefly watched his son leave the room and then turned his attention back to the news broadcast. *Look for another day of sunshine with increasing cloudiness by late day tomorrow. Monday will see rain returning to the forecast with unsettled conditions continuing until the middle of next week.* George hit the remote and tossed it onto the floor. "Damn the weather anyways."

"Something wrong, George?" June called from the kitchen.

"Oh, they're calling for some more rain again. What else is new? Those swaths were actually starting to dry again."

June finished up her dishes and entered the living room and sat down with her husband. They sat together in silence. June turned the television back on and switched the channel. "That's enough of the news for now?"

"Yes, sometimes I wonder if I should even turn it on. That sky looked pretty good tonight so who knows?"

The evening past slowly as the couple watched a couple of programs. They were eventually joined by the twins who sat down and entertained themselves with a game of UNO. Jim remained in his room. They exited the room by eight-thirty and headed to bed. By nine o'clock the house was dark and everyone was asleep; everyone but Jim. He had gone downstairs and had a little nap and then sat in the quiet of his room patiently waiting.

He lay on his bed feeling much renewed from his little cat nap. *Sometimes his parents just didn't get it. They might be worn out from the day's activities but they were not young anymore. The weather forecast looked lousy again so they might not even be harvesting next week. Meanwhile there was a perfectly good party going on at Megans and he might as well take it in. He should have invited Glen but had fallen asleep before getting around to calling him. Glen was fun to be with and a good friend but what he needed right now was his girl. If he was really quiet he should be able to leave and return without anyone knowing. What his folks didn't know would not hurt them.*

He quietly left his room and ever so slowly climbed up the stairs. He reached into the kitchen and grabbed the keys to the Ford and ever so quietly exited the building. The night air felt inviting as he carefully crept around the front of the house. The Ford had been left over by the fuel tanks which made it partially hidden by the garage. Jim opened the driver's door and inserted the key. *Here goes nothing he thought to himself as he turned the ignition.* The engine came to life and Jim put the transmission into drive. Slowly the truck drove out the laneway in the darkness of the night. He left the lights off until he was onto the front road and then he disappeared towards Royston.

13

The first rays of the morning sunshine were cascading through the bedroom window. A light breeze from the east had started during the night and it rattled the remaining dead leaves on the aspens. A few orange-colored leaves had floated down to the window sill and were dancing along the sill; seemingly attached to the wood. The noise awoke George from a sound sleep. He looked at the alarm clock. It was seven-thirty. He turned quickly to June.

"Wake up. Damn alarm didn't go off. Hey there, June. If you want us to go to church then you had best be rising and shining." George was hastily pulling on his clothes. "You can send the girls out to the layer barn. I'll get Jim up on the way out. It won't take long. Just have to get the eggs sorted. Are you listening?"

"Yes. Since when have you been in so much of a hurry to get to church?"

"Right now I need all the help that I can muster. Figure if the Good Lord looks upon us kindly it isn't going to hurt anything. I'm gone."

A still drossy June replied, "Don't you want some breakfast or at least a coffee?"

"Maybe a quick coffee, Hon. I'll get Jim up and catch it on the way out."

"Okay, I'll have it ready. Church isn't until ten. We'll be fine."

George walked into the bathroom and gave his face a quick wash and then decided to shave. He departed from the bathroom as the girls were rising in their room.

"Hey there, you two. It's time to get up and rolling. Give your Mom a hand and then head out to the layer barn."

"Morning Dad, we'll be there shortly," said Mary.

George proceeded downstairs and knocked on Jim's door. He carefully entered the room and turned on the light. Jim was still fast asleep in his bed. George slipped over to the bed and lightly shook his son's shoulder. "Hey there, sleepy head. It's time to rise and shine. We're running late here." Jim did not reply at first and George commenced to shaking his son in a more vigorous manner. "Come on there, Jim. I figured you'd be up and runnin' after getting to bed so early last night. Hey, let's wake up."

A very groggy Jim finally acknowledged his fathers actions and turned over slowly to face him. In a slow and painful manner he managed to squeak out, "Morning."

"It's time to get up. Your Mom will have our hides if we are late for church. I'll be upstairs. I'm going to grab a coffee first. You look like you need one too."

"Yes, I'll be up shortly."

"Since when have you been wearing your clothes to bed son. I know that you were tired last night but your Mom sure wouldn't approve. Are you feeling okay? You look pretty white. Christ, what is that smell? Did you not shower last night?"

"I'm okay. I'll be up shortly, Dad. You go ahead."

"See you in a bit then."

"Be right there, Dad. I'll just grab a quick wash."

Jim managed to pull himself upright and followed his Dad out the door. He headed directly for the basement bathroom and shut the door. He managed to get to the sink before his nose started to bleed. He splashed some warm water on his face. In the process he managed to slip against the sink falling to the floor. George burst into the room.

"What the hell? Jim, you're not okay." George yelled up to June. "Jim's got a bad nose bleed down here. Need some ice down here. June!"

George picked up his son and propped him up on the toilet. June was quick to arrive. She held an ice-cold cloth under Jim's nose. "Hold his head back, George." After several minutes the nose bleed was contained. "There, just keep your head back, Jim. What brought that on? That was a bad one."

"Don't know, Mom. I just felt it coming on when I was walking over here. I'm fine now."

"You don't look fine. What are you doin' wearing those clothes. I thought that you had a shower last night."

George looked directly at his son, "You look pretty pale son. Perhaps you had better just lie down for awhile and rest. Your eyes look mighty red. Did you sleep okay?"

"I'm fine, really. Maybe a touch of flu or something. There's always lots of stuff going around at school."

"Yes, you had better stay put this morning and rest," said June. "A rest will do you good. Just let us know if you get another nose bleed like that. You never get nose bleeds."

"Let me help you back to your room," said George. "Just take it slowly. Bring that cloth incase you need it again." George helped Jim back to his room and left him there with June. "I'll get out to chores. I'll grab that coffee and run."

George arrived in the kitchen just as the wall phone began ringing. He grabbed the receiver off the wall and answered, "Hello." It was Allan Heiner.

"Morning George, didn't expect to get you on the phone?"

"I'm just getting a coffee. We're running a bit late here. What's up?"

"Oh, nothin' much. Just wondering if you and Jim might want to go fishing or something this afternoon? I have to go back to the shop for a bit this morning for a customer but I'm free later."

"No church today?"

"Not today. Don't like it but I've got a little problem that can't wait. Anyways, are you interested?"

"Yes, we'll see how things work out here, Allan. Jim is under the weather this morning. We might have to slide into Royston later."

"Two days in row. You're setting a record, George."

"Don't understand, Allan. We didn't go anywhere yesterday. Must have been someone else?"

"Sure looked like your Ford. I just noticed it turning off Main Street when we left the theatre last night."

"Not here, Allan. We cleaned the broiler barn yesterday and lights were out early. Anyways, I gotta' run. I'll give you a call after lunch and let you know."

"That sounds good. I will be lookin' forward to hearing from you."

George slapped the receiver down and hurriedly finished swallowing the cup of coffee. It was getting cold and it was less than appealing. "Girls, are you ready?"

"They're already out," said June as she walked up the basement stairs. "Jim's sleeping. I'll check in on him later."

"Great. Allan asked us out this afternoon if Jim feels better. I'll see though. I should grease some machinery too. Well, I'm outa' here."

George walked hastily towards the layer barn. The east wind had gained momentum and it tugged at his ball cap. He pulled the brow down firmly to his head. For a fall morning the sun felt warm and inviting. *Three days without rain he thought. Surely the forecast was wrong. They really needed to get back at that harvest.* He briefly studied the yard as he walked. Everything looked where it should be. *Funny that Allan should mention the truck. It would be very easy to be mistaken. Those Fords were everywhere.* He shrugged his shoulders and entered the barn.

The Edwards family finished their chores, ate a light breakfast and dressed for church. At a quarter to ten the family, minus Jim, was on their way out the lane. George turned on to the main road and accelerated as quickly as was safely possible. He glanced down at the fuel gauge and made a mental reminder to fill the tank when they got home.

14

Jim awoke about eleven-thirty. He lay there in the silence of his room allowing his eyes to adjust to the dim light that entered from under his door. His nose was still tender to the touch but there had been no further occurrence of a nose bleed. He crawled off the bed, grabbed some clean clothes and slowly made his way to the shower stall. He undressed, turned on the hot water and stepped inside the stall. The warm water cascaded over his aching head and washed down his body. He would enjoy a long and comforting shower.

Once dried off he dressed, combed his hair and walked back into his bedroom. He turned on the light switch and glanced at his wall clock. The folks would be home soon but perhaps he had time to try Austaire. He picked up the receiver and dialed her number. The phone rang several times before a lady answered, "Hello."

"Yes, Mrs. Jamieson, is Austaire there?"

"No, we haven't seen her since last night. Probably stayed with a friend and who is this calling?"

"Jim Edwards. Could you let her know that I called when she gets back?"

"Jim Edwards. Yes, she has mentioned you. You are the farm boy. Yes, I'll let her know, Jim. Goodbye."

"Bye. Have a good day, Mrs. Jamieson."

Jim hung up the receiver and listened carefully. It was still quiet outside. He quickly dialed Megan's phone number. A drowsy Megan answered on the other end, "Hello".

"Hi, Megan, it's Jim. Don't suppose that Austaire is still there?"

"Yes, I think that I heard her in the shower. Do you want me to get her?"

"No, that's okay. Let her enjoy her shower."

"It was great to see you again last night, Jimmy. I trust that you made it home in time?"

"Barely, but I did. Folks let me sleep in because of my nose bleed earlier. It was a pretty bad one."

"Don't be concerned about the nose bleed. They will pass. It's all good in time. Anyways I should be getting on."

"Yes, my folks will be home from church soon and I had best be upstairs by then."

"Hey, Jimmy. Here's someone that wanted to say hi."

"Morning, Jim."

"Hi Austaire, you're lookin' good."

"Yes, I'm all showered up and looking for you. I got pretty wasted last night. It was another awesome party. You were your usual great self."

"It was just great to be with you guys again. Those parties that Meg throws are totally awesome. Her basement makes for the ultimate dance floor. What was the powder we took last night? Sure picked me up in a hurry. It was a real rush."

"Just have to condition yourself some," Austaire laughed. "Coke gives you such a great high doesn't it?"

"Well I'd better get, Austaire. I think I hear the pickup in the yard."

"Have a great one, Jim."

"Catch you tomorrow, Austaire. I've gotta' run. Bye."

Jim hung the receiver up just as the door to the back porch opened. He swept the comb once more through his damp hair. He stared briefly into his mirror and gave himself a nod of approval. Then with a burst of youthful energy he ascended the stairway just in time to greet his Mother.

"Hello, Mom. Sorry about missing church and all."

"That's okay. Are you feeling better? You look better. We thought that we might have to take you into emergency if that nosebleed had continued."

"It's all gone now. It's all good now, Mom."

"You still look pale to me. You had best take it easy today."

"Sure thing Mom, but right now I feel pretty hungry. Let me help you make lunch. It's the least I can do for missing church and chores this morning."

June looked solemnly at her son for a second. "Take care of yourself, Jim. I know that you've got growing pains but even youth needs its rest. We love you, son." She then entered the kitchen before turning around to look at Jim again. "Well, what are you waiting for?" June smiled at her son, "I can't refuse an offer to help get lunch ready, now can I?"

Jim stood on the steps for a minute and watched as his mother busied herself preparing lunch. She was totally a machine when it came to preparing food. *He thought how she seemed so at home in her element. He questioned her comment on looking after himself and getting enough rest. Did she suspect something and was keeping it to herself. Mom was like that sometimes.* He shrugged off the thought and started carrying dishes to the table. He was so totally hungry.

15

Monday morning had thrown a twisted wrench into the weather forecast. The low pressure zone had swept through the region during the night and unfortunately dusted the area with a light rain. But it was not to remain long as strong, westerly winds were once again the dominant force and the low lying clouds that had prevailed earlier in the day were quickly being blown to the east. Blue skies stretched far into the western horizon by noon. George sat down for lunch feeling content with the world.

"Damn it, June. I think that we're through the worst of it. That wind is blowing like crazy again. I'm going to try cutting wheat again tomorrow if it stays."

"Sounds great, Hon. September is creeping along. I just know that those west winds are a good omen. Praise the Lord. I had best get that garden cleaned up this week before we really get busy again."

"Yes, I can probably give you a hand this afternoon if you like? The kids can help us with the potatoes later. Talking bout' the kids, June. Did you notice anything disturbing about Jim yesterday morning? I mean his body odor. Probably wasn't anything. I just can't help tossing over Allan's concerns in my head. I know that he was feeling under the weather."

"Relax there, George. He just caught something. He probably was so tired on Saturday night that he forgot to shower. He did fall asleep with his clothes on. He had changed before supper but he may not have showered."

"You're probably right, June. He certainly wasn't feeling good."

"And he really made an effort to help me with lunch yesterday. He felt badly about missing church."

"You two certainly made a great lunch. Hopefully he got rested yesterday. We just might get busy here again by the look of that sky. Gonna' need him big time."

The afternoon went quickly as June and George gathered in the remaining rows of beets, carrots, and turnips left in the garden. The moist soil provided easy access to pulling the valued vegetables that June would preserve for the winter months ahead. George was just finishing carrying the last basket into the cold storage when the school bus turned into their driveway.

"Kids are home, June. We can get some of those potatoes dug before supper."

"Sounds good, George. I'll get the burlap bags from the basement."

George went to the shop to find the fork for digging the potatoes. When he returned to the garden area the girls were already chatting with their mother. Mary greeted her father with a hesitant, "Hi Dad, how was your day?"

"Fine, your mother and I have been busy with the garden. You girls and Jim can give me a hand with some potatoes before supper."

There was a brief moment of silence as the girls exchanged glances amongst each other and their mother. Susan blurted out, "Jim's not here yet."

"Come again? Did he miss the bus again?"

"He wasn't at the school when Monty arrived," said Mary. She quickly added, "He may be getting a ride home with Glen or something."

"Has he called?"

"Not yet. We've been outside all this time so I'd better check the answering machine. When he calls I'll have to go pick him up."

"Not today, June. When he calls I will go and pick him up. This is getting to be ridiculous. It's an everyday occurrence. Well girls you might as well get changed and we will pick potatoes until we hear from your brother." The twins walked quickly into the house leaving George and June alone in the garden. George watched them enter the back porch and then threw the garden fork deep into the soft soil. "Damn this foolishness."

"Oh, I hope that everything is okay, George. Anyways I had best check that answering machine."

"So help me, June. When that young lad gets home I'm going to tan his hide."

George heaved on the garden fork and almost broke a tang pulling it from the black soil. He commenced digging into a row of deadened potato tops, well blackened by the early frosts. He dug quickly and earnestly trying desperately to ease his tension and calm his temper. He shoveled the fresh potatoes off to the side of the freshly dug hill concentrating only on the job at hand.

The girls were quick to return to the garden and worked hard bagging the new potatoes. June came back from the house to give them a hand.

"There's nothing on the machine, George. I'm sure that he won't be long. It's not like Jim to not call. He would have called if he needed a ride."

"If he knows what's good for him he had better be getting home soon; real soon."

George had barely gotten the words from his mouth when Glen Rollins brown Ranger pulled into the yard. Jim jumped out of the pickup and waived goodbye to Glen while running into the house. Glen waived to the family from his open window and exited the yard leaving a light trail of dust behind him. Within five minutes Jim appeared back outside at the garden site. "Hi guys."

"Where have you been?" asked George.

"I just got a ride home with Glen. We were working on a project together. He offered me a ride earlier."

"Well, you could have informed us. We didn't know where in the hell you were. All you have to do is leave a damn message or give us a call at lunch or something."

"I didn't think that it mattered if I was home at my regular time. Monty knows that we older kids often find alternative ways home at night. God, you look like I've done something wrong, Dad. I haven't done anything wrong."

"Let me be the judge of that, Jim."

"Do you want some help or not? I just arrived home and already you guys are jumping on my back."

"Okay, enough of that in front of the girls. You and I can talk later. You can start carrying those bags into cold storage for your mother. I'll get back to digging. Okay girls, show is over. Let's get back to work."

"Dad, I didn't say anything."

"Jim, enough!"

One could have heard a pin drop in the silence that followed. Everyone returned to their assigned duties. Jim dug in his heels and lifted the heavy sack of potatoes over his shoulder and headed towards the root cellar. At seventeen he was very strong for his stature. He handled the eighty-pound sack with relative ease. George watched from one corner of his eye as Jim descended into the root cellar with his precious load. Perhaps he had been too strong in his words. Perhaps his suspicions were unfounded. June was probably right. Still they must talk later.

June went into the house to prepare supper around six. George finished his seventh row and stuck the fork into the ground. He watched with satisfaction as the twins jammed the burlap sacks with the newly dug potatoes and Jim continued to deliver the heavy packages into the root cellar. George counted the remaining rows. They were about 1/3 finished. It was time to perform evening chores in the layer barn. "Just finish up here kids. I'll get the layers tonight."

"Okay, Dad," said Susan. "We won't be long here."

Supper was not finished until almost eight o'clock. The girls had offered to help their mother wash dishes while Jim had left almost immediately after the meal to attend to his homework. George finished his second cup of tea and walked downstairs to Jim's room. He knocked on the door and entered his son's room.

"How's the homework coming?"

"Good, I've got a project I'm working on in art class. Wanta' see?"

"You bet. Is that an oil painting?"

"Yes, it's an abstract, Dad. What do you think?"

George briefly studied the starkly colored lines and images trying to make sense of the picture. *What appeared as a tree was forbidding and cold to him.* He managed, "It's very challenging. What is it?"

"It's a nature scene. It represents winter. The tree is death."

"Yes, it looks cold. Whatever happened to the nice scenes that you painted before? Many think that you have a real talent in art. This is pretty grotesque to me."

"It's just an expression. I'm expressing a feeling through the picture."

"You've got that right. I just find it frightening. Anyways, I came down to talk with you about today."

"You're not going to come down on me again over getting a ride with Glen are you? He has the Ranger quite often and he doesn't mind dropping me off. We're working on a project together."

"No, but you should of let us know what was going on. I know that you're busy with your school activities too. Let's start over here. How be we let you take the Ford to school during harvest? That will allow you to get in and back in good time and it gives you some flexibility. We will be getting back to harvest tomorrow and I just need to be able to count on everyone. We can make out with the old Chev if we need a part or something. I've already asked your Mother to let Monty know what we are doing."

"So, I take the girls with me?"

"Yes, just during harvest. Interested?"

"Sure Dad. Thanks. I know that it will help."

"Great. Just keep her fueled up so I don't have to worry about it and no foolishness, okay? The first time we have an issue it will stop."

"It sounds good here. So we are definitely starting up again tomorrow?"

"Yes, the weather looks good again. I'll start back at straight cutting wheat while the swaths dry. It'll be tough and we'll have to dry it so I'm counting on you to either take over the combine or run the grain drier."

"You can count on me."

"Well, I'd better leave you to your abstract. See you in the morning. Don't stay up too late."

"Night, Dad. Thanks again."

George exited the room and closed the door carefully behind him. *He was trusting that this would help inspire his son. He hoped that it would help*

Stephen Pain   **63**

with the harvest effort. In the meantime he was tired and anxious for sleep. He slowly walked up the stairs and headed across the kitchen.

June was on the telephone. "George just came upstairs, Elaine. Nice talkin' to you." She handed the receiver to George, "It's your mother."

"Hello Mom, what brings you on the phone at this hour of the night? Everything okay out there? Is Dad fine?"

"We are all fine here," answered Elaine. "Ronald and I just thought that we would catch you in at this time of the day. June tells me that the harvest is going slow but your weather is changing for the better again."

"Yes, it definitely looks better, Mom. We need a break now. So you two are well and life is good?"

"Oh yes. Anyways, I'll give you your father. He has something to ask you."

"You take care, Mom. Bye for now." George waited for a few seconds and then heard his father picking up the phone on the other end. "Good evening, sir."

"How's George tonight? You're probably headed for bed so I will not keep you long."

"That's okay, Dad. What can we do for you?"

"Your mother and I were wondering if you folks would like some visitors for Christmas this year. We haven't been out for awhile and we thought that perhaps it was due time. The kids keep growing on us. We know how hard it is for you to come this way. So what do you think? Would you have room for a couple of old farts out your way?"

George hesitated for a moment as he put the receiver to his shoulder and turned to June. "They want to come out for Christmas, Hon."

June beamed with approval and blurted out, "Of course, that would be wonderful."

"Are you still there, George?" Ronald waited and asked again, "George?"

"Sorry Dad, I was just talking to June for a second there. We would love to have you two out for the holidays. The kids will be ecstatic to hear the good news. When do you think you will arrive here?"

There was a slight pause at the other end of the line this time as Ronald cleared his voice. "We were wondering if we might stay most of December, George? Your mother can get a pretty good deal on some flights if we arrive early in the month. We just thought that it would be nice to have a good visit and not be rushed and then we could come home before New Years."

"That is simply wonderful, Dad. This is the best Christmas gift that we could ever ask for. We haven't seen you guys in ages."

"Well, I'd better run, son. This is long distance. Elaine will touch base with June once we have the tickets booked. We'll just rent a car out there so you don't have to worry about picking us up or anything. Good luck with the harvest. Good night, son."

"Thanks. Good night, Dad. Catch you later."

George set the receiver down and looked up at June. "They'll be here all December. You okay with that?"

June gave George a light hug and looked up into his dark eyes. "It's about time that they stayed out here for awhile. We'll give them some good western hospitality and have a very special Christmas together. To use Jim's expression, it's all good, George."

Mary had gotten up to go to the bathroom and looked across at her parents in the dim light of the hallway. "What's up?" she asked. "You two look pretty excited."

"Grandma and Grandpa Edwards are coming out for Christmas," said June quietly. "Actually, they will be visiting us for most of December. We just got off the phone with them."

"Wow. They're going to be here for Christmas," said Mary excitedly. "Just wait until I tell Susan. This is great!"

"Quiet now, Mary. Don't go waking her up," said George. "You can tell her in the morning." He glanced over at the kitchen clock. "Talking about morning, I think that we had all better get to bed. Morning will come soon enough for all of us."

The rooms in the house were soon filled with darkness. The excited family members initially struggled to fall asleep as the prospects of the impending visit filled their minds. They finally succumbed to the need for sleep and the household grew very silent. In the basement a faint light still cast a shadow underneath Jim's bedroom door. Inside the room the diligent artist continued with his abstract oblivious to the time. He had caught broken bits of the conversation upstairs and was excited about seeing his grandparents too.

16

Monday morning saw the Edwards's farm bathing in the rays of early fall sunshine. Jim had slept very well and was feeling on top of the world. His Dad had definitely surprised him with the truck offer and he felt a renewed sense of importance and responsibility. Jim had dropped the twins off at Royston Elementary and proceeded back to the High School. He parked the Ford and entered the school heading directly to his locker. In the midst of arranging some books Jim felt a tap on his shoulder and turned quickly expecting to see Austaire. It was Glen Rollins.

"Good morning. I didn't see you on the bus."

"Dad is letting me use the Ford during harvest so you will probably not see me on the bus. So if you are looking for a ride just holler. Thanks again for giving me a ride home yesterday. I would have missed the bus again."

"No problem. My Dad had asked me to pick up those parts so I had the truck. I'll keep your ride offer in the back of my mind. Have you got that English assignment for Miss Harris finished? I'm sure that it is due today?"

"Oh shit, I forgot about that bloody assignment. When do we have English?" Jim glanced down his timetable that was taped to the inside of his locker door. "We don't have English until this aft'. I've got a spare this morning. I'll get it done then. Thanks for reminding me."

"No problem there, Jim." Glen padded his friend on the back. "By the way how is Megan? Any parties comin' up?"

Jim smiled and turned towards Glen. "It seems like there is always a party. I think that they have another group hitting her place for Friday night. I'll let you know."

"Thanks. I'll tell you one thing. You sure have your hands full." The two boys smiled and then burst into laughter just as the nine o'clock bell sounded.

Jim's spare was just before lunch hour and he had gone into the cafeteria to work on the English assignment. He had not seen Austaire in class this morning and was wondering if she was ill. He wished that he had a cell phone to call her. That had been another heated debate with his folks. It had been made clear that a cell phone was definitely not in the budget this year. Austaire broke his train of thought.

"Hello, Jim. I looked all over for you. What's up?"

"I'm just getting this English done. You're late." Jim looked sincerely at his girlfriend. "So how you doin'? Your clothes are totally rad, but you look kinda' pale?"

"Yah, I'm fine." Austaire pulled her chair up closer to Jim and whispered in his ear, "I need to talk to you in private."

"It sounds important. Sure, but can it wait until lunch time?"

"Maybe we could go over to Dobeys and catch a bite now and talk before the crowd comes, Jim?"

Jim looked at his assignment and then looked up at his girl. "Okay, just let me drop these books in the locker."

Austaire leaned over towards Jim and planted a discrete kiss on his cheek. "I'll wait outside for you."

Jim folded up his papers and closed his binder. He hurriedly walked to his locker and dumped the books. The twosome left the school grounds and headed across to Dobeys. The place was still quite quiet and Austaire chose a stall near the back of the room. "Let's sit here."

"I'll be right back, girl."

Jim ordered a couple of Cokes with cheese burgers and fries at the counter and then returned to the booth and sat down. "So what's up?"

"Oh, I've got a little predicament. Megan's after me for some cash. I asked my folks for some extra last night and they wanted to know what it was for. They said that I already had used up my allowance and that I had to wait until next month. My bank account is basically zilch."

"I don't understand. We've been paying for our stuff up front. What else would Megan need some money for?"

"I just ran up a little tab from before. I was hoping that you would help me out. I usually find enough extra cash lying around the house but not this month. It's not Meg. She has to answer to Jason and I don't want to see her in tough. She only asks if she's short. It's kinda' awkward asking you."

The couple was interrupted by the waitress delivering their meals. Jim dumped ketchup on his burger and salted down his fries before continuing.

"So, how much? You sound pretty serious."

Austaire took a small bite from her burger and then looked up a Jim. "I need about five hundred dollars."

"Five hundred! Damn it, that's a lot of money, Austaire." Jim regained his composure and continued. "The folks give me a great allowance for helping out on the place. In fact Dad is giving me a bit more this fall since we don't have outside help but that's still a lot of money."

"It won't happen again, Jim. I just got behind more than I thought. You know what that stuff costs. I screwed up. You're all that I've got." Austaire looked longingly into Jim's blue eyes. "Please, I'll make it up to you." She rolled her tongue around her mouth. "I'll more than make it worth your while." She cast a silent smile at Jim. The stare lasted only a moment.

Jim smiled and then blurted out, "We'll have to get some money from my account. We can get it after lunch. I think that I am allowed that much in one withdrawal. I guess, we'll see."

"Thanks, Jim. I knew that I could count on you. It won't happen again. You mean the world to me."

"You too, Austaire. Eat up. We'll drive over to the bank and get the money. Best go now while the bank is open in case that damn ATM machine isn't working. That way I won't be late picking up the girls after school."

"You got a ride?"

"Yes, Dad said to use the Ford during harvest. I'll be driving in everyday. I drop the girls off and take them home with me."

"Wow, that's totally wicked. So what do we do this afternoon?"

"I should finish my classes today. I missed yesterday afternoon. I've got an assignment to hand in for Miss Harris." He looked down at his watch. "Shit, I'm not quite finished the paper yet." Jim looked back at his watch. "I'll finish it tonight and hand it in tomorrow. Piss on it!"

"Easy there, Jim. You just need some tender care. My folks are gone until four. I might even have a joint hanging around." She smiled at Jim and he returned the smile. They quickly finished their meal and headed back towards the school parking lot. They met Glen Rollins.

"Hi guys, eat early?"

"Yes, we have an errand to run so we best keep going. Do you need a ride later?"

"No, I'm fine. Nothing rushed to get home to anyways. Not like you. Sure is a nice day."

"Yes, it sure is. Anyways, see you later."

"Yep, see you in class, Jim. We have English together."

"Oh, about that, Austaire's errands might take a while." Jim cast a sly wink towards Glen. "Could you cover for me? I'll hand that assignment in tomorrow."

"I can hand it in for you if you want?"

"No, I didn't quite get it finished. If Miss Harris asks maybe tell her that I had to run home to help with harvest."

"Okay there, Jim. Enjoy your afternoon."

"Thanks bud."

Jim and Austaire left Glen and headed towards the pickup. The drive to the bank was fruitful and Jim was able to obtain the full five hundred dollars for his girlfriend. The ensuing afternoon was spent in the comfort of Austaire's room. At three-thirty sharp Jim left her place and headed back to Royston Elementary. The twins were standing out front waiting for him when he arrived. They climbed into the front seat of the Ford. "Hi Jim, you're right on time."

"You bet girls! Did you two have a good one?"

"School is school," said Mary. "And you?"

"It was just another day at Royston High. Well, we had better get this thing home. Dad is going to be waiting for us. It sure is nice out."

Susan was sitting beside her brother. She turned to him. "You been smoking again, haven't you? Your hair smells of smoke."

"Oh, give it a break, Susan. I've got more on my mind than a bit of smoke."

"Okay, Jim. It's your funeral. If Dad finds out that you are smoking he isn't going to be impressed."

"And Mom neither!" added Mary.

"Okay, enough of the lecture. Damn it you two are as bad as adults sometimes."

They all shared a little laugh as Jim maneuvered the pickup onto the highway. The drive home was uneventful with the twins filling the cab with idyllic chatter. Jim had time to revisit the pleasant activities of the afternoon in his mind. *If only they knew he thought to himself but they never will. Everyone deserved an afternoon like that once in a while. He could easily make up his classes later.* When he turned onto the south road he could see their John Deere slowly moving through a field of wheat. Limited amounts of dust were exiting the machine but it was threshing grain.

17

By Friday afternoon the harvest was once again in full swing. Although the grain itself was still damp and thus required mechanical drying at the yard, the straw was dry and flowing through the machine well. The winds had long left the area leaving blue skies dotted with billowing, white clouds in its wake. The countryside was alive with the sounds and movement of combines and grain trucks. The kids arrived home to a jubilant mother and father self-absorbed in the critical business of harvesting the crop. Jim walked over to June who was in the midst of emptying a grain truck.

"Hi Mom, I can finish that if you want?"

"Thanks Jim, but you had better go change your clothes first and then you can take the truck back to the field. I think that your Dad wants you to take over cutting while he starts up the dryer." June adjusted the flow of grain from the spout of the truck's box. She looked back up towards the girls. "Mary and Susan! You two can look after the layers for me. They're bringing the chicks tonight instead of in the morning so we will have to wiggle in supper early."

The kids quickly dispersed into the house to change while their mother finished unloading the truck. The girls were the first to exit the house and they headed directly to the layer barn to attend to their familiar chores. Jim reappeared around the corner of the house just as June was shutting down the grain auger. He sluggishly trod towards the awaiting grain truck.

"Hey there, Jim. Get a move on please. Don't go keeping your father waiting over there forever."

"Right Mom, I'm on my way. What time are the birds comin'?"

"About eight o'clock. It'll be dark by then anyways. I'll send some supper out to the field for you."

"That'll be great. I'm pretty hungry."

Jim mechanically climbed into the grain truck and started the engine. He ground the truck into gear and popped the clutch forgetting to release the parking brake. The truck lurched ahead slightly and stalled. June ran up to the driver's door of the truck.

"The hoist is still up. You've got to drop the box down."

"Sorry Mom. I was just cleaning the box out." Jim sheepishly pushed down on the control and watched as the grain box settled onto the truck frame. "I've got her this time. Well I gotta' get. See you in a while."

"Drive careful, Jim. You look tired again. That bug you have seems to be pretty persistent. I can make an appointment for you if you want?"

"Hell no, Mom, I'm fine. Don't even go there."

Jim smiled at his mother and then successfully edged the grain truck ahead and carefully turned onto the driveway. The dust drifted aimlessly into the air behind the moving truck as it sped out the lane with black smoke pouring out the exhaust stack. The field that George was harvesting was located only a couple of miles away and Jim wasted no time putting the International through her paces. He turned the unit into the field. He could see his father emptying wheat into the Mack tandem at the far end of the field and arrived there just as George was jumping off the combine. Jim pulled up beside the Mack and immediately shut of the International. He was just exiting the truck when his Dad spoke.

"Hey, let her idle for little. You know better than to shut off a diesel hot. What are you thinking?" George brushed past his son and started up the International. "The Deere is waiting for you, Jim. Just take it easy. Some of that tangled stuff is hard cuttin'. I'll bring the Mack back after I get the drier going. Should get a couple of loads before those chicks arrive? Now, don't just stand there. That Deere doesn't harvest grain standing still."

"Right on. Sorry bout' the truck. I'll watch for those tangled spots. Anyways, see you later."

George looked down at his son, "I'll just bring the Mack back to the field and leave her for you. Just leave the Deere here for tonight and be into the yard by eight if you can. Okay?"

"Sure thing Dad, Mom was going to send my supper out with you so just leave it in the cab."

"It's a done deal then. We'll see you around eight."

Jim walked to the green combine, climbed up the steps and entered the cab. He energized the threshing mechanism and pushed the throttle to full. A cloud of spent, black diesel smoke poured from the machine's exhaust as Jim mobilized the machine. He quickly swung the machine around in a tight circle. George watched in horror as the swift moving machine narrowly missed the parked Mack. He had no time to react as the combine roared into the field and began cutting the standing grain. The combine was soon hidden by a cloud of fine dust and shooting straw coming from the rear of the machine.

The truck delivering the new broiler chicks arrived just before eight o'clock. The girls ran out to the awaiting driver and directed him back towards the broiler barn entrance. June finished up some supper dishes and quickly joined them. George was in the midst of unloading Jim's first load of wheat having picked up the International from the field where he left the Mack for his son. Darkness prevailed now and the escaping steam from the grain drier dissipated upwards into the cool, night air. George finished unloading the truck, checked the drier settings and wandered over to the broiler barn.

June and the twins had already began the chore of unloading the cartons of broiler chicks and releasing them onto the fresh shavings. She smiled and looked up at George when he walked into the barn. "'Bout' time you got here. Jim not up yet?" She hurriedly walked back to the awaiting driver who was placing the cartons at the back of the truck. "It's getting pretty dark."

"He'll be up soon, June. He was making out fine when I went back for my load. You know Jim. He probably figured on filling that Mack up before leaving." George reached for a couple of flats of chicks. "Are the birds all here?"

"Yes, all twelve thousand of them. Girls are placing them. They love to handle those little chicks."

George glanced over at the girls. They were carefully dumping the brown flats of fragile, yellow birds into the bedding pack while maintaining a steady conversation. "Take it easy with those birds, girls. You'll bore them to death with your chatter." George gave them a quick smile and set down his load of flats beside them. He quickly exited the barn for another load meeting June as she entered the barn door with her arms full of boxes.

The truck was almost emptied by the time Jim arrived to help. George and June had acquired a good sweat from the multiple trips to and from the truck. The girls were swimming in a sea of the small, yellow chickens contained within the partitioned portion of the broiler barn. Jim grabbed a couple of flats of chicks and was greeted by his Dad near the barn door.

"Thanks for showing up. You need a new watch or something? Everything okay out there?"

"Sorry, but I plugged the damn combine header in one of those lousy draws out there. I didn't mean to be late."

"You should have stopped before it got too dark. It's hard enough doing those spots in the light. You get the truck filled?"

"Yah, I've got a good load on."

"That's great, we're almost finished here. Let's get those flats in before these chicks get bloody cold. No need of trying to heat the great outdoors too."

The family proceeded to finish the process of unloading the precious cargo into the barn. It was nine-thirty by the time the work was completed and the birds were safely placed in the confines of their new home. June and the girls left for the house while Jim and George headed towards the drier. The drier was into cooling stage but remnants of warm air still eased upwards into the frosty, night air. The two worked in silence as they unloaded the Mack's partial load of damp wheat into the wet bin. Having finished that operation, George shut down the drier's main fans and turned to Jim.

"Well son, don't know about you but this day is over for me. Tomorrow will come soon enough. I might try those barley swaths tomorrow. Be nice to get them cleaned up. Probably keep you cutting that wheat."

"That sounds good. Sorry bout' the delay. I didn't mean to plug the machine. It took longer than I thought to get that header going."

"Oh, I know. It can be a bugger in that down stuff. You should of quit and just come up for eight. No sense in fooling around in the damn dark. Well if you know what's good for you, I'd catch something to eat and hit the hay. We've got a busy weekend ahead of us."

"What no church on Sunday?"

"We'll probably get into church but I'm running in the afternoon. The church elders probably don't like it but they don't pay our bills."

"You don't think that they'll refuse your Sunday collection then?"

"No, I don't think so."

George and Jim shared a light chuckle as they slowly walked towards the house. The chill of the evening air was quickly descending on the entire area. The dew was already setting on the grass and it shimmered in the light of the half moon. It was still and calm and very quiet. In no time the Edward's household was also dark and quiet too.

June turned over on her side and briefly looked out the bedroom window, listening attentively. She stirred George from his sleep. He responded with a groggy, "What's up?"

"Just listen," she said quietly. "I thought that I heard something in the yard."

George slowly sat up in the bed and listened too. He whispered back to June, "I don't hear a damn thing, Hon. Not even a cricket chirping out there. The dogs are out running around. If there was something or someone out there they would be making a real commotion by now. Go to sleep."

"Yes, I don't hear anything now, either. I must have been dreaming or something. Weird how it awoke me and all."

George reached over and gave June a light kiss on her forehead. "Just get some sleep, Hon. Night now." He lay down in the bed and twisted himself under the covers. His exhausted body needed rest. June listened momentarily and soon joined her husband in deep slumber. Outside the quietness of the night was undisturbed. The dark night hid practically everything; everything but the dim shadow of the Ford pickup as it turned slowly and crept out the laneway.

Jim turned on the headlights once he hit the main road and continued on his way to County Road 22. He had one stop to make before he reached the highway. Glen was waiting by the road as Jim approached the Rollin's driveway. Glen quickly jumped into the truck. "Evening, thanks for giving me a call."

"I wasn't sure if you'd be around, Glen, but I thought that I'd give it a try."

"So where are we headed? Are we going to another Megan party?"

"Sort of but it isn't in town tonight. We'll pick up Austaire. She knows how to get there. Just relax and enjoy the ride. So talking about driving? Do you think that you can drive us back home? It'll give me a few more winks. I've got to thresh wheat tomorrow. So if you can kinda' watch the time for me and don't let it get too late."

"No problem there, Jim. You can count on me to get you back to my place and then it's all yours. Let's say that it's my gift to you. It's all good if we get to party."

18

The family was eating breakfast when Jim awoke Saturday morning. He looked down at his wrist to catch the time but his watch was missing. He rolled over on his side and observed the weak red lights on his clock-radio. It read seven-thirty. His eyes began to adjust to the comforting darkness of his room. The silence was broken by the audible conversation coming from upstairs. His mind left the confines of the bedroom and he was adrift on a cloud floating over a vast, dark chasm. It was cool, so very cool. Time was seemingly infinite. He was jarred to reality by Susan's voice.

"You awake in there?"

"Yep, I'll be right out. Any breakfast left?"

"We've all finished. Mom left cereal on the table. You better get up there quick. Mom and Dad and Mary have just left for chores..."

"I'll be right there. Consider it done."

"Brother, you sure have been acting weird lately. Dad wasn't impressed that you weren't up for breakfast. You still feeling sick?"

"Oh get lost, Susan. Tell Dad that I will be right out. I just over slept. Not the end of the damn world or anything."

"Okay, Jim. I know when I'm not wanted. See you outside brother."

"If you are lucky, girl? But only if you are lucky."

Jim crawled out of his comfort zone and waited until Susan had gone outside. He bundled some clothes under his arm and walked across to the bathroom. In minutes he was upstairs eating cereal and drinking hot coffee. Outside the birds were gathering on the electric lines in front of the house. He envisioned being able to fly like those birds. He stuffed a second bowl of corn flakes down and washed his dry mouth with another large mug of black coffee. The coffee was bitter but it was working as the caffeine slowly edged Jim's senses back to life.

"It's nice of you to join us. You awake now?"

Jim wrenched back in his chair almost emptying his cup on the floor. "Gee, Dad. You really startled me." Jim swung around to face his Dad who was standing in the kitchen. "Sorry about sleepin' in. I was more tired than I thought. Slept like a babe."

"Okay, enough of the small talk. That's great that you had a great sleep. Whatever you caught last weekend seems to be dragging out. We just got running ourselves for that matter. There was a light frost last night so the dew is pretty heavy."

"Yes, it was pretty chilly when we came in."

"Anyways, finish your meal and then we'll get the IH serviced. We'll have two machines running today."

"It sounds good. Be out shortly, Dad." Jim poured the last of the coffee from the pot and swallowed the black liquid. It was nearly enough to turn his stomach but he swallowed hard and felt the liquid nudge his senses up another notch. He would definitely sleep tonight.

The men spent the remainder of the morning servicing the harvest machinery and finishing drying the wheat from the previous night. The twins were actively entertained by the flock of newly arrived chicks while June attended to her house work. By eleven-thirty the autumn sunshine had eaten the dew away and the Edwards were able to resume harvesting.

George operated the second combine picking up swaths of barley while June hauled the harvested barley back to their yard with the International truck. Jim worked by himself straight cutting wheat with the Deere and hauling the wheat back to the wet bin with the old Mack. By late day the grain was piling up in the storage bins. Grain dust hung in the air like a gigantic veil as the roar from the lumbering combines echoed into the distant hills.

Jim starred blankly ahead attempting to fully concentrate on the header and reel as the Deere grunted ahead cutting the standing wheat. The setting sun was low on the horizon and it blazed directly into the cab of the combine. The air conditioner was locked on high as Jim tried to keep the cab as cold as possible. He continued to fight the drowsiness that had plagued him throughout the afternoon. The sunset rays played tricks with his tired eyes. Jim constantly fought the urge to shut his eyes. He reached up and turned the radio volume up a notch while he attempted to balance his coffee cup against the steering wheel of the Deere. He did not notice that the cutting header was precariously low to the ground.

The low cutting header suddenly dug directly into a knoll on the right side of the machine. The forward momentum of the combine twisted the steering wheel from Jim's hand causing the machine to violently veer to the right plowing the header into the ground. Jim's coffee cup was thrown directly into his face and he was momentarily blinded by the warm liquid. He missed the foot clutch with his first attempt. To make matters worse he pulled on the hydrostatic control which propelled the machine around faster. His second attempt to depress the clutch was successful and the growling machine came to an abrupt and noisy halt.

Jim sat shaking in the seat of the combine cab. His hands were glued to the steering wheel and it took great effort to reach over to the gear shift and put the machine into neutral. He shut down the threshing mechanism and killed the engine. It rocked to a stop and the cab became silent. Jim remained seated fearing the damage that had just occurred. He swallowed hard and gained enough courage to slowly climb out of the combine cab and down the ladder to the ground.

The right side of the header was buried in soil and bunched wheat straw. The front of the machine was a mixture of bent reel bats and twisted, crumpled metal that had once been a feed auger. Pieces of the cutting knife lay everywhere. Jim sunk to his knees and cried aloud, "How could this happen? Why me? Whatever did I do to deserve this?"

He regained his composure and slowly walked back to the edge of the field where the Mack was parked. The drive to the barley field gave little time for Jim to think. *The one thought that stuck in his mind was that if there was a God, then he must surely hate Jim.* He simply drove the old truck into the field where his Dad was threshing, parked the truck and waited for him to arrive. Jim sat in a time warp and watched as the approaching tractor and combine finally came to a halt across from where he was parked. Jim walked over towards his Dad and met him half way across the field.

"What's up Jim? You got problems?"

"Yes, I plugged up the feeder."

"Is it bad enough that you can't get her going? You've cleaned out plugged feeders before. Another hour and I'll have this piece done. We're makin' good time here. Are you sure that it can't wait?"

"It is worse than that, Dad." Jim burst into tears and started to tremble. "I wrecked the header. I hit the dirt in the sunshine. It just happened so fast and I didn't get stopped in time. It's a total mess."

"Damn it, Jim. Shit." George grabbed his son and held him by his shoulders. "It can't be that bad, son. Get a hold of yourself. Here comes your Mom now. We'll unload this bin of barley into the truck and then we'll go see what we can do."

"There is a lot of dirt and grain in the front of her, Dad. The reel is pretty bad. I'm real sorry."

"Just calm yourself. Damn it anyways. Step out of the way and let your mother drive the truck in here."

June pulled the International up beside the combine and George swung the unloading auger out across the empty box and began unloading the barley. It tumbled into the box creating great swirls of dust which rose high into the air.

"I've gotta' go over to the wheat field, June. Jim had a problem. Can you finish here? Just shut the tractor off when you're done. It looks like this day is finished."

"Sure thing, you okay there, Jim? You look like you've seen a ghost."

"I'm okay, Mom. I'm just so very sorry." Jim burst into tears again and June jumped out of the truck to comfort her son.

"It'll be fine, Jim. It can't be that bad. We're no strangers to fixing things. Your Dad will make it right."

"Jim, you go back to the house with your Mom. It's getting dusk anyway. You can unload that grain for her. Okay?"

Jim nodded his head in agreement and walked around to the passenger door of the International and climbed into the truck cab. He said nothing and felt content that he did not have to be around when his Dad saw the Deere. He sat in the cab with his head buried in his lap and wept.

"Take him up home, June. I'll take a look at the Deere. Sounds like I have a job for the morning. I've never seen him so distressed. Kid has me worried."

"Catch you in a bit then, George. Supper will be ready when you get back."

Jim watched as his Dad hurriedly walked towards the old Mack and eventually left the field. He sat waiting for his mother to finish unloading the barley. *How could this have happened to him? Perhaps it wasn't as bad as it first looked to him. Just chill out a little and this might pass like a bad trip.* The tractor was silenced and his mother jumped into the truck cab.

"There we're all done here, Jim. It'll all work out in the end. The Lord will see to that."

Jim said nothing but just looked out the dusty window of the truck with a blank stare. He sat motionless as his mother started the engine and carefully navigated the truck past the large swaths and out of the field. The ride home seemed endless.

The yard lights were on by the time they arrived home. June backed the International up to the auger and Jim commenced unloading the barley. He did not say anything as appropriate words eluded him. He continued to fight back tears and restrain mixed emotions of horror and fear. He stood in silence watching the warm kernels of barley flow from the truck spout into the grain auger. When the grain stopped flowing he cleaned out the corners of the box and walked over and turned the auger off. His Dad had not returned yet. The night air felt cold and forbidding. Jim ran into the house, quietly descended downstairs into his room and shut the door. He undressed and crawled into his bed weeping almost uncontrollably. Despite the emotional turmoil, fatigue quickly took its course and Jim fell into a deep sleep.

It was late when George arrived back into the yard. He had surveyed the damage to the Deere and attempted to dig out some of the grain and soil from the twisted header. June was waiting for him when he entered the house.

"How bad is it, George?"

"It's bad. She may be done for this year. I don't know yet. I'll know better in the light tomorrow. Suppose Jim is downstairs?"

"I think he is asleep. Didn't eat anything either. Just went directly into his room. Let him be, he's a mess."

"I don't know what the hell is going on with him, June. Damn it anyways. He's never screwed up like that before. He's always been so responsible."

"Let it go tonight, George. We all need some rest. Your supper is ready."

Jim never stirred all that evening. His sleep was deep and undisturbed. He floated down into a dark, deep chasm and remained there for the duration of the night. Outside a light breeze started to blow from the east. It intensified and then blew hard for about an hour and then it stopped. In its wake the sky turned into a mass of low lying stratus clouds that hid the half moon and the bright stars that had shone earlier. In the pale light of the yard lights a faint mist began to show. By three o'clock it was spitting rain.

19

George shut the door of the old Chev pickup, grabbed some tools from the box and slowly trod towards the Deere combine. Jim grabbed a shovel and followed quietly in his Dad's footsteps. A light mist was gently falling to the ground; more of a nuisance rain than anything but enough to dampen the landscape. It did little to help the depressing image presented before them. The two individuals said nothing to each other and earnestly commenced digging the compressed soil and wheat straw from the header of the broken machine.

About two hours later they had a formidable mound of material piled to the right side of the combine header. The twisted right side of the header and cutting bar were now clearly visible. After another hour of quietly digging and cleaning around the machine in the persistent mist, George finally spoke.

"Well, let's start her up and see if we can get her moved home. Go grab some chains and binders from the Chev to support things."

Jim nodded his head and walked back to the pickup for the necessary tools. The soil was lightly sticking to his boots. The moisture was accumulating on his ball cap and slowly dripping onto his face and jacket. George climbed into the Deere and carefully started the big diesel. It roared to life.

"Well, she still runs," George yelled from the combine cab. "At least you didn't break that part." He jumped off the machine and reached out for the chains that Jim was carrying. He roughly pulled one out onto the ground catching Jim's arm.

"You don't have to be so rough, Dad. You could have broken my damn arm.

"Better your arm than your head. Look at this damn mess we have here. What in the hell possessed you to do a thing like this?"

"Don't even go there. I didn't mean to do anything. If I didn't have to work so damn hard all the time maybe it wouldn't have happened at all. I just missed that knoll in the sunshine."

"Well you don't have to worry about the sunshine today do you? Look at the damn soil you moved. You were dragging that header forever. It's supposed to cut grain. Not be used as a damn bulldozer."

"Oh, I know, as if you never make a mistake."

"Shut your mouth, Jim. I make lots of damn mistakes. This is not a mistake. This is a damn wreck. You couldn't have done a better job here if you tried. The front of this machine looks like it was in a damn demolition derby."

"Austaire said that you wouldn't understand. You think that I have no feelings at all. I was a wreck last night because of this damage. I enjoy threshing with the Deere. You really think that I wanted this to happen."

"No, surely you've got more brains than that. And who the hell is Austaire?"

"She's just a girl that I know in Royston. Like whatever, as if she's any of your damn business anyways."

"She is now. All of your damn friends in Royston are my business. I'm not sure what went on here but I'm going to get to the bottom of it."

"Great, I'll let everyone know that my Dad thinks that they are responsible for a damn combine accident. Cause' that is all it was, just a damn accident."

"This was more than an accident, Jim." George looked menacingly into his son's eyes. "I personally believe that this never needed to happen. You let us down, big time. Enough of this chatter, all the chatter in the world isn't going to fix her or pay for fixin' her for that matter."

Jim did not reply and stood there patiently watching his father. George was now occupied with chaining up the header and supporting the broken and twisted pieces of metal. He methodically wrapped the chains around the header and then tightened them in place with the load binders. "Okay, Jim. You watch things as I see if she'll still lift up." George climbed back into the combine cab and carefully pushed on the hydraulic control for the header. It slowly lifted the damaged header into the air. "Put the blocks around the cylinders to support them."

Jim crawled under the machine and inserted the blocks. Hydraulic oil was steadily seeping from the cylinders but it was holding. "There, I've got it, Dad." Jim crawled back to the side of the machine and stood quietly by watching as George put the machine into reverse. The hydrostatic drive growled louder than normal, hesitated and then rotated the drive wheels. The big machine shook and slowly retreated from the site of the accident.

"I'll take her up to the farm, Jim. You take the Chev."

"Whatever Dad, I'll see you over there."

"June and the twins should be home from church by now. Don't go upsetting your mother anymore than she already is. I won't be makin' any speed records here. Just tell her that I'm on my way."

George slammed the cab door shut and carefully feathered the hydrostatic into forward. The machine willingly moved ahead despite the persistent growl that was so audible. George looked at the header and shook his head fighting off tears as his emotions struggled with the sight before him. He looked to the entrance of the field and watched Jim head onto the county road. The tire tracks over the wet soil were clearly visible from his vantage point. George turned on the windshield wiper and allowed the wiper to fully wash the windshield as the light mist persisted. He carefully maneuvered the machine through the damp field and headed home.

20

The last week of September turned into a living fiasco as the damp weather prevailed throughout the entire week. Jim and the twins had returned to using the school bus freeing up the Ford for their parents use. Jim received frequent rides home with Glen Rollins during the week but his parents were too absorbed with repairing the Deere to make an issue of it.

George dismantled the cutting header and the auger assembly. Many of the knife parts were readily available while most of the larger ones had to be ordered. June was kept busy driving to various machinery dealers obtaining the array of items required to repair the combine.

Friday night saw a major frost hit the area. By Saturday morning the sun was once again shining to the east and a light westerly wind was attempting to blow the remnants of the grey, cloud cover away. June and the kids had looked after the morning chores allowing George to continue with the combine repair.

In the afternoon Jim and the girls were put to work digging up the remaining potatoes and putting them into cold storage. George was in the farm shop when Allan Heiner drove into the yard. He glanced up and smiled as Allan walked towards him. "What brings you out this way?"

"How's George?

"I could be better. With this harvest going the way it is. But I better not complain. No one listens anyway."

"Yes, Sheila was saying that you had a wreck. I'm not a farmer but this weather is getting to me too. Looks like it may be changing though. Weather forecast sounded better last night."

"Let's hope so this time around. Another month of this stuff and we'll be done for."

"So what's yah' working on?"

"I'm just attempting to rebuild the feed auger. New tube is on back order so who knows when that'll come. Should have her finished tonight and then we'll have to wait for the new shaft. June got the reel bats and cutting parts this week so that's all finished."

"It sounds like she's on the mend again. Hopefully the backordered stuff doesn't take too long?"

"We tried to rent another header but can't come up with one and they want an arm and a leg for a new one. Know damn well what the banker would say about that anyways. We'll make out with what we have. So how's life at your end of the world?"

"Busy George, in fact I've gotta' run. Just goin' to the Laney place and thought that I would drop by."

"Thanks Allan, it's always a pleasure. You're always welcome here. Just don't bug me when I get back into harvest."

The two men shared a quick laugh and Allan turned to walk back to his car. "By the way, George, there was something else that I wanted to mention to you."

"What's that? You're getting forgetful in your old age."

"Yes, not sure but I could of sworn that I saw your Ford last Friday night turning off the highway into Royston. I worked late over by that new subdivision everyday last week and I was fillin' up at the Quick Gas store beside the turnoff into town. You know that I practically live in that little town. It just isn't big enough that people don't notice things. I know that I mentioned it before and I may be wrong this time too but it sure looked like your truck. Thought that maybe Jim was out on a date perhaps?"

"Bout' what time, Allan?"

"Oh, it was about ten-thirty or eleven. I worked late finishing up that job before the weekend. It looked like there were two people in the truck."

"Thanks. I know that he certainly hasn't been himself of late. However, we were in bed by ten or so that night."

"I've got to get. Let me know if I can do anything. Sorry that we missed fishin' the other weekend."

"Yes, Jim was feeling under the weather that Sunday. He had quite a nose bleed earlier in the day."

"June had mentioned it to Sheila after the service. Apparently he looked pretty pale too. He's okay now?"

"He seems better this week."

"I really must get, George. Good luck with the machine."

"Thanks. See you later, Allan."

George watched as Allan drove out the laneway. He looked over at the kids who were busily engaged in digging the potatoes. Jim was carrying a full sack across the lawn towards the root cellar. His brawny frame appeared as strong and determined as ever. The twins were chatting away as usual while they cleaned the freshly dug potatoes, struggling to keep up to their brother. *Should he confront Jim on Allan's suspicions once again? While the timing was possible why would his son head into town during a harvest night? Jim had gone right to bed that night. In fact he was the first to go. June did think that she had heard something in the yard though. It did seem like too much of a coincident.* George shrugged his shoulders and went back to his repair work. Meanwhile his mind worked overtime as he struggled to reason with his friend's concerns over his son's whereabouts and actions.

21

The sunshine and light winds continued into mid-week. George had resumed swathing grain with vigor as he attempted to get swaths ahead to thresh with the remaining pull-type combine. The process was slowed by wet soil conditions and tough straw but he was making progress. Meanwhile there was no news on the back-ordered parts for the Deere. By Thursday Jim and the twins were once again driving the Ford into school in preparation for hauling harvested grain.

Austaire had missed school on Thursday but Friday morning she was waiting for Jim when he drove into the school parking lot. She waved at him and ran over to the Ford as Jim was getting out of the truck. "Good morning, Jim. What a beautiful day. It's going to be warm today. How be you and I go for a picnic or something?" She gave Jim a big hug and planted a wet kiss on his right cheek. "There's lots more waiting for you."

"Morning, I missed you yesterday. I actually had to take in a full day of school." Jim smiled and Austaire let out a small giggle. "So you want to have a picnic do you? Like for real? It's getting a bit cool for that don't you think?"

"Megans away, Jim. My Mom is home today. I thought that we could get up into the hills and find a nice secluded and warm spot somewhere. It is going to be nice and sunny today. Besides, I've got my backpack full of drinks and eats and I got some goodies from Meg yesterday. I told her that we would pay her on the weekend."

"I thought that I told you not to charge that stuff. You've got to measure it out a bit. I know that's it's awesome and all but I'm not totally made of cash."

"Gee, Jim. Now you are starting to sound like my parents. I thought that you got your monthly allowance from your parents on the first of each month. I didn't mean any harm. I just thought that it would be okay."

"Oh, I'm sorry, Austaire. My parents have been on my case ever since the damn combine wreck. Anyways, time to leave this place. I know of a good spot out by McPherson Point by Wawa Lake. Can't waste all that preparation of yours now can we?"

The couple jumped into the Ford and disappeared out of the school parking lot. Jim paid no attention to the bus unloading students at the school entrance. He didn't notice Monty wave at him as he went by. Neither of them noticed Glen Rollins watching them leave the grounds as he arrived at the parking lot. There was no time like the present and for Jim and Austaire there was no concern for tomorrow.

The day turned out to be absolutely beautiful. The couple found a secluded portion of the beach by the Point and relaxed in the warm sunshine enjoying each others company and the golden weed that Austaire had purchased from Megan. By mid-day they were stretched out on an old blanket they had found behind the back seat of the Ford munching on snacks and sipping beer. The cool water of the deserted beach lapped up against their bare feet.

"Not bad for a Friday?" Austaire snuggled up to her boyfriend. "I wish we could just do this forever. You make me feel so awesome, Jim."

"It's all you, Austaire. You're right though. I could do this forever too. I'm getting fed up with the crap at home. If it's not the stupid weather then it's about the harvest and people figuring that they have to work all the time. I used to just figure that it was the norm but I know different now."

"Here draw on this, Jim and just chill out with me."

Jim inhaled the joint and relaxed as the enticing drug worked its wonders in his mind. He slowly exhaled and blew a thin cloud of the smoke towards Austaire. He passed the joint back to her so that she could enjoy it too. In minutes the world had slowed down to a crawl. There was only Jim and Austaire and the beach. Nothing else mattered. They enjoyed another one before Austaire slowly rose up and walked knee deep into the cool water. She was laughing.

"Come on in. It's really not that bad."

"Are you crazy, girl? Shit, it has to be freezing."

"Oh, come on in. You chicken? Bluk, bluk, bluk."

Jim watched as Austaire walked back to the beach and carefully undressed before him and then ran out and dived into the water. Not to be outdone he managed to do the same. The crippling cold was soon forgotten as the couple splashed in the cool, autumn waters of Wawa Lake. Jim reached out and grabbed his girl holding her tight to his body. "You're down right crazy. You know that."

"Yes and it's so wonderful, isn't it?"

"You're wicked, Austaire. I gotta' get out of this water before I'm frozen."

"You do look cold. I know a good way to warm you up."

The couple laughed and ran out of the lake as quickly as they had invaded it. The warm, autumn sunshine still shone directly onto their blanket and they lay there allowing the sunshine to dry them. They lit their last joint and lay there enjoying its pleasant effect on their minds. By three o'clock a light westerly wind was stirring little choppy waves onto their isolated portion of sand.

"Brrrr, you all dried off? I've gotta' get dressed before that wind freezes me up." Jim laughed at Austaire. "Hey there beautiful, are you coming?"

"Yes, that breeze is getting totally cool." Austaire started pulling on her clothes. "You ever think about the future much?"

"Once in awhile, I guess. Sometimes I think about what I want to do later on. I really don't know. Like anything in particular?"

"I mean like Megan has been after me to come live with her. She can get me work. My parents are old and they just don't understand anything. Most of the time I just hate them."

"What about school? You'd still graduate?"

"Meg didn't graduate and she does just fine. She treats me well. She treats both of us totally awesome."

"I know that Meg is great but don't you think that you should finish school? My parents are always on my case to end up better than them and not to have to work so hard. I'm beginning to believe them there."

"Your parents are basically idiots, Jim. Nobody should work that hard. They ask way too much of you. I don't know how you put up with it."

"Most of the time my folks are okay. Farming is all we've ever known."

"Come here." Austaire planted a huge kiss on his lips and the two embraced each other with a lightning grip hug. "We just need each other, Jim." Austaire looked into Jim's blue eyes and added, "And some really good weed."

The couple erupted into a spontaneous laughing fit that lasted several minutes. They frolicked across the course sand holding hands and tossing the brown sand into the cool breeze with their toes. They landed hard on top of the old blanket.

"It's a good thing that you had this blanket in the truck."

"Yes, Mom always leaves a blanket in there for serving supper in the field or whatever." Jim reached down and grabbed his wrist watch from the sand. "Holy shit. Look at the damn time." He burst into laughter. "The girls will be waiting on this hard working farm boy to pick them up from school." He sobered up as he attentively studied his watch as he put it on his wrist. "We've got to get."

The couple picked up their things remembering to dump the majority of the sand out of the blanket before they left their private beach front. They were still giggling when they hit the highway as Jim pushed the Ford into motion in the direction of Royston. He looked at the time on the clock radio. It said four o'clock. He pushed the Ford quickly down the deserted road.

"Take it easy there, Jim. You would think that we were late or something." Austaire looked at Jim and laughed loudly. Jim joined in with some more hearty laughter. He let Austaire out by Megan's turnoff and proceeded directly to the Elementary School. The twins were not in front of the school. Jim jumped out of the Ford and ran up the steps facing the main entrance to the school. In his haste he tripped and fell hard on his left knee. He rolled up his pant leg and sat for a moment nursing his scraped knee. He was startled by the sudden deep voice. "You okay there? That was a pretty bad fall."

Jim turned abruptly and faced one of his old teachers. "Mr. Yews. Jim Edwards. You taught me math in grades seven and eight. You probably don't remember me." Jim slowly stood up favoring his left leg. "I'm fine now. Are there any kids left inside? I'm here to pick up my sisters."

"Jim Edwards. Yes, you have two sisters in my class, Mary and Susan. No, everyone is gone, Jim. Classes were out early today. First Friday of the month you know. Buses were here by two o'clock."

"Shit, I mean sorry. Damn it, I forgot about that. So you think that they got on the bus then?"

"Can't be sure but I know that all the buses loaded students and left here for Royston High. Both schools share the same schedule for the rural students. Well it's been nice seeing you again, Jim. Good luck with that knee. It looks pretty sore."

"Yes, thanks for the help. See you around."

Jim hobbled back to the Ford and hastily headed for Royston High. Perhaps the twins had gone that far to catch a ride with him there. The parking area at the High School was vacant when Jim arrived. He visually checked the front foyer of the school but it appeared that there was no one around. Even the teachers parking area was void of vehicles. Jim turned the Ford around and hastily bid a retreat out of the parking lot.

The laughter that had existed only minutes before was now replaced by anxiety. Cold sweat appeared on Jim's face as it adopted a stern and empty appearance. He smelt his shirt sleeve and opened the side windows of the Ford enough to drive a cold breeze throughout the cab. He shivered in the cool air. He looked at his watch. It was now five o'clock. *What on earth was he going to tell them?*

His thought process was broken by the unmistakable sound of a police siren. He looked behind the pickup and saw the flashing red lights gaining ground on the Ford. He looked down at the speedometer. He was not speeding. *Had he been speeding and not noticed? Was it something else?* He smelt his shirt sleeve again. The perspiration gathered on his face as the patrol car approached the Ford. Jim slowed down the truck and began to edge over onto the shoulder of the road. The speeding police car sped quickly pass the Ford leaving Jim sighing in relief.

He laughed aloud and accelerated back onto the highway. The reality of his situation returned with a vengeance as Jim's mind was completely enthralled with his current predicament and what excuse he could give. *What if they had called the school? Did they realize that he was not at school as well?*

He could feel his pulse rising and his chest hurt as Jim turned onto County Road 22. In minutes he was driving up the lane towards their house. He pulled the Ford up beside the shop and ran into the house and downstairs to change. Nobody was inside and he stopped briefly to call Megan's number. Perhaps she would have a good excuse. He let the phone ring but to no avail. He hung up the phone without leaving a message.

He was walking up the stairs when June appeared at the top of the landing. She gave Jim a cold stare. "Where have you been? The twins were home early on the bus. They said that they didn't see the Ford in the parking lot this afternoon. What's up, Jim?"

"I'm sorry, Mom. I forgot about the time. I went out to Dobeys after school."

"It's not going to work this time, Jim. I called the High School and they said that you weren't in class today. The twins have been home since three. It's six o'clock. Where were you all day? Your Dad is furious."

"I just took the damn day off, Mom. I forgot about it being the First Friday of the month. What do you want me to say? I screwed up. What do you want out of me?" Jim brushed past his mother to head outside. He turned abruptly. "What do you guys want me to do anyways?"

"I guess you might as well take the Mack out to the field. Your Dad is working on the Augusta place."

"Fine, I'm on my way there."

Jim exited the house and briskly walked towards the Mack truck. He drove over to the Augusta place where his Dad was threshing swathed canola. Jim parked the Mack and checked the load in the International. It was almost full so he decided to take the load back to the yard. He noticed his Dad flashing the lights of the tractor but he was not ready to combat his father at this moment.

When he arrived at the yard he backed up to the auger and commenced unloading the canola. He noticed his sisters walking up from the layer barn and waved at them. He could see them conversing together. *Thanks for nothing girls he thought.* He watched the black canola seeds emptying into the auger hopper. They seemed to be falling into an endless chasm. *He felt like his life was like that.* While deep in thought he did not notice his Dad come into the yard in the old Chev. He didn't notice anything but the emptying canola until George touched his shoulder.

"Hi there, you weren't at school today?"

"No, I skipped with some friends. Sorry. It won't happen again."

"You're damn right about that. You are officially grounded. I've seen and had enough of this foolishness to last a long time. Until you've proven your trust again you are grounded. That's all I've got to say for now. I've got work to do. No more of this bullshit. You attend school and you come home. No more lies. Allan said he saw our pickup in town a couple of nights and I gave you the benefit of the doubt but now I don't know."

"What is it with Allan? Is he your spy or something? Perhaps Allan should look after his own business."

"That's enough about him, Jim. This is about you. Allan spends long hours in Royston at his work. He's just acting like a concerned parent and friend. I've got to get. You can bring the truck down after you're finished. We've got a busy weekend ahead of us."

"Fine, I'll work hard just like I always do. Hell, I just skipped one lousy day and the world is coming to an end. Give me a break here. I took my girlfriend to the lake, Dad. Yes, I have a girlfriend and she made up a picnic lunch and we played hooky for one damn day. It was one very nice day. I wasn't late getting home. Didn't you ever miss a day of school here and there?"

"We'll talk later. In the meantime I expect to see you and this truck back in the field soon."

George turned and walked back to the old Chev. Jim watched as the old pickup bounced out the laneway. He turned his attention back to the load of canola. He suddenly felt relief that the worst was probably over. *They would not discipline him too severely. They needed his help too badly. He smirked to himself at the thought of being grounded. What idiots they were? He would show them who was grounded. Perhaps Austaire was right. He loved his parents but they were becoming just domineering idiots. He still loved them but he cherished his freedom more.* Jim finished cleaning out the truck box and shut off the auger. He jumped back into the cab of the International and hastily left the yard. The engine responded to his heavy foot and the truck sped out the lane, leaving a trail of dust and black diesel soot in the air.

22

The weekend weather provided a golden opportunity to resume harvest with a vengeance. The westerly winds were slowly drying the multitude of grain swaths that lined many fields. By Sunday evening the long hours spent in the field were finally allowing the Edwards to make substantial inroads into their harvest. As dusk disintegrated into darkness Jim was unloading yet another load of damp grain into the wet bin for the grain dryer when his Dad pulled up into the yard. George walked over to his son.

"So how are you making out here?"

"Good, I didn't think that you would be up this soon?"

"Dew is setting hard tonight. Winds died early. It brings the dampness right out of the ground."

"Are we done for the day then?"

"Yes, you bet. Can you finish up here while I take a quick run through the barns?"

"Not a problem, Dad. Mom said that she had supper waiting."

"Yes, I'll have to make peace there with her too. She was upset that we didn't make church this morning."

"Yes, she mentioned that to me too. I just told her that you wanted to get runnin' early. She can get pretty worked up about that stuff."

"That stuff means a lot to her, Jim. Never forget that. But you're right. It worked out pretty good for us. We knocked off a nice chunk of ground this weekend. We're heading into the middle of October next week. We can't afford to miss any days now."

"Think that this is our Indian summer?"

"Let's hope so, let's hope so. If we get a couple of weeks of this we would be on the home stretch."

"No word on the parts for the Deere?"

"No, your Mom phoned again yesterday. Damn backorder on the shaft. I can't make one so we just wait."

The two stood there for a minute and watched the golden kernels of wheat pour into the hopper. Small traces of dust lifted upwards into the still night air. The darkness had brought quietness to the surrounding area with only the steady clang of the grain auger breaking the stillness. George turned to leave.

"You're just about finished, Jim. See you inside?"

"Sure thing, five minutes should clean her up. You don't want me to start up the dryer?"

"No, I may come out later. We'll see." George hesitated and then resumed looking directly at Jim. "You did well this weekend. If you promise me that Friday was just a freak thing then we should keep up with our program. You're right about one thing. I remember taking the odd day off school myself." The two shared a quick smile before Jim spoke.

"Sounds fine. It won't happen again. It wasn't like I missed much anyways."

"Just no more, Jim. Mom and I have enough to worry about getting this damn harvest off and paying some bills up. We don't need to be having you playing foolish games behind our backs. Your schooling is important to all of us and most importantly yourself and your future. You understand?"

"I understand, Dad. It won't happen again."

"Okay then. Seed your wild oats at another time. I'm counting on you. Hopefully, this weather gives us a break. See you in the house."

"Thanks Dad, I won't let you down."

George exited in the direction of the broiler barn while Jim finished unloading the wheat. By the time that George had finished his nightly check through the barns the yard was deathly quiet. He walked quickly towards the house. The wet grass marked his boots as he trod. He looked up into the star lit night sky and breathed the cool, damp air. The kitchen lights shone out into the front yard and he could hear June and Jim conversing as he neared the back porch. *His son was growing up faster than he would like but that was life. He mused about the thoughts of his son having his first steady girlfriend and spending the day on a picnic. He was almost envious.* George stopped for another moment to listen to the sounds of the evening before opening the porch door and treading quietly downstairs. He was hungry and very tired.

23

Jim was sorting out books for his afternoon classes when he felt the familiar tap on his shoulder. He remained kneeling against the locker and turned to gaze up at Austaire.

"Are you just going to stare there?" Austaire laughed as she watched Jim struggle with his books while attempting to maintain his balance and look at her at the same time. "You look like a circus juggler. So where were you on the weekend? You didn't call. Is everything okay?"

"Hell yes, girl. Sorry about not calling. I was pretty busy all weekend. I actually tried to call early Sunday but I didn't get anyone. Anyways, how're you keeping? You look fantastic in that outfit."

"Thanks. Sunday morning. No, I would have been at Megans. Good party there Saturday night. You missed a good one, Jim."

"My folks were pretty pissed at me on Friday night but things ironed out." Jim stood up and shut the locker door. "Dad was pretty happy with our progress over the weekend."

"Long as you keep them happy. You are way too devoted to that damn farm." Austaire leaned into Jim's chest. "How about devoting some time to us this afternoon? Folks are away today."

"I'd better not today, Austaire. I'm sort of on probation after Friday. They had called the school asking for me."

"And found out that you weren't there. That's too cool, Jim. By the way I need a few bucks for Meg. I was able to find some loose change around the house but I came up a bit short."

"How much is a bit short?" Jim whispered into Austaire's ear. "You know that we talked about this."

Austaire reached around and tenderly nibbled on Jim's ear before speaking. "Bout' fifty, that's all. Meg said that she could wait until Friday. There's another really big party this Friday. You've got to come to this one."

"You think so do you?" Jim smiled at his girl. "We'll have to see how my schedule is." Jim looked at his watch. "God, I've got to get to class. Tell you what. Let's leave after English. That'll still give us a couple of hours. I just can't be late to pick up the girls at four."

"Great, English it is then. Gotta' grab a book. See you in class." Austaire blew a kiss at Jim and left.

Jim watched for a moment as she walked away. He then looked through his text books and carefully set the Creative Writing one aside while depositing the others into his locker. *Tomorrow he thought. He'd catch them tomorrow.* In the meantime his thoughts progressed towards their time together after class. He could catch the ATM for some cash before they went to Austaire's house. He would then drive directly from there to Royston Elementary for the girls.

On Thursday, Jim and Austaire took in an early lunch at Dobeys before venturing over to her house. They had been so engrossed in each other that Jim did not notice the growing cloud cover building in the west. He did not pay attention to the light, easterly wind. Their only interest was getting from point A to point B in the most prompt manner.

At three-thirty he hopped into the Ford and headed towards the girl's school. He had enjoyed a pleasant shower before leaving and left the driver's window down enough to air out the cab just for extra security. The girl's were waiting in front of the school. The rain began to fall as they got seated in the truck cab. At first it came in little bursts and then it became stronger. By the time the kids had left Royston the windshield wipers were barely able to keep up with the downpour. The cab of the truck resonated from the noise of the pounding rain on the roof. They drove in silence knowing full well that this would provide yet another delay to their harvest.

Friday morning Jim and the twins took the school bus into Royston. The unwelcome rain event continued to shed moisture over the general area. Water was sitting in many low lying areas of the fields leaving swaths of grain soaking where they lay. The grey skies did little to enhance what was a depressing and forlorn sight. Jim approached Glen Rollins at his locker.

"Morning, you got wheels today? Got any plans for tonight, Glen?"

"Not really, Jim Boy. But I do have my Ranger." Glen was reading the excitement in Jim's eyes. "Got another party that you require a chauffeur for?"

"You got that right. I thought that with this rain I could just stay in later and was thinking that I could mention that I had a ride with you for tomorrow. Think that would work with you?"

"You don't have to break my arm, Jim. Your folks okay with this? There's certainly no problem here."

"Great, see you at Megan's around eight."

Jim waited until classes were finished before calling home on the public phone. He waited patiently while the phone rang on the other end. His mother answered, "The Edwards. How may I help you?"

"Damn it, Mom. Dad is right you certainly do that well."

"Oh my, it's you Jim. Is something wrong? Are you okay? Where are you?

"Slow down there, Mom. Everything is fine. Just finished classes and was wondering if I could go out with Glen tonight? He has the pickup in town and seeing as it is raining I thought that maybe I could stay over and come home tomorrow. What do you think?"

"I had better talk to your Dad. I don't think that it matters much. This rain is going to shut us down for awhile now. Your Dad is inside. Just hold it a second, son."

Jim could hear his mother talking to George in the background. Austaire had joined him and was teasing him by gently rubbing her hands up his side and gently tickling him. He was attempting to refrain from laughing when his mother came back on the phone, "Hello, Jim."

Jim blurted out, "Go ahead."

"What's so funny, son? Who else is there?"

"It's just Glen. Tell him to stop tickling. So what is the verdict?"

"Go ahead and enjoy the evening. Are you going to come home with Glen then?"

"He'll bring me out...I mean home tomorrow. I won't be late. Tell Dad to leave some chores for me. Well, I've got to run. Thanks again. Love yah, Mom."

"Love you too, son. Have fun."

Jim hung up the receiver and turned to Austaire just in time to burst completely into laughter. "Damn it, Austaire." He grabbed her lovingly and wrestled her gently onto the floor. "Had enough?"

"Never enough of you." She looked deeply into Jim's blue eyes and brushed his blonde hair with her one free hand. "Let's get out of here before we make a real scene."

The couple slowly got up from the floor. "I believe that you are blushing there, Jim Edwards."

"I probably am. As for the scene I believe that it is too late by the crowd that we have around us. It's all good, right?"

The couple just laughed and left the others chatting amongst themselves. They were definitely a thing now and to Jim it was the best thing that had happened to him in a long time; perhaps ever. He paid little attention to the dreary weather outside as they ran quickly across the school parking lot towards

Dobeys. Once inside they found their favorite booth and made themselves comfortable. After consuming a generous amount of burgers and fries they left Dobeys for Megans; stopping first to hit the ATM machine on the corner. Jim grabbed the cash and looked briefly at the receipt before tossing it away.

"Is everything okay, Jim? You look concerned."

"Don't even go there. Balance looks too low but you can never trust these machines anyways. We're fine. Well, let's make a dash for it."

"Yah, I tried to get Megan but couldn't get through. Her line was busy. We could take a taxi?"

"Glen could have been our taxi but I missed him. He'll be around later, for sure. While girl let's make a run for it."

The couple headed across town on foot, oblivious to the standing drizzle. The continuous dampness inhibited their progress as they splashed their way towards the south end of town. They laughed and giggled their entire journey there while taking extra care to splash through some of the larger puddles on the way. They arrived at the familiar tree lined dead-end street where Megan's townhouse was located. Jim looked up at the street sign.

"She lives on Aspen Grove, Austaire. You know I never looked at that damn sign before."

"Say what? Thirteen Aspen Grove. It's like a second home to me."

The soaking wet couple knocked three times on the door before waiting and then knocking again. They waited patiently for Megan to come to the door. With the rain intensifying, Jim carefully turned the doorknob. It turned easily and the couple opened the door. They walked into the refuge of the dark but dry room. It was quiet inside. Jim and Austaire removed their wet shoes and socks and quietly walked towards the kitchen. They were startled by Megan's voice coming from the top of the stairs. "Who's down there? I've got a gun."

"Hey, it's Jim and Austaire. We knocked but when you didn't answer we just tried the door and it was open. We didn't mean to surprise you."

Megan appeared at the top of the stairs, "Don't ever do that again. I can't believe that I left that door open. You can never be too careful."

"Sorry Megan, we'll be more careful another time."

"Well Jimmy I'm just going to have to get you to make that up to me." Megan began to laugh loudly. "Yes kids I believe that we will have to discipline you both. Lock that damn door and get your hides up here. Meg has something special for you two."

After securing the door the couple eagerly ventured upstairs. Megan was sitting on the side of her bed inhaling crack cocaine vapor from a heated, glass tube situated on the top of a small night stand. "Come and sit down and let's get this party happening. Sit down. Chillax. It's my treat!"

Jim and Austaire sat on either side of Megan. Jim took a deep breath of the intoxicant and sat back not knowing what to expect. His second attempt sent him whirling as the powerful and intense high began to infiltrate his body.

"Is it better than being at home, Jimmy?"

"No damn chores tonight, Meg." Jim jumped up and threw his arms in the air. "I could do anything right now. I am so, so invincible."

The high was a prelude to a night that allowed everyone to attain a level of enjoyment that left nothing unearthed. Jim did not even notice Glen arrive around eight o'clock. Neither did he notice Glen leave with a girl late in the evening. He paid no attention to the miserable weather outside nor did he awake early on Saturday morning. *He felt no guilt for his actions nor did he think about his parents. His thought process was driven by the drug experience only. He felt no remorse only freedom and satisfaction. Time became a blur sending him spinning on an endless wheel.* With little persuasion he continued to party with the girls throughout the following afternoon and long into the evening finally falling fast asleep in a slumber that left him dead to the world. It was late on Sunday morning when he finally came to the realization that he should be somewhere else. He washed and walked slowly downstairs. Austaire was in the kitchen.

"Good morning. What can I get Jimmy Boy today?"

"Nothin' much, girl. Is that tea you're drinking?"

"Yah, I made a pot. It's herbal. Good for you. Sit down and I'll bring you a cup."

Jim sat on the old sofa and looked around the room. It bore the scars of the weekend party. The room was arid and stuffy but it was acceptable to his nostrils. The darkness was comforting to his eyes. Austaire handed him a cup of tea. He slowly sipped on the beverage. It brought welcome relief to the dry linings of his mouth and throat. He sat in silence and sipped from the cup. "Good tea, girl. It tastes good."

"Lot's more there. Meg must still be out of it."

"I believe that she's still upstairs. We were pretty wasted last night. Damn this tea is good."

The couple could hear noise coming from upstairs. Within minutes Megan appeared at the top of the stairwell and carefully walked down the stairs. She had dressed in a light throw that hid nothing. She spoke first, "We'll have a hard time topping this party, Jimmy Boy. You two can like go forever."

"We've got a great teacher, Meg," said Austaire.

"Not talking this morning, Jim?" Megan poured herself a cup of the tea and sat down beside him. "How's my student this morning?" She laughed loudly.

Jim just smiled and continued to sip his tea. He finished his beverage and stood up. Suddenly from nowhere he realized what day it was. "Shit. It's Sunday. I've got to get home. Damn that Glen anyway. Can I use your phone, Meg?"

The girls were both laughing at this sudden outburst from Jim. They both reached out to him and pulled him abruptly down onto the sofa. "Relax, Jim. You can phone Glen in a bit. Just calm yourself."

"Megan's right, Jim. All you did was miss some chores and some crappy weather. Who gives a damn about that?"

"I had promised my folks that Glen would drop me off yesterday. This is a winner. I don't even know where Glen is?"

The sound of the familiar knocking on the door rocked the room. Megan meandered over to the door and cautiously opened it. Glen was standing there. "Morning folks. Is Jim still about?"

"Morning Glen, come in out of the wet. Jim was just talking about you. Come in before we all catch cold."

"Your folks called our place yesterday and I kinda' persuaded them into thinking that you were still asleep. Your Mom wasn't impressed but she said that with the weather and all it was okay for the day."

"Thanks, I'm going to be up the creek today but at least you patched up the situation. I trust that you can give me a ride home?"

"I'm ready whenever you are. Sorry that I couldn't stay the other night but hey duty calls."

Jim and Glen exchanged smiles and then Jim went looking for his jacket. He slowly pulled it on and pulled up the zipper. He gave Austaire a big hug, "See yah, girl. Wish me luck." He turned to Megan and exchanged another hug with her. "Well until the next time, Meg. It might be awhile."

"Like whatever, Jimmy. You're always welcome here."

"Thanks." Jim turned to Glen. "Well let's get this show on the road."

The boys walked out into the damp air. The sky was still grey and a light mist was falling. The pavement was wet and almost had a light shine to its surface. "It is damn cold out, Glen."

"Yes any colder and it could snow. Who knows this year?"

Glen dropped Jim off in front of the house. It was well after two but the Ford was still gone from the yard. Jim walked cautiously into the house and down into his room. He did not feel particularly hungry but he was still drowsy. The room provided a warm and inviting refuge from the cold air outside. Jim had a quick shower and put on a clean change of clothes. He sat down on the edge of his bed. *His thoughts were restrained. How was he going to explain this one? Did he even care? He totally looked after his duties at this end. It was only a weekend. It wasn't like he missed any harvest work.* He gently stretched out on his bed and closed his eyes. He did not hear anything and he remembered less. He did not dream. He just fell into a deep, deep slumber.

24

Jim slept for a couple of hours and then awoke suddenly as if he was being called from elsewhere. He crawled out of his bed and looked at the clock radio. It was just past four. He opened his door and heard nothing in the house so he decided that he might as well get started on the night chores. The air outside remained cold and damp and the sky was dreary and dull. Jim entered the broiler barn and went about his familiar routine of checking the drinking fountains and filling the feeders. He finished the broiler barn and proceeded to the layer barn to gather eggs. It was funny that the family was not home yet. It was not like them to be this late for night chores.

Darkness was falling when Jim left the layer barn. The Ford was sitting in the yard but he saw no signs of anyone. He swallowed hard and walked towards the house. He was half way there when his Dad came around the corner of the back porch. Jim stopped in his tracks, "Chores are all finished. You just need to do your walk through, Dad."

George nodded to Jim and walked quietly past him. He stopped before Jim had resumed walking and looked back at his son. "You had better come along, Jim. You and I both know that we need to talk."

"Okay, sorry about yesterday. Weather was bad so I didn't think that it was any harm."

"Just come along, Jim. We can talk inside the damn barn. At least it is warm and dry in there."

Jim dragged his feet but walked steadily behind his father. A light mist was falling and it glistened under the yellow light of the yard lamp which had just illuminated. The mist was very fine and the air was getting colder. The two individuals took refuge inside the front of the layer barn. Jim was the first to speak, "Eggs are all gathered. You should check a couple of hens in B row."

"Later Jim, I'll check the damn hens later." George turned and faced his son. They were about the same height now and he looked directly into Jim's eyes. "So are you going to level with me and tell me what the hell is going on? How come you never came home yesterday? You didn't even have the common decency to give us a damn call. Look at me when I'm talking."

Jim looked up at his Dad. "Sorry but I just didn't think it mattered. You know that I would have been home if the weather was better. Hell, it gets me down too. I should have called and I shouldn't of let Glen do all the talking. We were just buggering around over there."

"Okay, that's enough of this crap. Your Mom talked to Glen's Dad. You were never there this weekend at all. We know that you stayed in Royston Friday night and I suppose Saturday. I just need to know the truth about your whereabouts and what you were up to. Were you with your girlfriend? Start talking and start making sense."

Jim shuffled his feet and looked down at the floor. He watched a single fly walking around in front of him. He methodically crunched it with his boot. It was probably stupid from the cold weather.

"Look at me, damn it, Jim. Start explaining." George reached out and grasped Jim by the shoulders. "Hey, is anyone home in there?"

"Let go of me, Dad. Just let go of me." Jim backed away from the advances of his father and stood glaring back at him. "I went to a damn party in Royston with some friends. I stayed over and when Glen did not show up on Saturday and the weather was crap I just figured that it would be okay to stay. Glen picked me up this morning."

"And where in Royston were you and with whom?"

"I was with Austaire and some other school friends. We went to a house party, just dancing and the like. Glen was there Friday night but he left and went home without me. He was suppose to pick me up on Saturday but didn't."

"So does this Austaire have a last name?"

"Austaire Jamieson, I told you about her before. We are friends and she lives in Royston. Not that it is any of your business. I mean my friends are my own doings. I'll hang out with whoever I wish to."

"If your friends are making you lie to us and others then they are not going to be your friends very long. I think that we deserve a little better than a diet of damn lies. Why didn't you just ask if you could go to a party? Why didn't you just call and tell us where you were? What the hell did we ever do to deserve all these damn lies?"

"I didn't because I figured that you wouldn't let me go. I should have called yesterday. I'm sorry about that."

Jim and George appeared locked in mortal combat once again. Jim stood directly in front of his Dad awaiting the next round of accusations. *He thought how his Dad's words meant so very little. It was the typical parent refusal that they could not be wrong and that they could do no wrong.*

"Are you laughing at me now?" George reached across and grabbed hold of Jim by the shoulders. This time the hold was secure and meaningful. "This is not funny anymore. You are not too old for a good whooping."

"Just like in the good old days, eh Dad? You can just bully us kids around and make us do whatever you wish. What are you going to do, hit me? Is that what you are aiming to do? Go ahead then. Let the good times roll." Jim stepped back and brushed off his father's hand. He stood there defiantly awaiting his Dad's next move.

"Damn you, Jim. Whatever is going on inside you? You think that I like this situation? We used to be like buddies. Now it seems like I hardly know you."

"You only know this damn farm and these damn birds, Dad. We just come along as necessary baggage. Look I am sorry that I didn't call home and I will not lie about a party again. Okay?"

"Definitely because you are formally grounded this time. We will know your whereabouts and what you are up to. Your mother was so upset when you didn't even call her. Now get into the house before I say or do something that I'll just regret. Make sure that you talk with your mother. Tell her that I will not be long. She'll have supper soon."

Jim just nodded his head in agreement and turned away from his father. He walked quickly out of the barn into the darkness of the evening. The dampness that had appeared earlier was slowly transforming into a white mist. He reached out his open hand and allowed a few flakes of the wet snow to land on it. They quickly melted on contact leaving wet marks on his hand. He nervously reached up with his other hand and wiped a few tears from his eyes and walked slowly towards the house.

June greeted him as he entered the back porch. She smiled at her son but remained silent. Jim returned the surprisingly warm greeting, "Hi there, Mom. Sorry about not calling. It won't happen again."

"Are you okay, son? Is everything okay between your Dad and yourself? We just care, Jim. We just care so much about you."

"I know you do, Mom. Everything is fine. I just got caught up in a party. Sometimes I'm afraid to ask you guys because I want to go somewhere or do something and I figure that you won't let me. It won't happen another time, promise. It's all good. Well I had better get cleaned up. Looks like the school bus again tomorrow. It's trying to snow out there."

"Come and give your Mom a hug. Supper will be ready in a few minutes."

Jim reached over and hugged his mother. "I'm really not too hungry, Mom. I might grab something later. I just need some quiet for a bit." Jim turned away and proceeded downstairs. His head was in turmoil as a flood of mixed emotions created a formidable headache. He changed out of his chore clothes, washed and entered his room.

The dim overhead light was satisfactory for the moment. He sat on the floor and surveyed the contents of the room and what they meant to him. They increasingly represented a distant world that was quickly fading from the reality of his new life. *Austaire would have been proud of him when he stood up to his Dad. Jim no longer felt the guilt trip that had accompanied his actions previously but increasingly felt uncertain as to where his future lay. Did he really even belong here anymore?* Jim sat still for a while longer just enjoying the warmth and quiet of his room. He didn't have any homework since he didn't bring any books with him. He pulled up his paint easel and decided to paint for awhile.

25

George purposely dragged his feet as he slowly made his tour through the barns. All the chores had been performed to perfection. Even Jim's observation on the layers was correct and George had addressed the problem. He took one more glance across the flow of white bodies all nestled in for the evening under the dim lights and left the barn.

The crisp darkness greeted him with white flakes of wet snow floating onto the damp ground. If it got much colder during the night it would easily be white in the morning. George looked across the yard and gazed into the darkness. *Were Allan's concerns for Jim correct? Were they losing Jim to the lure of Royston?* He picked up a stone from the roadway and tossed the wet missile hard into the distant tree row. He listened as the rock hit the wood with a dull thud and tumbled to the ground and then he continued into the house.

Supper was a very quiet gathering. Jim did not come up for the meal despite several attempts to encourage him to attend. George decided it best not to push the issue but the empty chair sat as a constant reminder of the events of another disastrous weekend. The sparse conversation was centered on the weather and the state of their harvest progress. Even June's famous apple pie could not shake the gloom.

"Great pie, Mom," said Susan. "Should Mary and I start the dishes now?"

"How be you and your sister watch a program or something and I'll help your mother tonight?"

"Are you sure?" asked Susan. "We don't mine, Dad."

"No, you two relax. Have you got your homework done?"

"I'm finished," said Mary. "Thanks Dad. Are you coming Susan?"

"Lead the way. Thanks Dad. There's nothing else, Mom?"

"No. Thanks. It seems like your father wants to help with the dishes tonight."

George had already started to gather the dirty plates and carry them into the kitchen. He started the water running into the sink and made another trip back to the dinner table for more dishes. June glanced up at him as he loaded his arms again. "So what do we owe this occasion to?"

"Oh, nothing much, I just felt like washing dishes. Helps clean my hands up once in awhile."

"You wash dishes once in a blue moon, George. What's up?"

"Can't I just wash some damn dishes if I want? If it is such a damn issue I won't bother."

"Okay, okay, I was just teasing. I know the weather is bad but it isn't going to help things by us all clamping up like zombies."

George dumped his load of dirty dishes beside the sink and commenced washing them. He remained silent as he methodically washed and rinsed each piece and deposited it on the drying rack. He was half way through the exercise when the conversation resumed. "Are we doing okay?" He let a small crack of a smile migrate from his sober face.

"Looking fine, George." June grabbed one of his wet hands. "You're right, you should wash dishes more often. It is an improvement." She released his hand and went back to drying dishes. "So what did Jim have to say to you?"

George looked around the corner into the living room. The twins were engrossed in a movie. He looked back at June. "He was pretty defensive. He mentioned that Austaire Jamieson girl again and admitted to staying in for a house party. I told him he was grounded and he nodded and left. I'm sure this Austaire is his new found girlfriend but what I don't understand is why it seems such an issue to him."

"He seemed apologetic enough when he came into the house, George. I thought that he would have been hungry. Did he have the chores done?"

"They were done well just like Jim always does his chores. I don't know what to think, June. You don't think that Allan is right and Jim is associating with the wrong kids? Perhaps you should check and see how many Jamieson's are in the phone book and see if you can make contact with her parents?"

"Yes, I can do that. He certainly is off on his own thing lately. I'm worried about him."

"Me too. Don't go thinking that you have a monopoly on worrying about him. I told him that out there. I told him that he was still young enough to get punished but my threats did not have much effect on him."

"You didn't hurt him, did you? Nothing is accomplished by that and you know it. Both of you can be pretty obstinate at times."

"I didn't touch the kid. I felt like grabbing him and shaking the livin' fear of God into him. It was like it was going in one ear and out the other. I just don't know. All I know is that he has to become accountable again. What the hell did we do to deserve this crap? Why can't he approach us and just be honest and up front with us? All this sneaking around just isn't like Jim at all. He's completely changed of late."

"It'll work out, George. He is a good kid and he's undoubtedly got himself a new girlfriend and has got some adjustment to make in his life."

"Well he can remain grounded for awhile and let this weekend settle in. Anymore of this crap and I'll put a damn chain on him."

"Calm down, George. You're talking ridiculous now. By the way it may not be a great time to mention it but you've got a bank appointment on Tuesday."

"Yes, I almost forgot that. Gotta' go in and tell that miserable S.O.B. that all is fine and well despite this damn weather. If it keeps this shit up we won't have to worry about Jim staying in Royston because we will all be in there."

"It can't be that bad, George. We must be half way through the harvest and we always have the birds to support us. We are all praying for some better weather and the Lord will answer those prayers."

"And is he going to pay the damn land payment coming up at the end of the month too? If we hadn't busted that damn Deere we would be three-quarters finished now. Instead we are swathing everything and dumping it onto the damn ground so it can get soaked and deteriorate in front of our faces. Sounds like a hell of a plan to me."

George finished washing the last plate and pulled the drain plug to the sink. He watched in silence as the water cascaded down into the drain. *He too had that sinking feeling and despite all the encouragement and faith from June he was beginning to have sincere doubts about this year's harvest.* He finished wiping the countertop and reached for the cups to put them into the overhead cupboard. One of them slipped through his grasp and fell crashing onto the kitchen floor. He screamed, "Break, why don't you? Everything else is."

"Calm yourself, George." June started picking up the pieces and depositing them in the garbage can. "You won't make things any better this way. It'll all work out."

"Just like always, June. Hell this fall has been a receipt for disaster since September started." George cleared his throat and talked even louder. "It's bad enough that the weather is pure hell but we've had to contend with nothing but bullshit from our son and breakdowns from wherever. What is next? A damn earthquake?"

"George. Enough!" June's voice was rising to a level equal to her husbands. "There is no need for us to be having this conversation in this manner. The twins don't need this. They haven't done anything wrong. Jim's made some mistakes but he has also worked hard at times."

"That's the whole thing. He has worked hard at times and other times he is a damn, lazy idiot like the rest of those lame brain kids in Royston. Hell, even Glen Rollins has joined their ranks."

With that June broke down in tears. She fell destitute to the floor and sobbed almost uncontrollably. The twins appeared at the corner of the kitchen and Susan ran to her mother. "You okay, Mom?"

June made a valiant attempt to clear her tears. "Yes. Yes, girls, Dad and I just got carried away here. I'm sorry and so is your father."

The girls' eyes were fixed on their father. George looked back at them and knelt down by June and reached out to her with one hand. "Come on, June. I'm sorry too. It'll all be fine. Everything will work out." George turned to his daughters. "How be you two get ready for bed and we can have a card game or something before you go. We can all play together."

"Sounds great, Dad," said Mary. "Come Susan."

Susan followed her sister without saying anything. George looked back at June. The couple remained on the kitchen floor. George reached out again and June hesitantly allowed him to hug her firmly against him.

"Just don't allow yourself to get swept away by this, George. Promise me that you will not. I know that we've got some problems but I can't take the arguing."

George looked sincerely at his wife of twenty years. They had endured so much through those years and had always kept it together. *He admired her silent strength and feared the words that she had just uttered.* "I'm sorry Hon. I know better."

The couple rose from the floor together. They finished cleaning up the broken pieces and tidied up the kitchen counter. They worked together in silence remaining satisfied that the encounter was over and finished. The girls returned to the living room table with the "Sorry" game board. When George saw the game he nodded his head in approval. *He thought how appropriate and fitting it was that they should play this game at this time.* Meanwhile downstairs, Jim was quietly digesting the conversation he had just overheard.

26

The Edwards had awakened to a relatively pleasant surprise on Monday morning. The wet snow that was attempting to fall the evening before had stopped and the family awoke to a frosty morning with clearing skies. By mid-morning the sun was again attempting to warm the area with its autumn blessings. It was ten-thirty by the time that George finished up outside and came in for a coffee. June had just gotten off the phone and ran to greet him when he entered the back porch.

"Our parts are all in. Derrick Equipment just called and the shaft has arrived. We can pick them up anytime."

"Well hallelujah, Hon. Do you want to try Ben at the bank and see if I could see him today? Perhaps you and I could catch lunch in Royston? Then we could drive up to Grenick and pick up the parts and possibly catch the kids on the way home."

"Did you say lunch? Let me give that banker a call. Hopefully Ben has a slow morning going for him."

George disappeared downstairs while June scurried to the phone. George had just enough time to wash and change when June hollered down to him, "It's a go. We have to be in there by eleven-thirty."

"Great, we're outa' here. This day is looking better all the time."

"Just have some faith, George. I don't know the last time that we had lunch out together. This girl is excited."

The couple lost no time in getting ready and jumping into the Ford. The trip into Royston was even quicker as George pushed the speed limit to beat the clock. They arrived in front of the bank just in time for his appointment. He hurried into the bank with an earnest smile on his face. The appointment lasted only twenty minutes and he exited the bank still carrying the smile. June had picked up a few grocery items from across the street and the couple met by the truck.

"So are we still in business?" June smiled and deposited her bags in the back seat. "Was Ben in a good mood this morning?"

"Ben was Ben. He just had the usual concerns about cash flow and our needs going into the winter. He asked about harvest. He's okay with our progress. I guess we are not alone."

"Well, George Edwards, let's go to lunch. That's enough about money and banks for today."

George started up the Ford and backed onto the street. "So where are going to eat, Mrs. Edwards?"

"Formal, aren't we now. I don't know. Let's go to Dobeys. I've never been in there and the kids always rave about the burgers there."

George looked down at his watch. "It's noon now. It may be pretty busy."

"Let's try it anyways, George. We can always get takeout and eat on the way up to Grenick."

George headed straight to Dobeys and parked just up the street across from Royston High. The couple entered the establishment and surprisingly the place was not too busy. They sat down at a table and ordered their meal which the waitress delivered to them in short order. They were soon sampling their first sample of Dobeys cheeseburgers and fries.

"This isn't too bad, Hon."

"You look surprised, George. Jim talks about this place all the time."

George was just in the process of dipping a fry into some ketchup when he caught sight of Jim crossing the street in front of them. He nudged June with his arm. "Speaking about Jim, just look at who's comin' across the street. My bets are that girl he is with is Austaire. Did you ever check in the phone book?"

"Yes, this morning. Several names under Jamieson but I'll keep trying. Better hush because they are coming in."

Jim and Austaire entered Dobeys and walked back towards their favorite booth oblivious to the fact that his parents were in the building. They sat down and ordered their food while continuing on with their conversation. June and George finished eating and walked back towards the booth. They startled the young couple.

"Good Afternoon." George reached out to the girl with an open hand, "And you must be Austaire?"

Jim hastily swallowed his food and acknowledged his parents with a hasty, "Hi, what brings you guys here? I mean this is quite a surprise."

"Dad and I had an appointment at the bank and had to go for parts so we thought that we'd have lunch out for a change. You're right about the burgers. They were pretty good." June looked at Austaire and then back towards Jim, "So are you going to introduce us?"

"I'm sorry; Austaire meet my Mom and Dad."

Austaire casually looked up at June and George. She slowly finished one of her fries before speaking. "I've heard lots about you guys. Nice meeting you." She turned her attention back to the food on her plate.

"Did you say that you had parts in, Dad?"

"Yes, hopefully it's the correct shaft and I can get that Deere back running. Anyways, we had better get going and leave you two to your lunch. We can probably pick you and the girls up later after coming back from Grenick?" George looked directly at Jim and finished with, "See you about three-thirty in front of the school." George turned and left the booth. "Coming, June?"

"Yes, it's a decent drive up there. See you later, Jim and nice meeting you, Austaire."

Once outside of Dobeys George resumed his conversation with June as they walked towards the Ford. "I think that we pretty much surprised those two. That Austaire didn't have much to say. I don't think that she would have given me the time of day if she had the choice."

"Well at least we got to meet her, George. Perhaps Jim will feel better about talking about her now. She sure is a pretty girl."

"She's pretty something, June, pretty something. Anyways we had better get those parts picked up."

The drive to Grenick proved fruitful as the shaft and associated parts appeared to be the correct ones. A jubilant couple drove back to Royston High to pick up their children. They arrived in the parking lot about three-thirty and waited in the visitor's area. At quarter to four Monty's bus pulled up to the school and George walked over to the bus. Monty opened up the school bus door, "How is George Edwards? I haven't seen you in awhile."

"Isn't that a fact, Monty? I'm okay. Be a whole lot better if this weather turns around but I'm sure that everyone is saying the same thing. We just picked up some parts and can give the girls and Jim a ride home."

The girls had seen their Dad and were already in the process of exiting the bus. "Bye, Monty," said Susan, "See you tomorrow."

"See you, Monty," added Mary.

George watched as the twins headed towards the Ford. He then turned back to Monty who was now standing beside him. "Well, that is two out three. Jim should be here shortly I'd imagine."

"I never know for sure with Jim anymore, George. Seems like he has the truck a lot or he gets a ride with the Rollins lad."

"We've been letting him take the Ford pretty regularly during harvest."

"Yep, I see the truck around town quite a bit. He seems to be hanging out with a different group of kids than last year. You've got a good lad there.

Everybody says so. He always seems so quiet and polite. I've watched him grow up for many years now."

"Thanks. He's definitely growing up and changing. Believe me, Monty, this fall has not been fun."

"Just be careful, George. I see a lot of good rural kids get mixed up with some weird ones here in Royston. It's a small place but it seems to have more than its share of worms in the barrel if you know what I mean. I drive taxi at night and I see them at all hours walking the streets or getting rides here and there. Unfortunately, there seems to be a lot of dope on the streets of this town and I see lots of kids using the stuff. I must be getting old or something. I'm starting to sound like a cynical old man. Anyways, I'd better get back in the drivers seat before one of these characters thinks they can drive this damn thing." Monty turned to walk up into the bus. "Speaking about Jim, here he comes now. You take care now, George."

"You too, Monty. Nice talking with you."

Jim did not head towards his Dad who was standing by the front of the bus. Instead he chose to walk around the back of the vehicle and head directly to the Ford. George nodded to Monty and then turned and walked slowly towards the pickup himself. He noticed that Jim was not carrying any school books but dismissed the observation. George climbed into the Ford and the family headed home.

By Thursday, George had the Deere running again. Jim had worked faithfully with his father late into Monday night. June had assisted George on Tuesday and Wednesday as Jim indicated that he must work on another school project. He remained quiet and distant from the rest of the family and spent the majority of his time in his room. His appearances were limited to performing his regular chores and hastily partaking in the family meals.

George attempted to straight cut wheat with the Deere on Thursday afternoon. The grain was tough and still damp but the repair had been successful. George harvested as late as humanly possible considering the conditions and then dried wheat well into the night. The weather remained "iffy" but it was allowing some resemblance of harvest activities to resume throughout the area.

Jim was allowed to drive the Ford into Royston on Friday with strict instructions to pick up the twins and be home early. He did not disappoint. They arrived in the yard shortly after four o'clock. Jim dried grain for his father until nine o'clock. He easily caught up with the small volume of wheat that his Dad was able to harvest due to the poor conditions. By ten o'clock the heavy dew had long silenced all operations. The weary family was fast asleep. George had taken the precaution of putting the keys to the Ford in the night table drawer beside June.

Jim slipped out of the house about ten-thirty. He had once again been refused permission to slide into Royston for the evening. He hurriedly walked out the lane in the dark. The clear sky was ablaze with stars and he felt cold in his fall jacket. He watched with satisfaction as the lights of Glen's Ranger drew closer to him on the main road. It came to an abrupt halt and Jim jumped in. "You got the heater going in this thing? Damn it's cold out there."

"Good to see you too, Jim." Glen laughed at his friend. "It serves you right for wearing that windbreaker. It makes me cold just looking at you. So where are we headed tonight?"

"Girls are away this weekend but I thought that you and I could catch a couple of drinks or something. I've got a couple of joints with me too if your so inclined?

"Do you really think that we can get into a bar?"

"Don't really know but I guess there's no harm in trying. There are always some kids hanging out by the old pool hall. At least we can get inside there if nothing else. Anything is better than lying around at home."

"You're definitely right about that, Jim. Are you starting to warm up? This thing isn't fancy but it has a heater."

"Shit yah, Glen." Jim pulled out a joint and looked at Glen, "Do you mine?"

"No, its okay, I guess. Maybe just leave the window down some once we get into town. And please don't go blowing that stuff around a cop car. My Dad still uses this truck some and I don't need any problems with my wheels."

"No problem." Jim lit up the joint and began contently drawing its valuable contents into his lungs. He exhaled and blew a light ring towards Glen.

Glen looked at him and laughed. "You're getting pretty good at that. You best be careful or you will have us both stoned before we even get into Royston."

Jim laughed at the suggestion and turned to his friend, "Like totally wicked, Glen my friend. Let the party begin then for the night is ours."

27

George was in a much better frame of mind by Monday morning. The weekend had been quite productive and the family had worked hard to take advantage of the weather break. He had risen very early and performed some much needed maintenance on the feeding system in the broiler barn before addressing the normal morning chores. The kids had been up early candling eggs and preparing them for shipment. By ten o'clock the egg truck left the yard and George prepared for another day of slow harvesting. June came out to the shop and asked, "So do you want the good news or the bad news?"

George crawled out from under the combine. "So do I have a choice?"

"I'll tell you the good news first." June spoke in a jubilant voice. "I was talking to your mother earlier and the folks will be here during the third week of November and will stay until just after Christmas. They'll probably be here around the 20th depending on how long they stay in Ollen."

"That's great, Hon. So dare I ask about the bad news?"

"We need to go into Royston."

"Royston? What the hell for?"

"It's Mr. Erickson, the principal at the High School. He wants to see us prompt. Didn't say much but said he had to talk to us about Jim, directly."

"Can't you go in, June? I've got to get going here. Not much of a day again but I can go."

"He wants to see both of us, George. I told him that we would be in this morning. That way you can still run this afternoon."

George nodded his head in agreement and tossed the grease gun onto the bench. In short order they were both driving out the lane and heading towards Royston High. They arrived at the school and headed to the main office where June recognized the receptionist. "Good morning, Amy. George and I have an appointment with Principal Erickson.

"Hello June, it's nice to see you again. Have a seat and I'll let him know that you people are here. He's been expecting you."

The receptionist talked in private over the phone and then nodded to June. "He'll see you now. Just take the first door to your left."

"Thanks, Amy," said June, "Nice to see you again."

George and June walked down the short aisle and approached the doorway. It opened about the time they arrived. Principal Erickson was standing at the open doorway. "Come on in." He extended his right hand, "Pleased to meet you both again."

George and June shook his hand and then sat down in the rather cramped office. The furniture was functional but definitely not lavish. The chairs appeared well worn. His desk was piled with multiple folders. One folder was opened on his desk in front of his chair. Mr. Erickson ensured that the door was fully closed and then quietly sat down facing the anxious parents.

"You look like a busy man," said George. "I can appreciate that. What can we do for you?"

"Mr. and Mrs. Edwards, I asked Amy to call you in regarding your son."

"Call us June and George. I know that it's been awhile but we've seen you before. Jim's been in this school for three years now."

"Okay. As you know we have term reports due by December. It's been brought to my attention that Jim's grades are falling badly. His attendance at school has been particularly poor over the past month. I know that you folks are faced with a difficult harvest and that you probably require all the help that you can get but your son is becoming completely delinquent in his studies. You cannot continue to restrict him from attending school in an attempt to get work done at home. His absenteeism is completely destroying his progress at Royston High."

"What the hell are you talking about? Excuse the language, Erickson, but our son attends school every damn day. Our kids work hard. No doubt about that one but they do not miss school days. Jim has left home either on the school bus or with our pickup every day this fall."

"Your son is missing half-days of school on a consistent and regular basis. He has several full days missed. I have attendance records from all of his teachers."

"I know that Jim missed one Friday because he admitted to skipping classes that day and he was disciplined for it. It was a Friday a couple of weeks back. Other than that we have no knowledge of our son missing school."

"Then how do you explain these notes signed by yourselves indicating that Jim was required at home due to harvest commitments? Here look at these. Someone is not telling the truth here folks?"

"You accuse us of bloody lying and you'll wear a fat lip mister. Let me look at those damn slips."

George quickly studied the pieces of paper and passed them over to June. The couple shook their heads as they studied the writing and signatures. "It's not our writing. What the hell is going on here?"

"I'd appreciate it if you talk in a more comfortable manner or I'll have to ask you to leave."

"It's not our hand writing. Do you require proof?"

June interrupted with a more quiet tone, "So how bad are his marks?"

"According to this mid-term report he is failing in three out of six subjects and barely passing in those. We have a student capable of straight "B's" who is now failing half of his classes. It is my duty to insure that your son is not deprived of the opportunity to obtain his education here. I also have various reports of him dozing off in class and appearing in class in a manner that would suggest that he is not receiving adequate sleep or possibly nutrition. Two of these teachers have known Jim throughout his entire school attendance here. They are very concerned. If this situation is not corrected then I will be forced to contact social services. You cannot work your son and deprive him of his studies."

"Now listen here. Enough is enough." George attempted to lower the tempo of his voice. "We did not know that any of this was occurring. Jim has been acting very different this fall ever since he met that Austaire Jamieson girl and another girl from town. I can't remember her name at the moment."

"Excuse me but does Jim keep the acquaintance of Miss Jamieson. Her folder is on my desk as well. We are attempting to get in touch with her parents as we speak."

"I bet you that she has similar absenteeism and poor grades as well."

"It's actually worst, George. She may face being expelled if some of these suspicions are validated."

"What kind of suspicions?"

"I cannot expand on anything at this time but let me suggest that we have grave concerns regarding possible illegal drug issues."

June burst into tears at that moment. She looked at George and then directed her concerns towards Principal Erickson. "Please don't tell me that Jim is in trouble too. He is such a good boy. He always tries so hard. This is not like Jim. He has seemed so troubled at times this fall but for the most part he is our Jim. What can we do?"

George reached over and grasped June's hand. He studied her anxious face before turning once again to Principal Erickson. "Is Jim in school now? Can we address our concerns directly to him?"

"Jim is not in school today. It was brought to my attention early this morning by one of his teachers. I'm sorry but you two must attempt to correct whatever is going on here. I believe that you may not have realized what was occurring but now you do and you must correct this. I can haul him into my office first thing tomorrow morning and chat with him but for his own good you are going to have to take control."

George and June nodded their heads in quiet agreement. They arose from their respective chairs and offered a handshake to Principal Erickson. "Appreciate the conversation. We just wish that someone had called us earlier. We just didn't know. It's the end of October. Anyways, thanks again. Sorry if my feathers were ruffed earlier. We just don't go around lying to people."

Principal Erickson stood silent for a moment while attentively digesting the contents of the conversation that had just occurred. "I'll talk with Jim tomorrow. In the meantime you must talk with your son and get this matter corrected. Sorry to meet with you two under these circumstances but you are going to have to devote some real time and effort towards the well being of your son. My hands are tied here. I'm just trying to do my job and look after the educational progress of Jim. Good luck to both of you. These situations are never easy. Amy will give you my direct phone line if you wish?"

"That would be most appreciated," said George, "We'll be in touch for sure. Thanks again."

June added, "We appreciate your interest in our son."

June and George slowly walked back towards the Ford. They had both been hit with a log and they remained stunned to the realities of what the principal had just related to them. George quickly drove home and disappeared downstairs into Jim's room. He turned on all the lights and began exploring the shelves and cupboard drawers. He was not sure what he was looking for but he had to look. June heard the commotion coming from the room and entered it as well. "What are you doing, George. You can't just tear everything apart here."

"I'll damn well tear it all apart if I have too, June. You heard Erickson mention the trouble that Jamieson girl was in. She is behind all this. I just know it." George stopped in his tracks as he studied a small clay pipe that he had just discovered hidden in one of the drawers. He carefully smelled the odor from the empty bowl and handed the instrument to June. "Do you think that smell is from tobacco? I wish it was but I know damn well it isn't. That kid is experimenting with drugs as sure as I'm standing here."

George went back to his mission while June stood in the room. Tears had once again entered her eyes. She stood silently in the room and whispered a small prayer. She opened her eyes abruptly to George's next discovery, a small plastic bag that he suspected contained marijuana. He opened the bag and sniffed the contents. He handed the package to June and sat down on the bed. "He's been playin' a regular game with us. He brought this stuff into our own house. I want you to get hold of Allan and tell him what we have found and you had better find that damn girl's parents. We've got problems here. Just wait until that boy gets home. Son of a bitch."

"George, please don't start with that language. It doesn't help anything. Perhaps we should take time to pray for our son. I'm sure that it isn't as bad as it seems."

"I'm just going to confront him, June. He can't excuse himself out of this one. Just let the cards lie where they may. We've got to get to the bottom of this."

George walked out of the room and headed towards the change room. He had things to do but they were now overshadowed by this sudden turn of events. *Perhaps he could finish up his maintenance in the shop. That would allow him the opportunity to watch for Jim when he arrived home.* "I'm going outside, June. I won't be far. So much for harvest today."

June remained standing in Jim's room. Her eyes were unconsciously surveying the contents of his shelves and walls. She called George back into the room, "Jim has several things missing from his room."

"What do you mean missing?" George had changed and entered the room in his work clothes. "What kind of things?"

"His coin collection is gone. That autographed hockey jersey always hung over there. I don't see that school medallion that he was presented in Elementary and where are his good books? No one has been here. The girls don't touch anything down here. Is he moving stuff out of here?"

George gave June a resilient hug and held her firmly for a good minute. "It'll be fine. We'll work this out. I'm not sure how we are going to stop him from seeing those damn kids but we will. He'll see the wrong to all of this."

George backed away from June and then silently turned and left the room. He was frightened and furious at the same time. He walked out into the dull, afternoon sunshine. It was pale outside but it was dry. He should have been harvesting hours ago. Instead he was mulling options on how to contain his son and prevent this foolishness from going any further. He walked to the shop and grabbed the grease gun and a cartridge from the bench. He looked at the combine and in frustration tossed the cartridge hard against the shop door. The top burst open allowing the contents to partially spill. He stood there and yelled at the top of his voice, "Why in the hell us?"

28

George was finishing with his greasing on the Deere when he saw Monty's school bus stop at the end of the lane. He glanced again as the bus pulled away and then looked hard down the lane way. Only the twins were walking up the lane. Jim was not to be seen. George ran into the house and yelled at June, "Jim's not there. Did you have any luck finding that Jamieson household?"

June came running into the kitchen. Her eyes were full of tears. "Yes, I managed to get a hold of Mrs. Jamieson about three-thirty. Apparently she had spoken with Jim a couple of times on the phone but has never met him. She had just received the message from Principal Erickson and was going to see him tomorrow. She thought that it was Jim that has been influencing her Austaire. She was pretty upset and I got pretty upset. The long to the short of it was that it didn't sound like she knew much about her daughter at all. Sounds like Austaire stays with a girl called Megan a fair bit but they don't even know her last name or where she lives. Both the parents work out, George."

"Did you say Megan, June? Jim has mentioned Megan before. It sounds like they may have a common link."

"She was saying ugly things about our son. I had to hang up before I blew my top. I know that Jim is in trouble but it isn't of his own accord. I just know it."

"Well he isn't on the bus again, June. I just hope that he didn't get word that we were called into the school and decided not to come home or some damn thing. This is just getting to be ugly."

Susan opened the porch door and the twins entered the house. They greeted their parents and confirmed that Jim had not been anywhere near the school when Monty had left Royston High. George walked out of the house and headed towards the barns. He was half way across the yard when Glen Rollins pulled into the yard and Jim jumped out of the truck. Glen waved to

George and exited the yard. George walked quickly over towards his son. Jim stopped in his tracks as his Dad approached.

"Hi Dad, how come you're not threshing? You didn't have another problem did you? I see the Deere at the shop."

"I've got another problem but it isn't with the damn machine. You had best go downstairs into your room. Your mother and I have to talk with you."

"Now what's wrong? I wasn't late or anything. I was only a few minutes behind the bus. Glen enjoys me tagging along when he has his ride."

"Jim, your mother and I had to go in and see your principal today. We have to talk. Just go downstairs. I'll be right in."

Jim stood motionless for a moment and then willingly walked away from his father towards the house. George watched in silence as his son trod up the beaten pathway. He remembered when his son struggled to walk along those steps. *He could still envision Jim pushing a die-cast toy tractor along those old stones. It really wasn't that long ago. He was no longer that child. Where in the world had the time flown?* He watched Jim disappear around the house while he attempted to put his thoughts together. The autumn sunshine beat down on the brow of his cap. It almost felt warm.

The twins had disappeared towards the layer barn when George entered the house. He quickly changed and entered Jim's room. June and Jim had already been conversing. George looked directly at Jim and asked, "So how are we going to correct this mess?"

"Tried and sentenced already? I know that I've messed up but it isn't like it is the end of the world. I'll do better and get my marks back in line. Like I told Mom, I just got caught up in the fun. I can bring my marks back. If you guys just give me enough time to work on the assignments and I'll get to class. You'll see."

"Now look here, Jim. You've had time for school all along. You have always had time for homework and if you require more then it's a done deal. That is not the issue here. It's your new friends in Royston that are messing you up. You've got to promise us that you will quit seeing Austaire and Megan. I know that Austaire is your girlfriend but you will find another. These girls are nothing but trouble. It appears that your school work has suffered as a direct result of your relationship with these girls. You lie to your mother and you've made me feel like a tyrant in front of your principal."

"You don't give me a lot of time to myself, Dad. You expect us kids to work like adults all the time."

"I know that you work hard," June interjected. "If we had another option to get the work done this fall we would have taken it."

"Sorry, June, but I have to make exception to this damn talk for a second. I've got two questions for you, Jim, and the answers had better be good ones. What have you been doing during all the time that you missed classes and are you taking drugs with your friends?"

Jim stood silent for a minute. He looked around his room as if he was studying the contents. He then stared uneasily at the floor. The perspiration flowed from his forehead further exposing his increasingly pale complexion. His hands and legs shook as the tension of the moment took an extreme toll on his nerves. He blurted out, "I've been hanging out with some friends and no I don't take drugs."

George reached down onto the night table and practically forced the material he had found earlier into Jim's face. "And what the hell is this for then?"

"Have you been looking through my stuff? Like this is my room here. You've got no right to dig through my stuff."

"We've got every right if you are in trouble. Your mother tells me you've got personal things missing from here too. Are you selling them to support your friend's habits? Why are they gone?"

"You two are just too much. I can do whatever I want with my stuff and it isn't anything to do with you. This is personal. These things are mine. I can do whatever I please with them."

June interrupted with a stern but sincere voice. "Jim, we just want what is best for you. I know that you have things missing from your room. Your Dad found that pipe and bag. We all know that it isn't tobacco. This Austaire and Megan that you have been seeing are hurting you, son. You can't keep going like this. Look at you. The Lord will help us through this. Your principal and your teachers all care about you. You've got family and friends that will help. I pray for your deliverance from this evil that has infiltrated your life. It is much too precious to waste on drugs, Jim."

"Now look here, Mom. First of all I'm not some drug addict and secondly what my friends do is none of yours or Dad's business. If I was to take some pot or something then it is my business. I am old enough to decide. It really isn't a big deal. Lot's of kids take drugs. It is just the way it is. Your God doesn't give a shit about whether I succeed or not. Your God just continually makes life hard for us. You can pray about me all you want but I have had enough of that shit."

June's tears flowed down her face. She looked lovingly into her son's eyes. "Tell me you didn't mean that blasphemy. The drugs are talking now. The devil is working from within you." June reached out to her son but Jim stood back pushing his mother aside.

"I don't want your sympathy and don't need your damn God." Jim's eyes were ablaze. "Even Dad laughs about going to church."

"That's not completely true, Jim, and you know it. What your mother is doing is asking the Lord for help here to see you through your problem. We can get professional help with counselors in Royston or through your school. We just need to take the right steps to see that you get back on track. You've got to attend school regularly and get your marks back up. You've got to let Austaire and Megan and anyone else associated with them go so that you can get your life back to normal. Do you understand?"

"All that I understand is that you guys are jumping to a pile of conclusions and attempting to take over my life again. That is what you do. I can stand on my own two feet and make my own decisions. I'm old enough."

"You haven't been acting as if you are old enough for anything at times. While you remain a part of this household you will obey some basic rules and principals. You can start by apologizing to your mother and then by agreeing to a plan to get your life back together. Otherwise we have a runaway here and you are out of control."

"Bullshit, I have nothing to apologize to Mom about." Jim glared fiercely at his father. "God and I have nothing in common and I don't need him."

"I know you don't mean that, Jim," June cried. Her face was filling with tears. She reached out to her son but this time he abruptly forced her away and she fell heavily against the dresser. June lay trembling in the corner of the room.

Jim sneered at his mother and yelled, "You want the devil. You've got him."

In an instant George reached over and attempted to slap Jim. Jim shuffled to one side and in the ensuing scuffle they both ended up on the bedroom floor. George managed to spin his son over and grab Jim's left arm twisting it around his back. "Apologize to your mother. Now!"

"You're hurting me. Let go of me. I apologize to you, Mom, but it doesn't mean anything. None of this does. Now let me go before I report you or something. Let me go you damn bully!"

George relinquished the hold he had on his son and stood up in front of him. He looked at Jim and stammered, "You will change and you will obey. You can say goodbye to those damn kids in Royston. If we have to we will home school you but we will not stand here and watch you waste your life on those idiots. We will take you into school ourselves tomorrow morning and get this situation ironed out with your principal and teachers and counselors. Do you understand?"

George stood still for a moment. His eyes remained transfixed on his son. "Your Grandma and Grandpa are due to arrive in just a few weeks time and they will be staying with us through to Christmas. You appeared to be as excited as the rest of us about that. I want this mess corrected and a degree of normalization in our lives by the time they arrive."

George abruptly left the room and headed up the stairs. The backdoor to the porch slammed shut as he left the house. June was still shaking and quietly looked at her son. She wiped the tears from her eyes and slowly started to walk past him. "Please work with us, Jim? Don't allow others to do this to you."

"Just shut up, Mom." Jim got off the floor and proceeded to slam his door shut behind his mother. He then slowly sat down on the side of the bed. He wiped the perspiration from his face and lay down on the bed staring aimlessly at the ceiling.

June walked up the stairs and exited the porch. George was standing at the back of the house. June slowly walked up to her husband who was staring aimlessly into the farmyard. "You shouldn't have grabbed him like that."

"And he should not have mouthed off to you like that, June. Look how he pushed you. You could have been badly hurt. That person down there is not our Jim. I don't know the answers here but we have to start somewhere."

"Getting rough with him isn't going to help anything, George. I have never seen him like that. I pray that I will never see that again."

"I'm afraid that it's going to take more than just prayer, June. We will get him help tomorrow. In the meantime make sure that he stays in the house and make sure that we have all the vehicle keys in our bedroom."

"You don't think that Jim would take off do you?" June looked sincerely into George's eyes. "I am really afraid for him."

"I know, June, I know. So am I. If only I had listened to Allan's concerns earlier? I just never thought that Jim would be vulnerable to those kids let alone to damn drugs. Monty tells me the town is full of it. I've let this fester too long."

George looked towards the out buildings and noticed the girls leaving the layer barn and heading towards the broiler barn. He turned back towards June. "I had better help the girls finish up out there. It'll all work out somehow. Just keep an eye and an ear open." George gave June a firm hug. "We'll get through this, Hon. Not sure just how but we will."

He released his hold and turned towards the girls who had stopped to look at their parents. "Just be a minute, girls. I'm comin'." He quickly glanced at the combine sitting idle by the shop and shook his head. *This was becoming the perfect wreck. Could anything else possibly go wrong this fall? It would take a miracle to finish harvest now. It was almost a gift that they were even going through the motions. And what was to become of his son. Was he into drugs bad?* George felt lost and empty, grasping for anything in a world that he no longer knew. He picked up the pace and headed directly towards the broiler barn.

29

Supper was a muted affair with the twins making up the bulk of the conversation. Plans were made for the family to rise early and head into town together after breakfast and chores on Tuesday morning. Jim ate with the family but excused himself immediately after finishing his meal. He retreated to the sanctuary of his room on the premise that he would attend to his homework.

Jim awoke about ten o'clock and listened carefully. The house was quiet. He quietly dressed and then stealth fully grabbed his old duffle bag that he had packed earlier and tip toed up the stairs to the back porch door. He attempted to turn the door handle but it was locked. *No problem he thought to himself as he reached into his pant pocket and pulled out the spare key that he had kept.* Once outside he proceeded to walk out the lane and headed towards County Road 22. He lit a joint and inhaled the satisfying fumes.

He eventually reached the main highway and proceeded to walk towards Royston. The night was dark and cold and he walked briskly despite the weight of the old duffle bag that rested on his right shoulder. The highway appeared deserted and he walked in silence. In the distance a lone vehicle coming from Royston approached him. He watched it attentively as the bright lights came closer and then slowed as the driver undoubtedly saw him walking on the shoulder. The right signal light commenced flashing and the vehicle came to a halt on the shoulder in front of him. He ran to the red Honda and opened the passenger door. "You came. I didn't know if you were around or not but I left a message anyways."

"Normally, I wouldn't be around but Austaire called me today too. We were talking when you left your message. So don't just stand there. Dump your load in the back seat and get in. It's cold out there."

Jim hurriedly jammed the loaded duffle bag into the back seat of the car and seated himself beside Megan. "Thanks for coming, Meg. It would have been a cold walk into town."

"Like whatever, Jimmy. It's all good now."

"I didn't know what to do. Sorry to bother you and all. My folks and I had quite a heated conversation."

"Don't worry about it, Jimmy. We'll talk at home."

Megan made an abrupt turnaround on the highway and the old Honda was soon rolling back towards Royston. The couple arrived back at her townhouse and they disappeared into its warm confines. Jim was startled to see Austaire waiting inside when they entered. She immediately came over to him. "Hello there. Let me grab your bag there, Jim. Looks like you are moving in or something."

Jim let the old duffle bag fall to the floor and gave her a big hug. "You're the best thing that I have seen tonight or should I say second only to seeing Meg pull up on the highway." They all shared a light chuckle before Jim continued, "I didn't think that you'd be here too."

"I had to stay after hearing your message. So what's up?"

"Yes Jimmy, let loose with all the details for Meg here."

"Could I have a joint before I start Meg? I had one coming in but I really need to calm my nerves here. I'm pretty twisted right now. Everyone was so upset. It got pretty ugly at home. I've got paper but Dad found my stash at home and took it."

"There's fresh green in the kitchen," said Meg. "You're welcome to it, Jimmy."

"Thanks Meg. I just need to unwind some. I'm really messed up."

Jim wasted little time in the kitchen and soon returned to the living room. The threesome proceeded to get comfortable on the old sofas while Jim methodically made a hand roll and then contentedly lit it. He then proceeded to give them his item for item account on the confrontation that had occurred earlier in his room at home. The girls listened attentively and without interruption until Jim had finished with the details including his painful decision to leave home that night.

"I just could not stand anymore of that nightmare. They even locked the house to contain me." He pulled out his spare key. "They just weren't as smart as they thought." They all enjoyed a hearty laugh as Jim lit yet another joint and sat back in the comfort of the old sofa.

"So what's the deal with school now, Jimmy?" asked Megan. "You in trouble there like Austaire here?"

"They called my mother today from school, Jim. My folks were on my case about it when I got home so I left and came over to Megs. I'm going to stay here until we figure it all out. School really doesn't matter much to me anymore. I'm old enough to do whatever. Meg says she can get me work and help me out for now."

"So you're staying here?" asked Jim. "But what if your folks come for you?"

"My folks don't know this place and even if they did I don't believe they really give a damn about me. Meg says that I'm old enough to do my own thing. Just like you, Jim. I'm so glad that you are here. This is just plain awesome. Now we can begin to live our own lives and do our own thing just like we always wanted to."

"So tell me, Jim," continued Megan. "What plans do you have?"

"I don't know, Meg. I just know that I couldn't stay there. They were going to take me to the school in the morning for counseling. They even mentioned home schooling. Dad made it pretty clear that my days associating with you two were over. When he pinned me down and made me apologize to Mom he was really upset."

"So he had to pin you down to make you apologize to your mother, Jimmy?" asked Megan. She laughed and continued, "Too bad that you didn't crown him."

"I think that he was just trying to slap me but he missed and we ended up having it out on my bedroom floor. It seemed to happen."

"He hit you and wrestled you down to the floor. He has gone too far this time. Child welfare would love to hear about this whole deal. First of all your folks work you to the bone like child slavery and then they deprive you of school time and lastly your Dad beats on you. This just couldn't get much better, now could it?"

"It isn't really like that, Meg. You know how it is. I still think a lot of my folks but I just had to get away from them. They refuse to understand anything."

"Oh yes, dear Jimmy. Such wholesome parents you have. I've got an old friend that will just love hearing about your situation. I'm going to have to give Betty a call first thing in the morning. By the way have you got any change?"

"Just a few bucks but I've still got some savings. I would have received last months check this Friday. I probably should have stayed at home but I just couldn't imagine not seeing you guys. I sort of mouthed off to Mom and Dad was furious with me. He meant everything he said about not seeing you, Austaire. It was only going to get a whole lot worse out there. I was fucked." Jim drew back heavily on his joint and slowly exhaled the precious smoke. "I don't wish to make problems but I just didn't know what else to do but leave until things were sorted out. This just seems so right here and it is so wrong out there."

"Not to worry, Jimmy." Megan appeared delighted with the situation. "It's like totally all good. You did the right thing coming here. We will work this all out. I've got to make some calls in the morning. We'll get Betty to visit your principal and get all the details worked out. This will play out just fine. Just give it some time with a little outside help. You'll have this whole thing resolved in your favor. They'll be eating out of your hand by the time we're done."

"So who is this Betty?" asked Jim. He was now mildly stoned and felt increasingly comfortable and at ease. "How is she going to help me?"

"Just an old friend of mine," replied Meg. "Hell, we go back forever. I haven't seen her in awhile but it's time we renew our acquaintance. She's in the business of helping people just like you. She'll come around to our way of thinking real quick, I'm sure. Anyways, we'll worry about that in the morning. In the meantime you two need some beauty rest. Take my bedroom for tonight. I've got some thinking to do."

"We can go up together," said Austaire. "Just like always." Her dilated pupils blazed with excitement as Megan nodded and then pointed her towards the stairway. Austaire leaned against Jim and beckoned, "Coming? Meg will look after us. You'll see."

"You sure that you're not coming up, Meg? I didn't mean to make you loose sleep too. Like I really appreciate this and all but I'm not here to make trouble."

"You're not trouble, Jimmy. You guys are not taking my bed, you're sharing it." They all laughed at the thought. "I'm pretty much wide awake right now. Meg has some planning to do. You guys go chill out and don't worry bout' nothing. You okay now or do you need something else, Jimmy?"

"No thanks, I'm feeling much better. Fact is, I'm getting pretty much stoned." He laughed loudly and very slowly rose to his feet. "I'll just finish this while Austaire and I meander upstairs. I think that we can entertain ourselves for awhile."

Jim and Austaire laughed in unison and proceeded to make their way up the stairway. The giggles and laughter continued for awhile longer as the ecstatic couple re-shared the events of the evening with one another. Eventually their chatter subsided and the youthful couple fell into a harmonious and drug induced sleep. In the meantime Megan sat quietly by the kitchen table making some rough notes in an old binder. She occasionally snorted on the white powder that was conveniently sitting on a small plate beside her. She would call Miss Betty Oagle tomorrow morning.

It was almost time for the Edwards to rise and attend to their chores when Megan finished making her notes. She shut off the single light in the kitchen and quickly walked through the darkness of her townhouse upstairs to her bedroom. She stood at the open doorway for a minute and observed her new house guests before undressing. Then she carefully lifted the covers and snuggled in beside Jim.

30

George cast a sleepy eye towards the luminous dial of the alarm clock and rolled back over into the warm confines of their bed. His eyes came to rest on the white plaster ceiling. He lay quietly staring upwards, allowing the cow webs to clear from his head. The remnants of the headache from last night still attempted to dull his mind and he was content to remain motionless for the moment. He slowly turned his head to view the clock once again.

"What time is it, George?" June asked softly. "It still looks pretty dark out there."

George rolled back towards June and whispered, "Four-thirty, Hon. I couldn't sleep. I've just been lying here."

"How's the head? You seemed to sleep well after taking those painkillers."

"Its better, June, I'm amazed that I slept as much as I did. Hopefully, today will turn out better than yesterday. You call Principal Erickson first thing and we'll take Jim in and meet with him. We'll get this situation snapped in the bud before it gets worse."

"Jim scared me last night, George. It seemed like it was someone else speaking to us. He acted so different."

"He will come around now that the cat is out of the bag. We'll get him some help through the school or whatever it takes. I'm afraid that we are treading new water here. Anyways I might as well get up and get some chores out of the way. We'll want to get into Royston early. Maybe I'll even get some harvesting done later. That would be pleasant."

"Our prayers will be answered, George. I'm wide awake now too. I might as well join you. The kids will be up soon and I'll come in and make breakfast when they arrive. The morning air will do me good."

The couple dressed quietly in the relative darkness of the bedroom which was still slightly illuminated by the distant yard light. They walked softly through the kitchen and proceeded downstairs. In minutes they were both outside walking toward the barns. The ground was covered with a heavy, white frost and the crisp air served as a reminder of colder mornings to come. The naked skeletons of the aspen trees bordering the garden still clung to a few precious leaves but the bulk of their once green foliage had long been blown away by the autumn winds.

"It could be an early winter this year?"

"Maybe these frosts will keep the weather stable for awhile and let us finish harvest, George."

"I hope that you are right there. The days keep getting shorter but at least we haven't had any moisture to contend with in about a week now."

"I can look after the broiler barn and finish up later when we get back, June. You can send Jim over my way when the kids come out."

"Come here for a moment." June stretched out her arms inviting her husband closer. "Somehow this will all work its way out." The couple embraced each other with a warm hug. "The Lord will help us through this."

George looked into June's eyes. "I know, Hon. I know." He relinquished his hold on June. "Sometimes I just wonder why it always seems to be us that have these problems. Anyways I'd best get at some feeding." George turned and walked briskly towards the broiler barn. He looked up briefly into the dark morning air and inhaled a deep swallow of its crispness. The freshness revitalized his spirit and he entered the barn.

George went directly to his chores. He diligently walked through the still sleepy birds checking their drinking fountains and feed trays. Within minutes he was absorbed, as usual, in his work. It was almost six-thirty when George finished and walked back to the layer barn. He met June and the girls just as they were leaving for the house.

"Where's Jim? Did he not get up with you two?"

"We knocked on his door but didn't get an answer so we just came right out," answered Susan. "Mary didn't think that we should bug him after last night."

"Last night was just last night, girls. Dad and I will take Jim into school first thing this morning and we'll get this worked out. He's probably still upset. Anyways, let's get some breakfast."

The twins darted ahead of their parents and disappeared around the back of the house. By the time the couple entered the house the shower was already running upstairs. June washed quickly downstairs and headed upstairs to prepare breakfast. George shed his coveralls and then washed too. Having finished washing he walked over to Jim's door and knocked.

"Hey there, sleepy head, we missed you outside." George listened attentively and then slowly opened the door. "Just because we had a little disagreement doesn't mean that you can sleep all day." George reached over and turned on the light switch. He briefly stared at the empty bed and then walked to the bottom of the stairs. "Jim must be in the shower, June."

"Girls are in the bathroom, George. Jim is downstairs." June's face appeared at the top of the stairwell. "Jim's not upstairs."

"I heard you the first time around. He's not down here either."

"What do you mean? He has to be down there."

"He's not. His bed is empty." George walked back into Jim's room and June quickly followed. "See for yourself. He is gone. Maybe he left when we were chorin'. He can't be too far."

"You shouldn't have hit him," June shrieked at the top of her voice. "You should not have threatened him like you did. He's gone. Our son is gone." June beat on George's chest. "Now look at what we've done."

"Calm down, June. He may have gone over to Glens. Maybe he's headed for Royston and those damn girl friends of his? He won't be far. We'll get this settled big time. This has gone way too far. They've got that kid so damn mixed up with drugs and shit. Damn those idiots, anyways."

"Don't you swear about our son, George? We should have let him go to football. You were way too rough on him last night."

"Last night your son swore at you and basically denied your existence as a parent. There was no respect in his words last night. You know how he upset you. Calm down. This isn't going to help anything."

"How can I calm down? Our son has left." June's eyes were surveying the room. "His duffle bag is gone. He's taken clothes and left." She broke into tears and fell onto the bed. "Jim has left. He has left us." Mary was the first of the twins to enter the room.

"Where is Jim?"

"We don't know right now, Mary. Your mother and I will find him this morning. In the meantime you two go back upstairs and get some breakfast. Mom and I will be right up."

"It'll be okay, Mom," said Susan. "Jim will be back."

"Please don't cry, Mom," added Mary.

The twins both gave June a hasty hug before turning and heading back out of the room. In the process they both gave their father a blank stare before disappearing upstairs. June struggled to wipe some of the tears from her eyes. She looked up at George. "They know. They know it's your fault. You are just too demanding. This time you went too far." June got up and started across the room. George reached out to her but she avoided him. "Don't touch me." She promptly headed upstairs.

George sat down on the bedside and allowed his head to survey the contents of the room. He grasped the polished rock that sat on the dresser and studied it intently. He looked at the baseball trophy sitting on the shelf.

He glanced at camp photographs and the small photo album. He studied the paintings that adorned the one wall. The progression of his son's art over the past several years hung before him. He came to rest at the last grotesque painting and shed a silent tear. His head was pounding. He slowly placed the rock back on the dresser and left the room.

George walked up the stairs and headed straight into their bedroom. He grabbed the keys to the Ford and exited the room. He glanced quickly at the twins and June who were now seated at the kitchen table. "I'm just going for a quick drive. You girls can still make your bus and remember if you hear anything we must know about it. If he left this morning he can't be far. Perhaps you can call the Rollins quickly, June. I won't be long."

George dashed to the Ford and quickly backed into the yard and disappeared out the lane. Surely Jim had just left this morning. Perhaps he was still on the gravel road heading towards the main highway. It was a long walk to County Road 22 and even farther to the highway. The Ford swerved onto the gravel road and stones flew as George accelerated the truck. His heart beat faster and cold perspiration formed on his forehead. "Damn this foolishness anyways," he shouted as the frustration of the moment cast a sinking feeling in his mind. His head continued to pound as his eyes peered ahead of the Ford hoping to see Jim up ahead. He had no time to formulate what he might say. *He only wanted to have Jim sitting in the seat beside him and the two of them heading back towards home.*

It was about eight-thirty when George returned to the yard. June was waiting for him in the kitchen when he stepped into the house. He looked up at her while he removed his boots. "Any luck with the Rollins, Hon?"

"No. Glen hadn't heard from him at all. He said that Jim has been missing a lot of school, George. He knows this Austaire girl from school but he didn't seem to know much more. I called the school and we still have an appointment with Mr. Erickson at ten. He wasn't in yet so I didn't say much."

"Yes, I don't know what to do right now. I suppose that we should go in and see Erickson anyways. If Jim turns up at school then we can be there. I'm sure that he will turn up shortly. He couldn't have gone far."

"You had best get some breakfast, George. You must be starved. I'm sorry for earlier on. I should not have burst out like that. It's not like me to do that."

"I probably deserved most of it, June. God only knows what I deserve or don't. Anyways I will grab some breakfast and perhaps you can make a couple of calls. Maybe Monty might see him in his travels? Allan is in town all the time, too."

"Do we need to call Allan right now, George? Surely we'll hear from Jim later and we'll get this fixed up. He'll calm down and get in touch."

"Hopefully you're right, June. I've just never seen Jim like this. He hasn't been the same all fall. Anyways, we'll touch base with Erickson and perhaps we can make some plans for beginning counseling once we find him again. He was expecting us this morning at ten, right?"

"Yes, his secretary confirmed that time when I called."

George seated himself at the kitchen table and poured some milk on his cereal. He quickly devoured the contents of the bowl and poured himself another. His attention turned to the brightening morning sky. There was a light breeze starting to move the tree limbs. The grey sky had streaks of sunshine attempting to break through and reach the ground, casting shadows across the front yard. He shook his head in vain and swallowed the cup of coffee that June had just set down. The dull thud of his headache seemed to permeate his very soul. He slowly rose from the table and left for the bedroom to change into town clothes.

31

George and June arrived at the school early and managed to check with administration to see if Jim was in attendance. He was not. By ten o'clock they were escorted into Mr. Erickson's office. They exchanged greetings and then the principal quietly closed the office door behind them and sat down in his chair. He opened a folder on his desk and then looked directly at the couple. "So where is Jim? I believe that we had agreed to sit together. Apparently he is not currently in class."

George spoke first. "We don't know where Jim is at the moment. We were hoping that perhaps he was at school. He left home sometime last night. We confronted him with the issues that we had discussed with you and we haven't seen him since after supper yesterday evening."

June added, "He was quite upset about the whole thing but we never thought that he wouldn't at least talk with you. We suggested counseling and whatever else was required to find a working solution to this situation. Jim is a good kid and our only boy. He's just been acting strange all fall."

Mr. Erickson sat quietly for a moment before speaking. After studying the folder once again he looked back at June and George. "So you have no idea on his whereabouts. You said that he was quite upset with the outcome of your conversation with him."

"I had a chance to look around his room before he got home yesterday and I found a pipe that we believe he was using for smoking dope. I confronted him with it along with the absenteeism at school and his failing grades. It didn't go too well." George took a deep breath before continuing. "We believe that our son requires some outside help and that he has been exposed to drugs through some new acquaintances here in Royston."

"Jim just isn't the same," added June. "He seemed to defy us last night. He was not very interested in listening to us. We thought that today would be better in here."

"Look folks, I sympathize with your plight. However, I can't help you or your son until he turns up and comes forward. I'll probably have to report the issue to Child Welfare as a matter of routine protocol. I'll indicate a strong desire on your part to get Jim back into school. When he does surface again we can begin addressing the issues at hand. I'm sure that he will return home shortly. Unfortunately, we see this sort of episode all too frequently. Have you tried contacting his friends?"

June spoke first, "We tried one this morning but had no luck. I'm afraid that I didn't have much success trying to talk to Mrs. Jamieson yesterday."

"Yes, Austaire's mother. I spoke briefly with her yesterday. It sounds like they don't know much about the activities of their daughter. Anyways that is another matter."

"You mentioned Child Welfare," George interjected. "I don't understand what that is all about?"

"It is just a matter of routine that we would call them on an issue such as this. Not to worry, folks. We are all just trying to help here. Anyways, I think that we can conclude this meeting until another time when Jim is present. I trust that will be in the near future." Mr. Erickson rose from his chair and extended his hand. "In the meantime good luck and keep in touch. If anything turns up here we will be sure to call you folks."

George and June acknowledged Mr. Erickson and left the office in relative silence. The very mention of Child Welfare hung in the back of their throats. They spent the duration of the morning touring the streets of Royston hoping to spy their son at the next corner and bring him home. It proved unfruitful and a distraught couple returned home by early afternoon. June continued to make phone inquiries while George returned to Royston for the afternoon. First he went to the Credit Union and then he spent the remainder of the day scouring the streets looking for their son.

Darkness was falling as George arrived back in the yard. He briefly looked at the combine that remained parked by the garage. His eyes quickly scanned the barren yard and brushed past the remainder of the out buildings. Mechanically, he ventured towards the house. His mind was a virtual blank. Anger had been replaced by shock.

June heard him enter the back porch and came to meet him. The reality of the situation had hit her too. She attempted to smile as she greeted her husband, "Supper is ready. We were getting worried about you." She reached out to him. "The girls are waiting for you. Quick now before we eat it all on you."

George followed her to the table and sat down. The girls greeted him cheerfully and then the family bowed their heads for the blessing. It was Susan that spoke. "Dear Lord, please bless this food and this family. Please give my Mom and Dad strength and love. Be with my brother and keep him well for his return. Amen." Susan broke into tears.

June and George quietly sat back in their chairs and digested the simple prayer. Wet eyes remained as the food was passed around the table. The dining room light seemed to glow brighter than normal. It had a soothing effect on the family's wounds. The darkness that seemingly prevailed around them was being kept at bay. George felt his spirits being lifted by an unknown force. *It was a gift that he did not deserve but he was grateful for the tranquil feeling that seemed to spread around the table.*

An eerie and uncomfortable calm had settled over the Edwards's household by the weekend. They had still not heard from Jim. Despite all her phone calls and the good will on many folks part June could not obtain any leads on the whereabouts of their son. It was like he had disappeared from the face of the earth. The grey mist that appeared by late Saturday almost seemed a fitting conclusion to the week.

32

The sun broke through the cloud cover on Monday morning and once again spread its autumn rays across the Edward's farmyard. George had finished up with the morning chores and had just begun to grease the grain dryer when June came running out into the yard. She paused for a second to locate his whereabouts and then promptly marched over to the dryer. "We've got to go into town."

"Right now? Can I finish greasing this thing?"

"Finish quickly and then we have to leave. It's Jim and we are to meet with Child Welfare in Royston."

"You talked with him! What's goin' on?"

"Not exactly, George. It sounds like Jim will be there but we are to meet with Child Welfare this morning. She didn't give any details but we've got to get."

"What he can't talk with us? What the hell does Child Welfare have to do with this?"

"Remember when Mr. Erickson mentioned that he would have to make a statement or request or whatever he was talking about. It's probably to do with that. It's a start. At least we get to see Jim."

George crawled out from under the grain dryer and wiped his hands on his coveralls. "Be right there, Hon. So where did you say we were goin'?"

"It's at the Government Office on Main. That's all I know. We go to the third floor and ask for Miss Oagle."

"Wonderful, a damn social worker."

"That's enough of that, George. I just wish for this whole thing to end."

The couple arrived at the government office by eleven o'clock. They reached the designated floor and waited for Miss Oagle to show. After waiting for about an hour a red-haired lady in her early twenties came over to them and introduced herself. She directed them into a small room that contained only a table and few chairs. June and George sat down and waited in anticipation as

Miss Oagle opened a file and sat down on the opposite side of the table. She passed a form and a pen to the couple. "I'll need you to fill this out, please."

"And just exactly what is this?" asked George.

"It's a registration form. We just need some information on you folks in order for us to commence with this case. It's pretty self explanatory. Just fill in the blanks as directed."

"I thought that Jim would be here," said June. "We understood that we would get to see our son."

Miss Oagle studied her notes for a minute and then addressed June and George. "Mr. and Mrs. Edwards, I'll try to keep this as concise as possible. You may not be aware but your son, Jim Edwards, is now a registered client of this agency. I am his case worker. I am here as his formal representative to establish some guidelines with you, his parents, and to eventually work out a formal resolve to his case. It is hoped that in due time that you will be able to meet with Jim. In the meantime you will meet with me and I will serve as your son's liaison officer."

"I still don't understand all of this," said George. "You are telling us, his parents, that we cannot see our own son. We have spent the majority of a whole damn week sitting and wondering where he was and whether he was okay or not and you tell us that we get to see you instead. What is going on here?"

"Your son has filed a formal complaint through this agency towards you, Mr. Edwards with Mrs. Edwards named on the complaint as well. It is deemed necessary in such cases to isolate the child from his parents until such time that we feel that it is safe for visitations and eventually to allow normal parental exposure to the child. Jim has been billeted out in a friend's home for the time being. He will remain under my observation until this investigation is finished. At this time there are no formal charges being laid against you and we hope that this does not occur. However, until the investigation is complete there will be limited if any visitation or exposure allowed. Am I making myself clear on the severity of this situation?"

George sat stunned in his chair and looked down at the table. June was attempting to hold back tears as Miss Oagle attempted to resume with her conversation. George spoke first, "I don't mean to pry, Miss Oagle, but just what are we being investigated about? Just what is the complaint?"

"It has come to our attention that Jim is failing classes at school due to his absenteeism deemed necessary to facilitate work at home. As well we have complaints of physical abuse and time restraints that have arisen over several occasions from continuous farm labor being asked of the child. There is also mention of a physical altercation occurring last Monday. Jim is seeking protection from the possibility of further incidents. At this early stage of the investigation I cannot make any further comments. I will note that a friend of your son saw fit to contact this agency and formally initiate the complaint. I have known this individual for many years and will personally vouch for her. I have met with Principal Erickson and have received limited information from him at this point."

George remained speechless and seemed incapable of talking. It seemed like a large ball was imbedded in his throat. June sat sullen but managed to commence talking. "So what are we are being asked to do? What are we suppose to do here? How do we go about getting our son back?"

"We look forward to your co-operation in this investigation. I will be out to your residence during the next week to see how things could be improved and what possibilities exist. We will eventually require a formal contribution towards a support allowance for Jim unless this can be settled quickly. I will be in contact with you once the details have been concluded. In the meantime I will ensure that your son receives adequate care at the location of his temporary billet. He will be under my observation and I will meet with him periodically as his case develops."

"And school?" asked June. "Does he return to school?"

"We will strive to have him back in classes as soon as possible. That is certainly a primary goal. Until he has stabilized from this trauma I am recommending that he remain at his billet home. Mr. Erickson and I will determine when it is appropriate for him to return to formal classes. In the meantime, I will make arrangements for him to have access to a limited amount of homework."

George finally recovered his vocal cords and blurted out in quick succession, "And what about the drugs. Our son has been transformed into something that he is not because of exposure to illegal drugs. We found evidence of it at home. We confronted him with our discovery last Monday." George took a deep breath. "He has been meeting with an Austaire Jamieson and a Megan. They are the reason behind his missing school and carrying on. This Megan sounds like a real winner but we do not know her last name or where she lives. Our son has become messed up with drug people. That is the main issue here. What are you going to do about that? Seeing as you are now apparently our son's guardian?"

Miss Oagle remained quiet for awhile as if George had struck a sensitive nerve somewhere. She appeared flustered and shaken by the accusations. It required a minute but she regained her composure and addressed George's conversation. "I am not familiar with any such people or of the potential for drug abuse at this time. I feel confident that as this investigation continues that all the facts will be known and that we can arrive at a suitable solution. Now if there are no more questions I would suggest that we end this meeting."

"So we are to go home and simply wait for your calls with regards to our son and trust in you for his well being?"

"That is correct, Mr. Edwards. Might I suggest that if you had maintained acceptable and normal relations with your son then possibly none of this would be happening? I do not relish coming into broken families and seeing twisted lives. It is my job to attempt to find discovery for all parties and hopefully arrive at a common denominator. My caseload is unfortunately very large. Nevertheless, it is my first priority to protect the child. In this case that means your son. I will be in touch."

Miss Oagle arose from her chair and briefly extended her hand to both June and George allowing a light handshake before exiting the room. June looked completely washed by the conversation that had just occurred and she remained seated in the wooden chair. George got up and offered to help her. "Come on, June. It's time for us to go."

"It is not time for us to go, George. I want to see Jim. This is not right."

I know, Hon. We've done what we can for now. Miss Oagle has made it completely clear on who is in control at the moment. Come on. Let's get out of here."

The couple slowly exited the stark room and walked towards the elevator. George pushed the button for the first floor while he continued to assist June with one arm. *He had never seen her like this before. She appeared broken and disenchanted.* The reality of the past few minutes was slowly sifting into both of their heads. The sullen couple exited the building and made a slow walk through the parking lot towards the Ford. They had almost reached the truck when Allan Heiner drove up beside them and rolled down his window. "So what's up with you too?"

"I can't talk right now, Allan. We just got out of Child Welfare. It's not good. June here needs to sit down."

"Sheila said that you had called earlier, June. She asked me to drop by if I was near. I am so glad that I caught you two. We need to talk but you're right, not here. Feel like following me out to the house?"

"We're not going to be very good company, Allan. Perhaps we should talk at another time." George stood by the side of the Ford and solemn tears began to flow down his face. "I'm not too sure just what to do right now. Damn it all, anyways. Perhaps if you guys feel up to it; we could sure use another shoulder right now. You are on our way home."

"Just follow me out. I'll call Sheila and she'll have tea ready. What time do the girls get home?"

"Not till four-thirty, Allan," said June in a weak voice. "They get off the bus about four-thirty. We'll have to be home by then for sure."

"Then let's get. You two look like you need a friend and I guess that Sheila and I are just going to have to do." Allan smiled politely and then closed his window before slowly pulling up to the exit for the parking lot. June and George pulled in behind and proceeded to follow him. They barely said a word as the conversation from the meeting still settled in their minds. It was like a lump of coal had been inserted into their throats and even breathing was difficult. George just mechanically followed his friend along the highway and into the Heiners yard. *Both he and June needed the gift of friendship at this time. Allan could be a real pain in the neck sometimes but both him and Sheila could always be counted on when the going got tough.* The waters ahead looked mighty turbulent at this moment in time.

33

Sheila was waiting for them when they drove into the Heiners front yard. She ran out to meet June and assisted her into the house. George and Allan stood by the side of their trucks for a moment and then proceeded into the house. "Tea is on fellows. We're in the front room."

George sat down beside June. Sheila was in the process of pouring everyone their tea when June burst out, "We've lost our son. We've lost him."

"What in the name of the Lord do you mean, June?" asked Sheila. She reached down to comfort her friend. "What's happened?"

"It's Child Welfare. They are investigating us. They believe that we are bad parents and they have taken our son away from us. They've got a case worker investigating us." June swallowed a small amount of the hot tea. "Jim has filed a complaint against us."

"A friend of Jim's apparently initiated the whole thing," added George. "I think that I have a pretty good idea who but I have no way of proving it. They have him at a friends place in Royston. Jim has been missing a pile of school and his marks are terrible. I found drug paraphernalia in his room last week. He has got himself mixed up with some bad stuff in town and they have managed to turn him against us. I know. I know, Allan. I ask way too much of those kids of ours. But this is not just our Jim doing this nor was it Jim that spoke back to his mother last Monday night. He's in trouble and I didn't see it. You warned me several times and I didn't heed you. I was too busy trying to do my own thing. Now we're in a mess and I fear for his well being."

"So they are investigating you?" asked Allan. "At least they didn't try and lay charges your way. That Child Welfare can be a scary thing. We've had a couple of experiences from those people with members of our congregation. They may mean good but most of those case workers are idealists that feel that the world must conform to their ways or else. So you found evidence of drug use?"

"Yes, I'm no expert but I know what I saw, Allan. Jim has got himself involved in more than he can chew. I just know it. He found himself a new girlfriend and from what we can find out she has nothing to do with her folks either. At least her mother doesn't appear to have the faintest idea of what she is up to or even where she goes. Apparently this Austaire girl is in trouble at the High School. We met her once in Dobeys and she seemed quite distant from us. And then there is this Megan. I don't know just what all her connections are with Jim but I have this feeling they're all bad. That's about all I know right now."

"So what is the plan?" asked Allan. "Where do you go from here?"

"We don't know," answered George. "I know that everyone will blame me for this episode but that isn't going to help my son. For now I guess we just wait it out until we hear more from Miss Oagle."

"That's the case worker," added June. "She is quite young but seemed nice enough. Not overly friendly though and she certainly wasn't prepared to tell us anything. It was like we didn't exist anymore; at least when it comes to Jim. Well George, we had best get going. I don't need anyone else complaining about our parental abilities."

"Yes, the girls will be home and we had better be present when they walk into the yard. In the meantime, thanks guys. I needed someone to lean on."

Allan walked over to George and gave him a large hug. "Don't you be giving up? This is bad but it will get better. You look after those girls and that damn farm of yours." Allan smiled, "You know what I mean. Look after what you can and let the Lord help us out here. In the meantime I'll keep my eyes open in Royston. Perhaps I'll see Jim around or something."

"Don't get yourself in trouble if you do," said George. "He's different at the moment. But if you do see Jim and can talk with him, then great. He's not been impressed with your observations of late. Please tread lightly if you see him."

Sheila and June exchanged hugs as well. "You take care, June, and if there is anything that Allan and I can do, you know enough to ask. I'll keep in touch. It'll all work out. The Lord works in mysterious ways. You'll see."

"Thanks, Sheila. Thanks for everything; both of you. We'll keep in touch. We'll keep you abreast of everything. In the meantime just float a prayer our way."

"Catch you later, Allan."

"We'll be in touch, George."

June and George walked out to the Ford and climbed inside. They waved to their friends and George carefully backed the Ford out the lane and onto the highway approach. In no time they were on County Road 22 and well on their way home. June looked across at her husband. "I don't blame you,

George; even for the other night. I know that you were just doing what you thought was right."

"Thanks but I know that you do. I blame myself so it doesn't matter. What matters right now are those two girls of ours that are getting off that bus up ahead. Somehow this whole thing is going to blow over. Maybe they'll arrest me and get me the hell away from all of you." George hesitated for a moment. "I didn't mean that, Hon. We'll beat this just like we have to beat every other damn thing that happens around here. In the meantime we'll just try our best to keep strong."

"What about your parents, George? They are going to be out here in a couple of weeks." June looked inquiringly at her husband. "I guess that I'd best give Elaine a call and fill them in. It's only right that they know."

"Yah, you'd better explain things to them, June. Tell them their son has blown it again. I hope this doesn't stop them from coming. I hate the thoughts of them arriving into a mess but I wouldn't mind them around right now. Perhaps Jim will be back by then. I really doubt it but who knows."

George waved back at Monty as they met his school bus on the gravel road. He quickly approached the lane way and pulled the truck to a stop beside the twins who had waited for the Ford to arrive. He watched in the rearview mirror as they piled inside the back seat. June turned to chat with them as they continued up the lane way. Once in the yard they quickly abandoned the truck and followed their mother into the house. George turned the ignition off and sat in silence looking around at the farmstead. *The strife of mice and men he thought. He had committed his entire working life to this damn piece of ground and for what?* For the first time in ages he felt genuine remorse for being there.

34

Jim awoke early on Saturday morning and carefully made his way downstairs to Megan's kitchen. He was starving and the fridge contained much less than what he was used to at home. He grabbed a jug of milk and set it on the table. Soon he was devouring a large bowl of corn flakes. He had never been a huge fan of cereal but this was going down well. He got up and plugged in the kettle to boil some water for tea and then sat back down to finish his breakfast.

After breakfast he walked back upstairs and proceeded to shower. Austaire was still sleeping and he did not wish to wake her but he had an appointment at nine that he must attend. He finished in the bathroom and carefully crept back into the bedroom to grab some clothes. He was almost dressed when Austaire stirred and twisted around in the bed. She managed a very groggy, "So why are you up so early?"

"I've got to meet with Miss Oagle again. I told you that yesterday but you probably weren't listening."

"That's too bad, Jim. With Meg away we've got this whole house to ourselves. It's totally awesome, don't you think?"

"You just rest, girl. I shouldn't be that long. Have to meet her at the Government Building for nine and it's a bit of a walk from here."

"You could take a taxi over or something."

"No, the walk will do me good. Besides I've got to watch my money for now. Meg says that I will be getting some support soon. She's known this Miss Oagle for quite a well. It sounds like they go back to public school. I'll pick up some cash from the bank after my little meeting. Did you say that Meg will be back tonight?"

"She said that she is throwing a special in our honor tonight, Jim. Imagine that. She should be back from the city around noon."

Austaire shifted over to the edge of the bed and sat up with the comforter loosely draped over her shoulders. "So what do you think?" She looked intently at Jim. "Are you sure that you have to leave this early?" A huge grin spread across her face. "It's still pretty early. You can walk pretty fast if you have to."

Jim straddled Austaire and held her tight against him. She returned the move by grasping onto his muscular frame and wrapping her legs around his firm torso. Jim looked deeply into her blue eyes and the couple kissed. The kissing led to an extended embrace and before long they were actively engaged in love making under the warmth of the comforter. It was almost eight when Jim turned and looked back at the clock. "Shit. I've really got to get." He turned to Austaire and gave her a big kiss before jumping out of the bed.

"You could share one of these with me before you leave." Austaire had picked up a joint left from the night before and was in the process of relighting it. "Makes for a good morning fix." She laughed loudly. "You could probably share one with Miss Oagle or whatever her name is."

"Oh yah, I'm sure that she would be impressed with that. She's definitely too much of a prude for that. It's hard to imagine that she and Meg were close at one time. Can't see what they had in common." Jim laughed at the thought of her puffing on a joint. He finished dressing and blew a kiss at Austaire. "See you in a bit. Wish me luck down there."

"Good luck. You get back to me quickly now."

Jim turned and gave Austaire another big grin before he left the room. He flew down the stairs and quickly put his shoes on. He grabbed his jacket and left the townhouse. Outside it was grey and cold. Damn it was cold. He ran for awhile and then maintained a fast walk in an attempt to keep warm. He looked at his watch and kept up the pace. It was almost nine when he arrived at the Government Building. He ran to the elevator and headed for the third floor.

Miss Oagle met Jim as he got off the elevator. She greeted him and then directed him to the meeting room. Jim entered the room and sat down to wait for her. He looked at how stark the room was furnished. *It felt empty and unfinished. It definitely was not made for comfort but in many ways it seemed to suit Miss Oagle. She was rather plain in appearance.* She entered the room and shut the door. "So how is Jim this morning?"

"Great, I was worried that I was going to be late but I made it on time. It's a pretty good walk."

"You walked here? Wow! You should have called the taxi."

"I'm just watching my pennies and all. I know one of the taxi drivers and I'm sure that I'm not very popular with him right now. He knows my Dad well. Besides other than the fact that it is cold out, I really enjoyed it. So what is this meeting about?"

"You know that I met with your parents this week and I probably will be going out to the farm in the next week or two. We are assessing your economic situation and will be issuing a statement to them on your behalf. In the meantime I assume that you have adequate lodging at the home of Megan Italaze. She assured me of that when she made her statement on your behalf."

"It's all good. She treats me like totally fine. I've known Meg for several months now. So how long does all of this take, Miss Oagle?"

"I will endeavor to have your funding finalized within the month. I'm afraid it all takes time. In the meantime if you require anything please call me, okay?"

"Sure thing, so how did you and Meg come to know each other?"

"We practically grew up together in Ollen. We went our own paths after High School. I went to college and she entered the retail sector. We met again about a year ago shortly after I arrived here. I really don't know much about her anymore but she was always a great friend. I'll have to get over and see her sometime."

"Yes, Megan looks after everyone," said Jim issuing a wicked grin.

"Now back to our conversation, Jim. We need to get your schooling on track again. Mr. Erickson and I have decided that you should resume classes as soon as possible. I was hoping that you could start attending classes on Monday. How does that sound to you?"

"Yah, I'm fine with that. So I just go to classes and continue on?"

"Principal Erickson wishes to see you on Monday morning concerning formulating a plan to get you back on stride."

"So I see him first?"

"He is expecting you first thing on Monday morning."

"And what else?"

"We have to begin discussions on what you feel is wrong with your family life and how we can correct it."

"Like me working all the time and not being allowed off the place. My parents are strict and confining. They're not bad people. Their just old fashioned. My Mom can be great but she makes out like everyone must be religious like her. My Dad can be okay too but most of the time he is only interested in his work and telling everyone what to do on that damn farm. And just don't make him mad because if you do watch out. He's got a temper that will crucify you."

"I'm sure that I will learn a considerable amount when I visit your farm. It will surely be a learning experience. I don't know much about the rural lifestyle. I'm sure that in time we will get a plan together that will facilitate your return to your home."

"And what if I do not wish to return?"

"I know that it is the wish of your parents to have you back home again. They seem very concerned about your well being. After I'm finished with my investigation the material will be turned over to my supervisor. The department will then determine a plan to reunite you with your family. If in their opinion that is not an option then we will have to examine other alternatives. At your age this process can become fairly complicated and drawn out. In the meantime I wish to meet with you every Saturday morning at nine to discuss your progress and share my findings with you. Sound okay?"

"It sounds totally awesome. So can I go now?"

"Unless you wish to sit and talk more about this issue and your family relations then you can go if you wish? It would be nice to resume our earlier conversation but if you wish to discuss things in depth at a later time then I completely understand. You've experienced a considerable amount of trauma and you need some space."

"Yah, I promised to meet someone later so I should be getting. I'll see you next week and I'll come prepared to talk lots then."

"Sounds good and don't forget school on Monday."

"Yes, Principal Erickson on Monday morning." Jim extended his hand to Miss Oagle. "Thanks, Miss Oagle."

"You can call me Betty." She smiled at him. "You're going to see a fair bit of me in the next while."

"See you then, Betty. Bye."

Jim turned and walked out of the office. He headed directly for the elevator. He could not get out of this place fast enough. He found it stuffy and nauseating. *He mused in his mind the thought of Miss "Betty" Oagle pulling back on a joint and let a silent grin expand across his face. How on earth did she and Megan ever come to be friends? She probably didn't have the faintest knowledge on the lifestyle of Megan and he certainly wasn't going to expand on it. She looked like she needed to let her hair down. That bun was absolutely ugly.*

In no time he was out of the building and on his way to the Community Credit Union. He knew that his parents had created a savings account there for him ages ago. He entered the building and walked up to the clerk. She politely asked, "May I help you sir?"

"Yes, I would like to withdraw some funds from a savings account. It's in the name of James Edwards. I'm sorry but I don't have the account number with me but I do have I.D." Jim quickly shoved his driver's license to the clerk. "I just forgot to bring the bank book. Sorry."

The clerk immediately began examining the list of accounts and finally pulled up the one in question. She looked up at Jim, "I'm sorry sir but this is a joint account. You will have to get one of your parents to co-sign a savings withdrawal on this account. There is certainly no problem with a withdrawal at that time."

"Oh. Okay then. I'll get it another time. Thanks anyways."

Jim grabbed his driver's license and stuffed it back into his wallet. He quickly walked across to the Community Bank and inserted his bank card into the ATM machine. He withdrew two-hundred dollars and examined his balance. He had less than a hundred bucks left. *If only Principal Erickson had not called his folks until this week. He would have had his farm allowance from the previous month. He had a few items left in the duffle bag that he should be able to sell.* "Damn it anyways," he muttered aloud. *Hopefully Betty would work fast and have his support payment approved. Perhaps he would have to look for a part-time job to tie him over.* He turned to leave the ATM access and starred directly into the eyes of Allan Heiner. He managed a sheepish, "Allan. It seems like you are my shadow of late. How you doin'?"

"I'm better than some people that I know."

"I don't understand."

"You know very well what I'm talking about. We had a sobering conversation with your folks this week. What in the name of mother earth is going on? Your folks deserve better than this, don't you think? Your mother is worried sick and I've never seen your Dad like this."

"Yah right, I've heard it all now. Look I'd like to chat but I've got to get going and by the way I'd really appreciate it if you'd just mine your own damn business. They got you spying on me?"

"It's a small town, Jim. People bump into each other all the time. If you ever feel like a chat you know my number. I'm in town five or six days a week. We've always got along well in the past. I guess that I'm kinda' guilty in not keeping up with our conversations. So say do you have wheels? Can I give you a lift somewhere?"

"No thanks, I'm just going to the south end." Jim caught himself and eyed Allan. "I mean that I'm just walking to the south end of the street here and I have a ride coming. But thanks, anyways."

"Anytime there, Jim. Anytime."

Jim brushed past Allan and quickly headed south on Main Street. He walked briskly and then darted down a side alley making sure to take periodic glances behind him. Once he assured himself that the going was clear he hurriedly made his way back towards the South End of town. He would be glad when this foolishness was over and he had complete freedom. *He despised Allan for accusing him. What did Allan know anyways? Allan was full of the same religious crap as his mother.*

Jim ran the majority of the way back and was short of breath by the time he turned onto Aspen Grove. He slowed down to a quick walk and headed down the street. Megan's familiar, red Honda was parked by Number Thirteen. As he got closer he saw her carrying some bags into the townhouse. She shouted down the street, "Hi there, Jimmy. Can you finish bringing the rest of the stuff in for me?"

Jim squeaked out a weak, "No problem." He was still breathing heavily when he finished carrying the last of the bags inside. He took off his shoes and jacket and fell onto the trusty, old sofa.

"You look tired there, Jimmy. What you've been up to?" Megan rubbed on Jim's shoulder. "You managed to work up quite a little sweat there. Have you been runnin'?"

"Yes, I had a meeting with Betty earlier this morning and I just felt like a good run coming back. You have a good trip?"

"Always Jimmy, so how did your meeting go? Is she going to look after you?"

"Yah, it just takes time. She said that the support thing would happen fairly soon. In the meantime I'm supposed to start school again Monday. I'll see about that one when Monday comes."

"Oh no there, Jimmy, you'll do what they ask of you. It's important that you keep up appearances; at least until they get your support coming. Whatever she asks you will attempt to do for now. You've got to keep Betty happy. So where is Austaire?"

"She's probably upstairs? She was there when I left this morning. She may have gone back asleep. Want me to check?"

Megan sat down beside Jim and nudged close to his left side. She wrapped her right arm around the back of his head and whispered into his ear, "You know what I want, Jimmy. Let her sleep." She smiled and then commenced kissing him. She pulled a small bag out of her jean pocket and carefully dug out two small capsules. She swallowed one and then offered the second to Jim. "Swallow hard and enjoy the ride." He eagerly put it into his mouth and swallowed it.

It was later in the afternoon when Austaire managed to come downstairs. Megan and Jim were drinking herbal tea and sharing a joint in the kitchen. Austaire reached over to Jim and gave him a light kiss on his cheek and softly said, "Hello there. It smells nice in here." She sampled the lit joint before sitting down at the table and pouring a cup for herself. "So how was your trip, Meg?"

"Good, I think that I've made a connection for you, Austaire. I've got a couple of clients that showed an interest." Meg looked calmly at Austaire. "You have told, Jim?"

"No, we haven't discussed anything."

"Told me what? I'm all ears." Jim took an extra deep drag and slowly released the contents into the room while smiling at the girls. "I get the feeling that I'm missing something here."

"It's nothing that can't wait." Megan spoke with authority. "Austaire can chat with you later. Now we have to get things ready for a party tonight. I've got many special guests coming to celebrate. It's your breaking away party. Both of you are crossing the dimension. This one is my treat."

"Like totally, Meg?" asked Jim. "We owe you so much already. I'm going to be tight until my support comes through but I can help out." Jim reached into his jean pocket and pulled out some bills.

"Put it away, Jimmy. You'll need it later when I'm not feeling so generous." Megan's dark eyes twinkled. "Perhaps we can get you moving some stuff around the school later or something. We'll have to talk about that sometime once everything has settled down for you. We are not going to talk about such things today. It's all good out there for both of you. Meg will see to that. In the meantime we all need some good laughs and some real fun. Did you unload the cartons in the trunk of the car too, Jimmy?"

"No, I just got the bags from the back seat. I didn't look any further."

"Well you better just get out there and grab those boxes. I didn't buy all that booze for nothing. Besides I've got a special surprise for both of you as well."

Jim hurriedly exited the kitchen and quickly put on his shoes. In no time at all he had unloaded the trunk of the Honda and brought the valuable cargo inside. He carefully emptied the cartons and placed the valued contents on the kitchen counter and into the refrigerator. He surveyed the cargo and came to a quick conclusion that Meg was definitely pulling out all the stops for this party. He was excited already and it hadn't even begun.

"So who are these special guests that are coming tonight?" Austaire finished her tea. "I'm curious."

"Tonight you will just meet some elite friends of mine. Possibly even a client or two might make it. There's nobody from Royston High tonight." Megan looked into Austaire's eyes. "It'll give you some new acquaintances. Jason will be here. You guys remember Jason?"

"The candy man," Jim laughed. "Sorry, but I remember you calling him that on the first night that I met him."

"You're probably right, Jimmy. Jason never ceases to surprise. He has promised something very special for tonight. I know that he will not disappoint."

"I can hardly wait, Meg." Austaire wrapped her arms around Megan and then turned to leave the kitchen. She slowly started walking towards the upstairs stairway. "I think that I need a nice, warm shower." She gave Jim a

tempting wink as she passed by him. "My back could use a good rub too."
He just smiled and followed in her footsteps. *Now this was how life should be
he thought to himself as he eagerly looked up the stairway. This was like living a
dream. And the best was still to come he thought.* His creative juices were already
churning.

35

"Hey there, sleepyhead, it's time to wake up. Do you know what the time is?" Susan turned from the living room sofa where George lay and shouted, "Mom, I can't get Dad up. Not even a budge."

"You don't have to yell. I'm right here." June walked into the room and sat down on the edge of the sofa. She looked down at her drowsy husband who was managing to open his weary eyes. "It's about time you woke up," she said in a very soft tone. "We were beginning to think that you would sleep all day."

"What time is it?"

"It's almost ten, George."

"Ten o'clock." George pushed himself and he abruptly sat up in the sofa. "Why on earth did you let me sleep so late? You guys have to get to church and the chores."

"Chores are done. The girls and I just finished. I should have just let you sleep but I thought that you might want to tarp up the load on the Mack."

"What, is it raining again?"

"No, it's snowing. It's been coming down since we started chores." June put her arm around her husband's left shoulder only to have George suddenly pull himself aside. "What is it, George?"

"It's just my side, June. It started hurting last night. I just get these stinking pains bolting through my left side just like now." George slumped over allowing his head to touch his knees. "It hurts like hell when it strikes."

"Come into the bathroom and let me take a look. You've got to get those dirty clothes off anyways. You know better than to leave them on."

George gingerly walked into the bathroom and allowed June to assist him in removing the work clothes. "You've got yourself a rash, George. How long have you had these blisters on your side? It looks something like chickenpox. How long have you had this?"

"For a couple of days now. I figured that it was just from the dust or something but it sure is itchy and it seems to feel worse this morning. Damn it, June, I just feel like I could sleep all day."

"God only knows that you could use it. You simply can't keep working without rest. In the meantime let's get you cleaned up and I'll call the Emergency in Royston and see what they say."

George stepped into the shower and carefully ran the water over him. The reddened blisters felt like they were on fire and he carefully dabbed a wet cloth over them in lieu of the running water. He stepped out and equally carefully dried himself and put on the fresh clothes that June had left for him. He briefly stared into the medicine cabinet mirror. He could not remember the last time he hurt like this.

June shouted from the kitchen, "George. They want to see you in Emergency. Get your coats, girls. One of you get the truck keys for me. Are you ready George?"

Normally George would have resisted but today he did not have the stamina or the desire. He sat on the passenger side of the Ford and simply watched the road as June drove into Royston. The snow was still coming down and the landscape was quickly turning white. *He had forgotten to tarp the truck but he knew that he would have ample time later to dry what was already as tough as nails.* At this moment in time he simply did not care about too much. He was tired and hurting and fell asleep before June had turned onto the highway.

When the family arrived home from Royston it was late in the afternoon. The snow had stopped and the skies had partially cleared leaving the area enveloped in a cold, winters landscape. The twins left the house to start their chores in the layer barn while June made George comfortable in their bedroom. George was drossy from the medication and was soon fast asleep. The telephone rang just before June was leaving to join the twins at the barns. She stepped back into the kitchen and answered it. "Hello, oh hi there, Sheila."

"Hello June, I figured that I had better call and see if everything was okay. We were expecting you guys for lunch and when you weren't at church."

"I'm so sorry, Sheila. I honestly forgot about lunch. We had to take George into Emergency this morning."

"Is he okay? Did he get hurt?"

"It's nothing like that, but he is very ill. They diagnosed him with shingles. He's just exhausted. I hate to say it but this snow is probably a good thing. He's got a bad rash down his left side and he's just beat. They gave him a prescription of acyclovir to take. Hopefully, it will all pass in a couple of weeks."

"We'll pray for his quick recovery, June. I knew that something was up. I'll let Allan know. Oh, by the way, Allan saw Jimmy yesterday."

"In town? Did he talk with him?"

"Yes, he was at the bank ATM. Allan gave him quite a surprise. They didn't talk much. Allan said he was pretty defiant. Allan offered him a ride but Jimmy declined. Apparently he mentioned something about the South End. Anyways, I will not keep you any longer."

"No, I had better get out and see how the girls are making out. Thanks for the info. I'm so sorry for forgetting about your luncheon, Sheila."

"Not to worry, you undoubtedly had your hands full. You've got plenty on your minds already. Wish George a quick recovery for us. I've heard that shingles is quite painful. I'm sure that Allan will pay him a visit."

"Thanks Sheila, take care."

June hung up the telephone and quietly walked back to the bedroom. George was fast asleep. She quickly turned around and headed back to the porch stopping only to put on her rubber boots before heading out to the barns. Outside her breath left a frozen, white vapor as the dusk was quickly turning into darkness. Isolated flakes of snow sparkled in the reflection of the yard light as her boots crunched through the growing snow pack on the ground. It was mid-November and it felt like this snowfall was going to be around for awhile.

36

George sat quietly at the kitchen table and watched the twins walk out the lane to wait for Monty's bus. He sipped at his warm tea while digesting the winter's landscape through the picture window. It had stayed cold for a couple of days now and many were wondering if it was actually going to stay. His line of thought was broken by June's voice as she sat down at the table with her coffee.

"Staring at it won't make it go away."

"You're right there, perhaps it really doesn't matter that much anymore. I guess that we had better be thankful, anyways."

"So how're you feeling? You seemed to sleep better last night. You don't really have to get up early and go out to chores. The girls and I can manage. You've got to let the medication work."

"I'm okay. Surely I can manage to do a few chores. I'm sore and tired and taking it pretty easy. It's almost like a holiday." The couple shared a smile and a chuckle. "Besides we've got broilers to leave next week and hopefully I'm getting over this crap by then."

The kitchen phone rang and June got up to answer it. George sat back in his chair and listened to the muted conversation. In no time June had sat back down at the kitchen table. George looked across at her, "Anything important?"

"It was Miss Oagle. I guess that she wishes for us to pay her another visit next Wednesday. Apparently she wants to review her findings from her visit on Monday and she will have their proposed support figures ready. I told her that we would be there for one o'clock. She said that Jim had returned to classes yesterday. Not much more."

"I can hardly wait for that meeting. She sure seems intent in her ways. It seems like Jim is too. I mean as far as staying in town and away from us or should I say me."

The conversation was interrupted by the telephone once again and June hurried back into the kitchen to grab the receiver. She answered the phone on the run and brought it back to George. "It's for you, it's Allan."

"Good morning, Allan."

"Good morning, George. How you feelin'? Hopefully I'm not interrupting anything too important."

"Oh, about the same, thanks. It'll just take some time to clear up. June and I were just discussing our upcoming meeting with Miss Oagle. So what're you up to?"

"I'm just heading to a job site. So how did your meeting with her go on Monday?"

"She came out and sat here and pretty much told us how to run our business and how to look after our children. I know that she has good intentions but she has no idea of what a farm is about."

"So, she wasn't impressed?"

"I don't think that she even knows what a bird or a kernel of wheat is. So I guess we learn next Wednesday how much they deem is necessary to support Jim in his new lifestyle. We're pretty much buggered, Allan."

"Look, George, that's what I'm calling about. I've got a good friend in Royston that I've been talking to with regards to Jim. He'd like to help if he can. I mentioned him to you before. He's a constable in town and well aware of the growing drug problem at the High School. Anyways, he'd like to meet with us. Roy is a good guy, George. I think that you need to listen to him. If Jim is into the drug scene like you think he is then you really must hear Roy out."

"Sounds good, Allan. We sure appreciate all this but I'm not too sure just what he could do. It seems like our hands are completely tied at the moment."

"Just give him a listen, George. You free tonight?"

"Time is something that I've got plenty to spare right now, Allan. Just give me a place and a time."

"Just meet me at our house around seven. Okay? Gotta' run guy."

George heard the line go blank and he clicked his phone receiver off. He looked across the table at June who was eagerly awaiting insight into the conversation. "Allan wants me to meet with him and a constable from town tonight."

"What about, George?"

"Not exactly sure but it seems like this constable would like to help us. I'm not too sure just where this is all headed, June, but I've got to check out what he has to say. It's my fault that all of this has happened. I fear that Jim is messed up with some pretty mixed up people. I'm sorry but I get this terrible feeling that if we just let Child Welfare run over us then our son is as good as gone."

June stared across the table at George and watched in silence as the tears began pouring from his eyes. "You can't keep blaming yourself, George. Look at yourself. You've got to look after your health too."

"My health doesn't mean damn if I loose my son over this. I'm just so sick and tired of this whole damn mess. If only I'd listened to Allan earlier then we probably would not have been in this pickle now. I've got to listen to this Roy chap. Maybe he can help. In the meantime I need to have a rest."

George rose out of his chair and slowly walked back to the bedroom. He felt nauseous and dizzy. He stopped at the bathroom and pulled off his shirt. He carefully applied some petroleum jelly to the red bumps that filled his left side. He gently pulled his shirt back on and popped another acyclovir into his mouth. In seconds he was fast asleep on the bed.

Allan and George arrived at the Pioneer Coffee Shop in Royston around seven-thirty and promptly made themselves comfortable in a booth towards the back of the establishment. Shortly after the waitress had brought them their coffee a large, bald-headed man approached their table and turned towards them. "Good Evening."

"Good evening. Sit down. We've got a coffee waiting for you. Roy. This is my friend, George Edwards. George meet Roy Warrack."

"Pleasure, Roy."

"Likewise, George, I'm sure."

Roy sat down across from George and methodically began stirring a creamer into his coffee. He sipped a small portion of the hot liquid and then sat back in his chair. He looked directly at Allan and George and spoke in a quiet but stern voice. "This is all completely unofficial. We are just sharing some thoughts here, gentlemen. Allan tells me you've got a problem with your son, George."

George proceeded to deliver an itemized account of the troubling events of the fall to Roy. Allan did add a few comments as George updated the off-duty constable. However, for the most part he remained a silent listener as George poured out his heart to Allan's friend. It took a couple of cups of coffee before George eventually ran out of words. His explanation of the happenings of the past few weeks seemed of special interest to the constable.

"Allan suspects that Jim is in the South end of town. You mentioned a Megan a couple of times, George. I think that warrants a follow-up. The drug situation in this town continues to worsen. We nab kids on possession all of the time but it means nothing. If we cannot get to the sources then we do not achieve anything." Roy stopped for a moment and cleared his throat.

His began to speak in earnest. "I'm afraid that I have to agree with your fears regarding the drug consumption, George. You may very well have other problems with regards to Child Welfare and your farm situation. I sympathize with you there but that's your own fight." He swallowed the last of his coffee. "However, I do believe that you have a much worst problem on the horizon here. It sounds like your son has completely changed in the relative period of a few months. If he is not removed from this setting then it will probably only worsen. If he is exposed to regular consumption of illicit drugs then you run the risk of him eventually becoming addicted."

George broke into the conversation, "This is all reassuring, Roy, but you are not telling me something new. We don't even have access to Jim. Child Welfare has him. We cannot touch him even if we could locate him. They aren't even listening to me. In a few days time they are going to ask us for formal monetary support. Miss Oagle has no intentions of returning Jim to us, at least in the relative near term."

"Do you love your son, George?"

"What kind of a question is that, Allan?"

"Then listen to what Roy has to propose."

"Look, George. Allan and I go back a long ways. Our families have mingled together for a decade. Allan tells me that you are a decent guy and that you have a loving family. I lost a nephew a couple of months ago to a cocaine overdose. I watch kids laugh about our warnings when we give our presentation at the High School. Let me do some digging and searching around. If the occasion arises perhaps I can deliver Jim back to the farm. It would only be temporary until Child Welfare learnt of the action and hauled him back but it might give you time to act."

"I don't understand, Roy. What do you mean act?"

"You've got to get Jim away from here. If you sincerely believe that your son is in danger then you had better act quickly to remove him from this whole scene. I can't guarantee anything here but if something should happen then you would have one chance and one chance only to get him to somewhere safer. Are you prepared to do that? Are you prepared to risk the wrath of Child Welfare? Can you get him out of here if we are able to deliver him?"

George appeared stunned from the words. The table remained quiet as the three men looked at each other waiting for someone to break the silence. George finally spoke, "I am, Roy. I mean, yes. We will try. I've got folks back east. Mom and Dad are actually due here soon to stay until Christmas. I know that they will help." George began to perspire heavily. His head was spinning and he felt another bout of nausea coming on.

"You okay there, George? Perhaps we had better end this conversation for now. Allan had better take you home."

"Yes, come on there, George. We'll get you out to the truck. Thanks, Roy."

"Hey, anytime, Allan." Roy leaned across the table to George and grabbed his right hand. "We'll make this work for you guy. You hold in there. I know it's tough. Kids get lost to drugs everyday. It's just so easy out there. Unfortunately, our system often protects those that prey on the good ones but every once in awhile we get lucky. Have faith."

George managed a weak smile. "I certainly appreciate all of this, Roy. June and I want our son back but more important we want him to have a proper future. That's our biggest concern right now. We will do whatever it takes to accomplish that."

Roy silently walked away from the table. Allan helped support George as he struggled to get onto his feet. "Damn it, George, you've got to get feelin' better. You're too damn heavy for me to drag around like this." Allan smiled at his friend and the two of then slowly exited the coffee shop.

Later that night George spoke with his parents, Elaine and Ronald, on the telephone. June had already kept them informed on the drastic events of the last two weeks. George talked in confidence regarding the recent conversation he had shared with the constable. They agreed that the circumstances were indeed dire. Their flight out was scheduled for Friday and they would come directly to the farm from Ollen. They agreed to help in whatever capacity was possible irregardless of the outcome.

37

On Friday afternoon, June and George were walking across the yard after finishing some chores when they noticed a red car heading south along the side road. They stood quietly and watched the red, rental car turn into their laneway and slowly approach them. The car came to a halt beside the Ford. Both doors opened simultaneously and an older couple appeared. George walked over to Ronald and gave his Dad a welcome handshake before heading to the open arms of his mother. "You look good, Dad. You came so quickly."

"We figured that you guys needed us sooner versus later." Ronald looked at George, "You look horrible, son."

"Well I certainly feel better now that you two are here." George proceeded to give Elaine a big hug. "It's great to see you, Mom."

Elaine returned the embrace. "We wouldn't have missed coming." She smiled at her son. "You could have ordered some warmer weather for us though."

"It's just been a cold fall, period," said June. "Did you two have a good flight?"

"Three and a half hours and we were sitting in Ollen Airport and it took a couple of hours to drive here. Roads were good. You sure look like winter though." Ronald walked back to the trunk of the car and proceeded to grab their travel bags. "Your mother packed two big suitcases. You'd think that we were stayin' for a year. After our conversation the other night we weren't sure how long our visit was going to be."

"We can only hope for the best right now, Dad. Here let me grab one of them. Damn they're not just large; they're heavy too."

June and Elaine made their way towards the house while George and his father stood in the yard looking across the white fields. A light, north wind spread a chill over the barren looking landscape. "Come on, Dad. Let's get you inside before you catch a chill out here."

"So how are you standing up?" Ronald looked caringly at his son. "Shingles are no laughing matter for someone as young as you."

"I'd feel a whole lot better if we could end this debacle. It knocked the stuffing out of me for a bit."

"I warned you about demanding so much from those kids of yours. When are you going to realize that they are just kids? Jim is such a good boy. I can't even imagine what it took for him to actually leave. Hopefully, we can help everyone out here?"

"Please, not now, Dad. Hopefully, we'll come up with a solution before too long. Damn it's getting cold out."

Inside June and Elaine had sat down around the kitchen table and were catching up on family news from back east. Ronald and George removed their boots and jackets and joined them. The kettle began to boil in the kitchen and June got up to prepare tea.

"So when do the girls get home?" asked Elaine. "We're so looking forward to seeing them."

"They'll be here pretty soon," replied June as she brought out cups from the kitchen. "Monty is pretty prompt with his bus schedule."

George sat the tea pot down in the center of the table. "We'll just let this seep for awhile." He looked up at his folks. "You don't know how much this means to us. We don't know if Constable Warrack will sight Jim or whether he'll come up with a plan to actually get Jim out here. But if it happens we now have a route away from here if needed. I'm desperately sorry about all of this but I am truly grateful that you choose to come despite our mayhem. Perhaps if Jim gets a chance to talk with you two it will help. We have no idea of the outcome or whether anything will happen. For now we just wait and hope for the best scenario. In the meantime we welcome you to stay for as long as possible. Perhaps we shall have Christmas together yet?"

"That's why we are here, George," replied Elaine. "Your father and I are here to help and we are here for Christmas. I think that I'm ready for some tea."

Elaine stood up and began filling the cups and handing them around the table. "This smells good, June."

"Thanks, its herbal blend. We like it." June passed around a plate of cookies and sat back down to enjoy her beverage. "Eat them up. The girls are sure going to be surprised when they get home."

"So you didn't tell them we'd arrive today?" asked Elaine.

"No, they have been so excited about you two coming out for Christmas. I think that they have been expecting next week so this will be a little surprise for them. It's been a tough fall on them, too. This whole thing has been hard." June broke down at the table and began to cry. "I just hope that we can get our Jimmy back to us. I just pray that he will be returned."

George walked over to comfort June while Elaine and Ronald sat in quiet. He looked out the window and noticed that the twins were already on their way up the lane. "Twins will be here pronto." He sat back down and sipped his tea. "So have you got return tickets already or what did you do there?"

"Our flight is scheduled to leave Ollen on December 28th," said Ronald. "If something changes before then we will just have to work around it. It seems like they only needed a days notice for most flights in the immediate future. Once you get near Christmas then it's a different story. The fare rates change, too."

"Don't concern yourself with the tickets, Dad. We'll look after that if something happens that necessitates changing from your original booking. Right now I'm just hoping for an opportunity to get Jim. I'm still hopeful that once he sees you two that he will come around. He has always loved you guys greatly."

The twins stepped inside the porch door and took no time to shed their coats and run to greet their Grandparents. The atmosphere in the room was quickly uplifted. George watched as Mary and Susan enthusiastically chatted with Ronald and Elaine. *He wandered how Jim would react to seeing his Grandparents? Hopefully, he would exhibit a portion of the same compassion. Would they even be given the opportunity? Would they still be able to celebrate Christmas together?*

He continued to sip at his tea and reveled in the joy of the moment. *It was great to see his folks. They had not been out for a visit in years. Why did it have to be under such circumstances? He knew that his father would hold him accountable for whatever transpired during their visit.* His aching body served as a constant reminder of his predicament and of the delicate situation that possibly existed in the foreseeable future.

38

Jim watched with limited interest as Miss Oagle gathered her notes together. He glanced down at his watch and realized that he had been with her for two hours. She had been late for the appointment and his patience was quickly dwindling. The barren room was becoming way too uncomfortable. He was wasting valuable leisure time. Austaire and Megan were driving to the city later tonight and he wished to spend some time with his girlfriend. Miss Oagle finally spoke, "Well I think that we've got most of the bases covered, Jim. This session has been most productive for me and I trust for you too."

"Yes, I feel like I've pretty much spilled my guts for you, Betty. You know as much about me as I do now." Jim smiled at the caseworker. "You sure know how to get a guy talking. It's all good, I guess?"

"It's more than just the conversation, Jim. You've opened up to me as a person as well. That is so very important. It is so very important that I understand from your perspective if we are to eventually make inroads into restoring a family relationship that is beneficial for you."

"So you are going to see my folks next week?"

"Yes, we have an appointment scheduled. In the meantime I want you to continue on with your life. It sounds like you are adjusting well."

"Yah, Megan is super good to me. It's an awesome place."

"And your school work is starting to come? I want to see more progress there but I understand that it will take time."

"Like whatever! You're reminding me about missing some damn classes last week. We already talked about that."

"No need to be defensive, Jim. You're right and we did already chat about your school attendance. Mr. Erickson and I will continue your monitor your progress and we will review it in a couple of weeks."

"We aren't meeting next Saturday?"

"No, I'm off next weekend. I've got you scheduled for a visit in two weeks time. We should have your support details settled by that time as well."

"So, I don't see you until then?"

"Not unless you need me. You have my number. I've got several cases on the go. Not that it makes you less important but my caseload is pretty full." Miss Oagle pushed back her chair and got up. She walked towards Jim and extended her right hand. "You're doing great, Jim. Do you need a ride back to your billet?"

Jim shook Betty's outstretched hand. "A ride would be great."

Miss Oagle dropped Jim off at the corner of Aspen Grove and he watched her drive off. It was almost four o'clock and the sun felt nice on the side of his face as he walked down the street. He noticed an unfamiliar vehicle parked across from the townhouse but paid little attention to it. Megan knew many people and there were always people coming and going on the weekends. He walked up the sidewalk to number thirteen and entered.

"Hey, you forget how to knock?" snapped Megan. She got off the sofa and walked towards him. "I'm going to have to teach you some manners there, Jimmy. You always knock, remember!"

"Sorry, I didn't think that I had to anymore. So who's here?"

"Oh, just a couple of client types that I know. So is that nice caseworker lookin' after your interests for you?"

"I guess so. She sure is nosey. Plus she was late, again. Anyways, I don't see her for a couple of weeks."

"So have they got the support arranged? Like show me the money."

"It should be all arranged by then. She promised me that it would be. She is meeting with my folks this coming week. So what are you up to? Where is Austaire?"

"She must have just stepped out for a bit, Jimmy. I'm not too sure."

"You guys still leaving for Ollen tonight?"

"Yep, you'll have the place to yourself for a couple of days, Jimmy. You've got your key?"

"Yes, so where are your guests?" Jim glanced into the kitchen. "Are they downstairs? Okay if I join them?"

"Not right now, Jimmy. It's a private thing. How be you just stay here with Meg." She walked over to him and wrapped her arms around him. "How be you and I go upstairs and have our own little party?"

"I was hoping to spend some time with Austaire this afternoon."

"Whatever, so I'm not good enough now?"

"You know that it's not like that. You're the Queen, Meg."

"So, are you comin' up or not, Jimmy?" Megan's eyes glittered. "You can see her later."

"Okay, so do you think that Austaire will be long? She didn't mention anything to me earlier."

"She'll be here when she gets here. Boy you sure are one for questions today?" Megan laughed and then slowly headed towards the stairway. "Are you comin' or not?"

"Be right there, Meg." Jim walked into the kitchen. "I'm just going to grab a drink. I'm thirsty."

"Bring one for me too, then Jimmy. I'll be upstairs getting comfortable." She bewitchingly blew him a kiss. "Don't keep me waiting too long."

Jim opened the refrigerator door and grabbed a couple of beer. He could hear muted laughter coming from the basement. He and Austaire had set up their room downstairs and he was a little annoyed that someone else was down there. *It seemed strange that Meg was not with them but hey it was her house.* He shut the refrigerator door and headed upstairs.

The following hour passed quickly as the two individuals were trippin' and loving in an endless wave. *It was always so great with Megan. She was pretty hot and tempting. She was a phat.* Jim was slowly adjusting to the white powder. It no longer seemed to burn his nostrils like it once did. It gave him the ultimate high. *He felt supreme and powerful. He enjoyed the immediate and intense rush.* Meg just capped it all in one fine package. He could chill out with her anytime. Life was so awesome and it could also be so very wicked.

Audible voices suddenly ascended from the living room area. Megan crawled out of the bed and hurriedly dressed. Jim was content to simply watch her. She reached over and gave him a kiss. "You just keep comfy, Jimmy. I just have to let them out." In a whirl she disappeared from the room; firmly closing the door after her.

Jim could still hear the muted voices and decided to investigate on all this secrecy. He tip toed across the floor and carefully opened the door just a crack. His senses were burning. Megan was talking to a couple of young men whom he had never seen before. Suddenly Austaire appeared from the kitchen. She was dressed in her bathrobe. He watched in silence as she walked over to one of the guys and gave him a huge hug and then kissed the other. She then quietly and quickly disappeared downstairs. Jim softly shut the bedroom door and went back to the bed and lay down. His eyes filled with tears. *How could she of done that? What else where they hiding from him?* He focused on the revolutions of the white ceiling fan and he lay there awaiting Megan's return. The door downstairs closed and footsteps ascended the stairway.

"So, how you doing?" Megan walked into the room and sat down beside him. "How be you and I and Austaire catch a bite out tonight? She'll be ready…I mean back soon. Or we could order pizza if you want?"

"You were right the first time. She's already here, Meg." Jim sat up and looked directly at her. "I saw her downstairs. So who were those guys? Austaire was here all along wasn't she?"

Megan sat silent for a minute and gazed down at the floor. She slowly turned and looked at Jim. "Sorry, Jimmy. I should have told you before. Austaire has her own life too. You both do. Hell we all share around here." She snuggled in beside Jim. "It's not like you don't, Sunshine?"

"So how long has this been going on? I just thought that she was my girlfriend. She never let on that anything was going on."

"We all have our friends, Jimmy. Life is to be enjoyed. Now just chill out and relax a bit. What, you jealous or something?"

Jim's head was swirling. He felt hurt but most of all he was annoyed. "She lied to me. Both of you lied to me. Why did you do that?" He jumped up from the bed and proceeded to dress. "I care about her and I thought that she cared about me. I thought that we were a thing."

"And you two are, Jimmy. What about us? How do you think she feels about us? You seem quite happy to party with me. What the hell difference does it make?"

"You're different, Meg. You're our Meg. You're the Queen." Jim finished dressing. "I thought that Austaire was my girl."

"Now you are just being plain stupid, Jimmy." Megan stood up. "We party here and we have fun. I have my client's interests to look after too. You know, show me the money. Austaire knows that. You'll be eighteen soon. Stop acting like some prudish kid."

Jim stood at the doorway staring at Megan. "I'm just going out for a bit."

"What about supper? You've got to be hungry. I know that I certainly am."

"Maybe I'll just get my own tonight. I just need a little breather."

"Fine then, be like that. Austaire and I have to leave for Ollen soon. I know that she'll want to see you before we go."

"Well maybe I just don't want to see her right now. I've got to go." Jim walked over to Megan and kissed her lightly on the forehead. He looked almost apologetic but his eyes still contained remnants of dried tears. "I just need some space right now. Okay Meg?"

"Sure, you get yourself that space. If I don't see you before we leave then we'll see you on Monday. Okay? You okay, Jimmy? It's all good. You'll see in time. You'll be stoked to see her."

"Yah, whatever, Meg." Jim nodded his head in agreement and turned and left the room. He softly trod down the stairs and put his coat and shoes on. Austaire was moving around in the basement but he made no attempt to see her. Instead he grabbed a couple of beers from the fridge and left the townhouse.

The street lights dimly lit the street as the growing darkness of early evening spread across the town. It was cool but not as cold as it had been most of the week. The air felt almost inviting. Jim cracked open a can of beer and proceeded to walk down Aspen Grove and headed towards Main Street. *Maybe some of his friends might be at Dobeys? Perhaps he could give Glen a call.* He hadn't talked with him in awhile. Jim tossed the empty beer can into a vacant lot and proceeded to open the second. *Damn Austaire, anyways. Damn her. Make a fool of me would she?*

It was almost eight when Jim returned to the Aspen Grove. Megan's red Honda was gone and the townhouse appeared pitch black inside. He dug into his pocket and found the door key. He inserted it into the door knob and quickly opened the door. The warmth of the room felt inviting and he threw his coat onto a chair and deposited the key on the coffee table. In minutes Jim was comfortably stretched across the old sofa watching hockey on the television and consuming cold beer. He made a trip downstairs and returned with his stash of pot. The room became a haze of light blue as Jim drew back on a joint while consuming beer on the side.

By the time the hockey broadcast was finished he was completely thrashed and was becoming quite bored. He called Glen Rollins but only got his answering machine. *Damn that Glen anyways he thought. Where on earth could he be? He never went anywhere on his own. Maybe he had a girl on the sly too.* What Jim needed was some action. His mind was still active but it was running in slow motion. The world had descended into creep gear. He drew back on what was left of his joint and savored it. *Perhaps he could get into the Roadhouse? He'd got in there before. Lot's of kids from school got in there. It wasn't too far from here; only a few blocks. He had no company here. Perhaps he might find someone to party with at the Roadhouse. He'd show the girls. Yes, he could do with some quality company. He did have the townhouse all to himself. This night was still very young and definitely not to be wasted.* He smiled to himself and then he laughed loudly. *He was pretty much wasted.* He pocketed a couple more beer from the refrigerator. With a stoned smile on his face he stumbled out of the room and quietly left the townhouse; slamming the door close behind him.

39

Constable Warrack was dispatched after the Royston Police department had received a call from the Roadhouse shortly after midnight. Apparently, an underage youth had attempted to enter the establishment and was refused. The intoxicated youth had remained seated on a bench at the front of the Roadhouse and continued to act in a drunken and disorderly manner. It appeared to be only another routine Saturday night call for the constable.

He turned into the parking lot and immediately saw the youth in question sitting out front. He parked his car and proceeded to walk over to the unsuspecting individual. He stopped in front of the boy and asked, "You got a name son? I think that it is time we took you home."

The weary eyed youth cast a stoned look in the general direction of the police officer. In a slurred voice he answered, "Name is Jim Edwards, sir." His blurred vision was playing tricks on him. He looked again at the constable and managed, "What can I do for you?"

The name shot through the constable's head like a hot iron. This was the kid in question that he had discussed with Allan and George. The denim clad youth that stunk of alcohol and marijuana held little resemblance to the starry eyed boy that his father had described. Allan had given him a photo of Jim but the constable didn't require it now.

"So where do you reside, Jim?"

"I'm at thirteen Aspen Grove."

"Well how be you and I take a little drive over there. We've had a complaint son and you can't stay here."

"Oh, I can walk there just fine." Jim managed another very slurred, "Thanks, anyways."

"Look, I can drive you there or I can take you to the detachment but I will take you. Do you understand?"

"Yah, sure. Like whatever, officer, sir."

"So you think that this is pretty funny?" The officer struggled to help Jim up. "You realize that I could take you in to the detachment and book you. You're in no condition to laugh at anything right now, son."

Jim said nothing and allowed the officer to place him in the back seat of the cruiser. His head was spinning and his blurred vision hindered his actions. He felt like he was dreaming and he applied a very limited sense of reality to the situation. He sat quietly with a stoned smile glued to his face. The constable backed the cruiser out of the parking lot and then drove to thirteen Aspen Grove.

Constable Warrack pulled up in front of the dark townhouse and parked the cruiser. "It looks like everyone is asleep inside. I'll walk you to the door."

Jim exited the cruiser and very slowly meandered his way towards the front door. He tried the door handle and realized that it was locked. Jim then attempted to find the key in his pockets but could not locate it. His head was spinning and he leaned against the door for support. The urge to throw up could not be restrained and he spilled much of the contents of his stomach on the front door step.

"Look here, son. You're in pretty bad shape. Perhaps we had best get someone up in there if you can't find the key." Constable Warrack began knocking vigorously on the wooden door with his right hand. "Open up, it's the police."

"I'm by myself. I can't get in without my key." Jim threw up again and fell down against the doorway. "I don't feel so good."

"Look, I can't leave you here, son. I can take you to the detachment and you can stay overnight in the drunk tank or I can take you home."

"This is my home."

"I mean your proper home, son. You have parents waiting for you. You're sick. You badly need some help."

Jim violently vomited again. His forehead was wet with perspiration. His legs were weak and the officer had to support him in an attempt to keep him on his feet. Slowly they made their way back to the cruiser where the officer managed to steady Jim while opening a rear door. Jim was almost delirious as the officer settled him into the back seat.

Constable Warrack secured his passenger and then got into the front of the car. He called the dispatch and informed them that he was taking the youth out to his home after an attempt to enter a friend's house in town failed. It was a judgment call on his part in lieu of taking the lad back to the detachment and putting him in a cell overnight. He described the boy's condition as serious and that parental care was definitely required. In no time the cruiser was speeding towards the Edwards farm as per the directions that he already knew.

George and June were awakened by the steady knocking on the front door of their home. George crawled out of bed and threw on his bathrobe and slippers. He carefully walked to the front door and turned on the front light before opening it. Officer Warrack stood on the front porch staring directly at him.

"Good evening, I've got your son in the cruiser. He's pretty much incapacitated at the moment. He's sick, George, damn sick. We received a call from the Roadhouse and I found him outside the premise. He had locked himself out of the house on Aspen Grove so I told dispatch that I was bringing him home."

George followed Constable Warrack out to the cruiser and assisted the officer in carrying Jim into the house. Jim was basically out of it and he made no attempt to resist their assistance. George and the constable dragged him into the front room and removed his disgustingly, dirty jacket and jeans. June had overheard the conversation and was in the room assisting the men. They wrapped Jim in a blanket and placed him on the sofa where he was seemingly content to fall asleep in a drunken, stoned slumber. June sat down beside her son. Tears steadily flowed from her eyes.

"I've got to run, folks. You realize that Child Welfare will be looking for him eventually and they will probably come for him. We've done nothing wrong here. Jim could have been sitting outside that townhouse in a delirious fever by morning." Officer Warrack looked directly at George. "Get him away from here and deal with them later. It's pretty obvious that they haven't got a clue as to what's really going on. I wish you success. Some prayers got answered here tonight. Look after your son."

George cast a quick eye at June and she briefly looked up at him before directing her attention back to Jim. "I don't know how to thank you, Roy. Thank you for bringing him home."

"Just don't let me down. Get him the hell away from these people. I'm thinking that we will be paying a visit to a certain townhouse in the South End soon. You do not want your son involved. Watch him closely tonight. He's in rough shape. If he gets worse you may have to take him into emergency. Hopefully, he'll just sleep it off."

George extended his right hand to the officer and they exchanged a brisk handshake. "Thanks again. We'll give it our best from this end. My folks are here to help. Good night, Roy"

"Good night, folks."

Officer Warrack then turned and headed out the front door. George stood at the doorway and watched silently as the cruiser left the yard. He stood on the porch and continued to watch the headlights until they had disappeared into the darkness. He then entered the house and methodically proceeded to securely lock both entry doors. June was sitting on the side of the sofa gently cleaning Jim's face and stroking her son's golden locks of hair. She had covered his forehead with a warm cloth. Jim was dirty and pale. He stunk of alcohol and pot and vomit.

June looked up at George and quietly asked, "What has become of him? How could those people allow this to happen?"

George slowly sat down on the floor beside June and his son. "I'm responsible for this. If anyone allowed this to happen; it was me. I'm sure that Miss Oagle had no idea of what was going on. In time she would get to the truth but what would happen to Jim in the meantime? That is why we can't leave him here, June. Roy is right. He'll just fall in with more of the same."

"Perhaps when Jim talks with Ronald and Elaine it will be better," said June.

"Possibly but I can't see him changing just like that, June." George was developing a cold sweat on his forehead.

"Are you okay?" asked June. "You look almost as pale as our son."

"I'm fine. I just wish that there was another way but I can't see any." George looked hesitantly up at his wife. "We've got to get him away from Royston for good. This is our chance. Like Roy said prayers have been answered tonight. When Jim awakes in the morning and is aware of what is going down he is not going to be happy. Somehow we have to convince him to go back east with his Grandparents. Otherwise, take a good look at your son because it may be your last."

June's face turned blank at the thought. She bowed her head in a silent prayer. George got up and turned off the lights. He then returned to his position sitting on the floor beside the sofa. *The darkness was comforting. It was amazing that the commotion had not awakened the girls.* The furnace cut in and warm air was sent spiraling into the room. Its warmth tempted George's weary eyes to close but the adrenaline flowing in his veins was too strong. He was on guard and it would be a sleepless night.

40

Jim awoke to the sounds of Radio 61, Royston, on Sunday morning. He cautiously opened his eyes fully expecting to awaken in a cell. His memory was cloudy but he definitely remembered being put into the police cruiser. It still took a minute before he came to the full realization that he was back at the farm. He slowly rolled over on the sofa and gazed around the living room. His dreary eyes became fixed on Elaine and Ronald. He slowly pulled himself up into a sitting position and uttered, "Grandma and Grandpa."

"Hello, Jimmy," said Ronald. "It's good to see you again."

"Hi son," added Elaine, "How are you feeling this morning?"

"Okay, I guess. What brings you this way? I mean I'm surprised to see you guys."

"We came out for Christmas," replied Elaine. "We arranged this about a month ago. I'm sure your parents told you. It's great to see the twins and we're especially happy to see you, Jim. Come give your Grandma a big hug."

Jim slowly stood up and reluctantly walked over to Elaine and gave her a hug. "Good to see you, Grandma." Jim walked over to Ronald and extended his right hand. "Good to see you too, Grandpa. I'm sorry but I had forgotten about you coming for the holidays and all."

Ronald gave Jim a vigorous handshake and then resumed with the conversation. "We're especially happy to see you, Jim. We didn't know if we would or not. We know that you've been having some problems. We're here to try and help."

"Like whatever. I've pretty much got things squared around again. I don't live here right now. I guess Mom and Dad have told you the whole tale. Anyways, I'll be getting back to town soon. I'm staying with some friends in there. I'm not exactly sure how I managed to get out here last night. It sure wasn't my idea."

"A constable from town brought you out. According to him it sounds like those people may not really be your friends," said Ronald. "We came here to

171

help out. Your parents want us to take you back east with us and get you away from the drugs. Your Mom and Dad are very worried about you."

"Don't even go there, Grandpa. This is nothing to do with you guys. What goes on between my parents and I is nothing to do with you. I've just decided to move on to something better. Once Betty gets all the mechanics in place I will be set up. I don't belong here anymore and I certainly am not going back east with you two. Why would anyone expect me to do that? Why would I want to do that?"

Elaine and Ronald stood there in silence as Jim exited the room and walked into the kitchen. The porch door opened just as Jim was preparing to walk downstairs. The twins ran into the porch and stood looking at him. "Hi Jim," said Mary, "It's great to have you home again."

"Have you seen Grandma and Grandpa?" asked Susan. "Isn't it great that they're here to visit?"

"Yah, it's just awesome. Have you seen my shoes?"

"I think that Mom put them downstairs in your room after she cleaned them up," said Susan. "We've really missed you, brother."

"Well, I can't really say the same. I just need some clothes and my shoes and I'm out of here." Jim headed downstairs. "Don't know why that cop brought me out here but I'm sure as hell not stayin'."

"You were sure sick last night," said Mary who had followed her brother downstairs. "We are all worried about you. Why don't you let Mom and Dad help? Grandma and Grandpa are here to help too. Are you on drugs, brother? Is that why you act so weird?"

Jim turned to his sister. "I don't need your damn help. I am doing just fine without any of you." He glared at both of the twins. "Now just leave me alone or you will really see something. Maybe you're the weird ones? I'll just get cleaned up a little and I'll be out of here."

Susan ran up the stairs and out of the house. She was crying when she ran into June's arms. "Jim doesn't want to see us, Mom. He's getting ready to leave."

"He is going to leave, Susan. We are sending him back east with Grandma and Grandpa."

George left the layer barn and noticed June and Susan behind the house. He walked briskly to them. "What's up? Is Jim up, Susan?"

"Yes and he's pretty angry. He's getting ready to leave." Susan began crying in her Mom's arms. "Why does he hate us so?"

"Jim doesn't hate you, Susan," said June. "It's not him talking right now. Right now he is upset and confused and needs our help."

"I'd better get in there, June. Somehow we have to convince him to go with the folks."

"I'll be right there, George. Don't do anything stupid. Try not to upset him more than he probably is. Please."

George ran towards the back of the house and entered the porch just as Jim was walking up the stairway from the basement. The two stood still for a moment just eyeing each other before George finally broke the silence. "Good morning, Jim. It's good to have you home again."

"I'm not sure how you managed to get me out here, Dad, but I'm sure as hell not staying here."

"I think that you brought yourself out here, Jim. The constable said that you were locked out of your place in town. You were very sick when you arrived here. You still look mighty pale. You're lucky that you didn't spend the night in a jail cell."

"I wish that he had put me in a cell. I don't belong here anymore."

"I'm afraid that you are right there, Jim." George stood tall in the entrance to the porch. "But you sure as hell don't belong in that drug house in Royston either. From the sounds of it your friends that live there are going to get a visit from the authorities in the near future and you will not be there when it happens."

"You have no idea what kind of people they are," shouted Jim. "You have no idea what you are talking about. According to you none of my friends are good enough for you high and mighty types."

"Not if they are just a bunch of dropouts and dopies, son." George struggled to maintain his composure. "Right now you are going to get cleaned up and packed and we are sending you away with my folks. We've got to get you out of this whole mess before you are lost to the world."

Jim burst out laughing just as June entered the porch. He looked up at his mother. "Good morning, Mommy Dear. Your devilish little son is home for a visit. Don't worry cause' I'm being whisked away to Never, Never Land and away from all the bad people."

"It's okay to release your frustrations, Jim," said June in a quiet tone. "The Lord knows that it is only the drugs talking right now. After you get some help it will all work out."

"I have got help in Royston," screamed Jim. "Can't you stupid people realize that? When Miss Oagle gets wind of this you are going to be in a world of trouble. You can't hold me and you can't make me do something that I don't want to. God damn it." He calmed down and a smile crept across his face. "You guys really break me up. How be you just let me go and I'll forget all about this little caper of yours?"

George stood firm on the landing to the porch. "I'm terribly sorry son for not preventing all this and for allowing it to occur but we are not going to stand here and allow your life to be wasted by others." He walked down towards Jim. "You are going to leave with your Grandparents if we have to tie you in that damn car. You will fly back east with them and you will start afresh and break yourself from the drugs and alcohol that you have become so accustomed to consuming."

"You are utterly mad. All of you are." Jim stood on the stairway and turned his head to the ceiling. "So you say that I am to leave with my Grandparents. Suppose I leave them too? Suppose I go back with them and then what?" He glared back at his father, "Do I get put in chains?"

"No, Jim," said Ronald who had come to the stairway with Elaine. "We start putting your life back together. You get rehab assistance if needed. You return to proper schooling and you become the old Jimmy that we all love."

Jim started up the stairs, brushing his way past his Grandparents and headed towards the phone. "I'm going to make a phone call and you people are just going to watch." He picked up the receiver and began to dial.

George had followed Jim and promptly pulled the phone from his hand and slammed it down hard on the table. "You are not calling anyone and you are going to do as you are told. Sorry son, but that is how it's going down." He reached out to Jim but Jim backed away and stood staring in disbelief at his father.

"I can have you arrested for this. I can charge all of you. My rights are being infringed upon big time here. You have completely gone off the deep end this time. I was willing to work with you guys before but now you have crossed the line."

"You will do what you must, Jim. You've been fed all sorts of cheap talk, I'm sure. Right now we are doing what we feel we must for your own good. If I must fight others to defend what I believe is for your well being then I will. You were brought here by an officer of the law in lieu of facing charges for drunken misconduct. Even Miss Oagle will have to respect that action. The occupants of the house that you left last night will be receiving a visit from Royston's finest in the near future. Your life is being consumed by drugs and by idiots that really don't give a shit about you. Hopefully, someday you will understand."

"Right now we need you to shower and get cleaned up, son," said June in her usual quiet tone. "I'll get clean clothes for you and then I'll help you pack. Your Grandparents already have a flight scheduled."

Jim stood in solemn silence. Everyone had gathered around him and he felt threatened and cornered. He threw up his hands in despair and looked around at his audience. "Okay. You win. I'll take a free plane ride. A little visit back east isn't the end of things. I could probably use a little vacation." He looked directly at George. "But when Child Welfare brings me back here you are going to wish that you never tried this maniac stunt. You are in a pile of trouble old man." Jim then turned to his Grandparents. "I'm sorry for all this. I really am. I'll go back east with you if it pleases you. I can visit some of my cousins back there but I will not be staying long. I'm no kid anymore. You'll see."

With that Jim turned and entered the bathroom. Within minutes the shower was running. June headed downstairs to complete the packing that she had started earlier. George headed for the spare room to gather his folk's bags and then promptly headed out to their car. The twins gathered around their Grandparents and shared some last minute conversation and then helped their Grandmother prepare a Sunday lunch. No one would leave on an empty stomach.

Jim enjoyed the lunch immensely. One downfall of living in Royston was definitely the food. *No one could compete with his mother when it came to filling one's stomach, except perhaps his Grandmother.* If he had felt better he would have enjoyed it even more but his stomach was still quite upset from the night before. Despite the earlier comments and negativity the conversation around the dinner table remained upbeat and encouraging. Jim listened to the family chatter but remained distant to everyone. *It was like they existed in a different world; a world where he no longer belonged. But if the cops were going down on Meg's place then whatever. As for Austaire perhaps she should just go back to the city and stay.*

After lunch George carried Jim's suitcase out to the rental car and the family gathered around to say their goodbyes. Jim stared into the horizon as the twins and their Grandparents exchanged loving hugs. For them it was a terribly short-lived visit. He glanced at his mother and father when they said their premature goodbye to his Grandparents. And then it was his turn to join the spectacle.

"Take care, Jim," said Mary, "We wish you the best."

Susan stepped forward and said, "I love you brother and I know that you love us too." Jim issued the twins a blank stare and they both stepped away from him.

June grasped her son and gave him a warm hug and lightly kissed his cheek. "I'll pray for you. We wish you well and we will miss you greatly. Please try to understand that what we are attempting to do is through our love for you." Tears began to envelope her face as Jim failed to show any response. "If we are wrong then we wrong because we care greatly for you and your well being. I love you son."

Jim stared at June but said nothing. *It was touching he thought but he would not give into her. In a week or so he would be back in Royston and they would never touch him again. But for now he felt it advantageous to go with his Grandparents and leave this place for good. Besides it might be safer in the short haul. He would find new friends and a new supply of drugs elsewhere.*

George was the last to say goodbye. He looked solemnly at Jim and simply uttered, "Take care son. Be good for your Grandparents and give them the respect they deserve. I am very sorry for all of this and I truly wish you well. Please give things a chance out there. You owe it to yourself to just give it a try."

"What, no handcuffs? You shock me," ushered Jim in a defiant voice. He shuffled towards the car and added, "Oh by the way you look terrible. You sick or something?"

Jim then opened the car door and jumped into the back seat. He abruptly closed the door shut. His eyes remained focused towards the laneway as Ronald shifted the vehicle into gear and slowly drove it out of the yard. The remaining members of the Edward's family stood calmly waving goodbye to the occupants of the disappearing vehicle. The forlorn expression on June's face told it all. Their faces were wet with tears as they all succumbed to the reality of Jim going away. Hopefully, this action would lead to a Christmas season that they would share together under more pleasant circumstances. The car tires shuffled a light dust into the cool air as the rental car disappeared out the laneway and onto the County Road. It took little time for the car and its occupants to vanish into the western landscape.

41

Child Welfare received a call from Megan Italaze on Tuesday morning informing them that Jim did not come home on Monday night. Miss Oagle called Mr. Erickson and discovered that Jim did not attend school on either Monday or Tuesday. She promptly called the Edward's home. George happened to be in the house at the time and answered the phone with a weak, "Hello."

"Is that you, Mr. Edwards? It's Betty Oagle calling from Child Welfare in Royston. Would Jim happen to be out there?"

"No he isn't," George swallowed hard. "Is there a problem?"

"We can't seem to locate him. Have you seen him recently?"

"Now we both know your position on that one, Miss Oagle. However, I must acknowledge that we did see Jim on the weekend. He was brought out to the farm by a Constable Warrack after he was found intoxicated outside a bar in town on Saturday night. It was a matter of him coming home or spending the night in a cell as apparently he had locked himself out of his billets house. He was very sick when he arrived here and June looked after him. We haven't seen him since late Sunday morning."

"Oh, I'm sorry. He was okay, then. You have no idea of were he went?"

"You can get all the details of Saturday night from the Royston Police, Miss Oagle. As for his exact whereabouts at the moment; your guess is as good as mine."

"You haven't heard from him, then?"

"No, but perhaps you should try asking those two girls that he had been hanging out with. I believe that their names were Megan and Austaire. I mentioned them before to you. Perhaps they would know?" There was absolute silence at the other end of the connection. "Are you still there, Miss Oagle?"

"Yes, yes, of course. I'm sorry about that. I guess I'll have to dig a little deeper here. If you hear anything please call me. You still have my number?"

"June has your business card. When he turns up will you contact us or at least keep us informed? I thought that you were his acting guardian? He was in really bad shape when he was dropped off here the other night."

"I'm sure that he will turn up promptly. He is probably staying with some friends. I will keep you informed. Goodbye for now, Mr. Edwards."

"Goodbye, Miss Oagle."

George hung up the phone and looked up at June who had been following the conversation. She smiled at him and said, "I didn't know that you were such an ambassador. It sounded good from here."

"They'll catch on soon enough and my name will be mud. For now she can scratch her royal head. It's funny but when I mentioned Megan to her she seemed to fade for awhile. I think that Miss Oagle knows her. There's a connection somewhere."

"And now you are becoming a detective too. Wow. You never cease to surprise me, George."

"I remain convinced that those two girls had a dramatic influence on our son. Someone exposed him to the drugs. Ever since Jim started seeing that Austaire things just went downhill. Talking about downhill have you heard anything more from back east?"

"Not since your folks called and said that they had arrived safely back home. Do you think that Jim will stay there?"

"Don't know, June. You pray and I'll hope to God that he does. Hopefully some strong family influence and professional help will eventually bring him around. If he shows back here it's all over."

George was slowly starting to recover from the shingles attack and by Friday afternoon he was starting to feel more like himself. Not the serious conversation with the banker on Thursday or the light snowfall that night could stymie his steady recovery to good health. He was in the yard emptying feed into a storage bin when Allan Heiner drove into the yard. He shut off the tractor and walked over to greet Allan who had jumped out of his truck.

"Boy, you move pretty fast for an old guy, Allan."

"I've got some pretty interesting news for you, George. This is between you, me and the gatepost but I had to come out and tell you in person."

"Tell me what? Damn it guy, you look like you just won the lottery or something."

"We sort of did. You remember that Jim took Roy back to the townhouse on Saturday night; the one he couldn't get into. Well they started watching it Sunday."

"Who was watching it, Allan?"

"The Royston Police, George. They started a stake out and they raided it last night. Roy couldn't give me all the details but he said they arrested a dealer that they have been trying to pin for some time and a couple of others including the girl that rented the place. Roy was ecstatic. You were right about the place. They found lots of illegal substance including pot and cocaine. Her name was Megan Italaze."

"Shit, Miss Oagle mentioned a Megan and Jim mentioned a Megan. You don't suppose that it was her?"

"Jim was living there, George. They found some of his stuff in the basement. Megan was a drug push. It appears like Jim was unknowingly assigned to a drug house by someone from Child Welfare. This Megan girl owned the damn house."

George stood still and remained stunned by the news that Allan had just delivered. June wandered out from the layer barn and crossed the yard towards the two men. The two of them began to laugh as she got closer. "So what is so funny out here?"

George extended his arms and gave June an immense hug. "They caught them, June. They caught them. Jim won't be going back to Megan's place no matter what. They arrested her and others last night. It was a drug den, June."

It was June's turn to smile. "Oh my! Praise the Lord for providing a means to get our Jimmy out of there." Her smile quickly turned into tears of joy. "You were right, George. Both of you were right. All of you were right. God Bless that Officer Warrack."

"So how's Jim doing?" Allan looked sincerely at the couple. "Have you heard anything?"

"No. Not anything at all. I guess that no news is good news for now." George shook his shoulder and twitched. "He's in good hands. Hopefully it all works out for him."

"Well keep in touch with us. I've got to run guys. Give Sheila a call sometime, June. She asked me to tell you that. Take care."

"You too, Allan and thanks for the good news."

"I thought that it might make your day. See you guys on Sunday probably."

"We certainly will," said June. A large and very pleasant smile was expanding across her face. "It's time for us sinners to get back to attending church with the rest of you. I'll give Sheila a call too. Bye for now."

June and George waived goodbye and watched as Allan left the yard and headed out the laneway. In the distance they could hear the roar of Monty's bus as it turned onto the side road. Allan had just turned up the road when Monty turned into the laneway and dropped off the twins. The couple stood together holding hands and watched their daughters walk towards them. The day was ending well. Hopefully, it was ending well for Jim too.

The Edward's had a busy Saturday cleaning up the broiler barn after loading birds on the Friday night. George had kept expecting to hear from Child Welfare or worse yet see Miss Oagle and company cruise into their yard but it did not happen. The Edwards attended church services on Sunday and enjoyed a leisurely luncheon and afternoon visit at the Heiners. June checked the answering machine when they returned but it remained blank. It was an uneasy peace.

They had just finished lunch on Tuesday, one full week since hearing from Miss Oagle, when she finally called again. June had picked up the telephone and greeted her. After a brief conversation she brought the receiver out to George and handed it to him. "She wants to speak with you, George."

George hesitantly grabbed the telephone and answered, "Yes, Miss Oagle."

"How is Mr. Edwards today? Your wife tells me you are recuperating from a shingles attack."

"I'm much better, thanks," answered George surprised at this sudden interest in his health. "What can I do for you today?"

"You lied to me sir. Last week when I asked you if you knew where your son was you indicated that you did not know. Apparently you did."

"If I remember correctly I said that I did not know the exact location of my son and I did not. So what's up?"

"If you caught the local news on the weekend you probably know that there was a major drug bust in Royston last week. Unfortunately certain individuals that were associating with Jim have been arrested as a result of that investigation. We also received word this morning from a drug rehabilitation center that your son is now registered as an outpatient. Apparently he is registered under the direct supervision of your parents, Ronald and Elaine Edwards."

"That is wonderful news, Miss Oagle."

"You act surprised."

"Some of this information is new to us too."

"I want to apologize to you, Mr. Edwards. It appears that we acted incorrectly with both you and your son. You are guilty of hiding information from us but I fully understand the motive now. I judged too quickly and I had no idea of the trouble that Megan was in. She had become a very different person than the girl that I knew back in the city. If it makes you feel any better I am be reprimanded for not researching her properly from the start. It looks bad on all of us. I doubt if you will hear anything further from me and I wish you and your family all the best."

"I appreciate that. We realize that you were just following the book and performing your job. Perhaps in the future you will take more care before you jump. I don't envy your job at all."

"Goodbye, sir."

"Goodbye to you, Miss Oagle."

George turned the phone off and placed it on the kitchen table. "It sounds like they're giving up on us, June. It also appears like things are happening for the better back east. Let's just hope that it continues."

"I'm proud of you, George." June gently rubbed his shoulders with her hands. "We have much to be thankful for."

"It still never needed to happen, June. I've probably lost my son forever. He'll never look at me in the same light again. Somehow I know that I'll never see him here again. I can say I wished I did that or this forever but it will not bring Jim back. All I can hope for now is that he gets back on the straight right of way and starts building for his future again."

"You don't know that right now. All we can hope for is that he becomes Jim again, George. Sometimes the Lord works in mysterious ways."

George sat still remaining content to stare out the dining room window. The snow covered lawn and barren trees served as stark reminder of a season gone. He attempted to envision what another year might bring. *He thought of the sweat and toil and the often pointless and futile efforts to generate an income and stave off the creditors. And to often no avail as nature took back what she had given. Perhaps Allan was right and this whole process was damned from the start.* And now George had lost his only son and perhaps the very essence for remaining here.

42

The house exploded to the sound of the Heiners arrival on Christmas morning. Their girls had entered first and the twins whisked them off to their bedroom to examine gifts from Santa. June walked to the back entrance and greeted Allan and Sheila with a robust, "Merry Christmas!"

"And a very Merry Christmas to you," said Sheila. "Here you can take these if you wish?"

"I told you not to bother preparing anything."

"Oh, it's not much. I had to bring something."

"Merry Christmas, June," said Allan. "Santa's here."

June returned from the kitchen and reached out to Allan. "Here let me take some of those. Boy, it looks like Santa has been pretty busy here. Just put your boots anywhere, guys." June hastily carried some gifts and set them down in the kitchen and returned for their coats. "Here, let me take them for you."

"Is George still outside?"

"No, he was up early and decided to have a catnap after breakfast. He's just in on the sofa, Allan."

George was just stirring when Allan walked into the living room. He glanced up at his friend and smiled. "What is all the commotion about here?"

"Good morning there, George. Merry Christmas to you!"

George stood up from the sofa and walked over to Allan's outstretched arm. He grabbed it and the two exchanged a hearty handshake. "Merry Christmas, Allan!"

The twins ran into the living room. "Can we open our gifts now?"

"I guess we had better get down to business here," said George as the girls bounced around him. "Get everyone in here and we'll get started."

It took little encouragement to have everyone seated in the living room. In no time the room was in complete disarray. It filled with torn wrapping and packages scattered everywhere as the eager participants dwelt on the excitement of the gift opening. Even George could not resist getting into the Christmas spirit as the room filled with laughter and joy. The space surrounding the base of the Christmas tree gradually emptied as the torrid pace of opening packages took its toll.

George grabbed the last gift and handed it to June. "Here you open this, Hon and I'll go grab the camera." He walked into the bedroom and quickly returned. "Okay everyone, let's have a big smile." The flash illuminated the room as George took a couple of photos before setting the camera down on the coffee table. His mind gravitated to the fact that one family member was missing. He quietly sat down in his chair and observed the festivities.

"You okay there, George?" June had noticed the expressionless look in his face. "Is something wrong with the camera?"

George had no time to answer as the ringing of the telephone suddenly filled the room. June carefully meandered around the girls and answered it by extending a pleasant, "Merry Christmas!"

"Merry Christmas, Mom," said Jim in a rather sheepish tone. "I just wanted to call and wish everyone a Merry Christmas."

June walked into the living room and looked at the girls chattering to each other on the floor. "Just keep it down girls. Okay?" She looked at George. "It's Jim."

"You still there, Mom?" asked Jim. "Did I catch you at a bad time? I can call back if you wish?"

"Oh no, Jim. The Heiners are here spending the day with us." June slowly sat down on the sofa. The room was suddenly quiet. "So how are you keeping, son? It's so great to hear from you."

"I'm well, thanks. I'm back at school now and starting to settle in here." Jim hesitated and cleared his voice before continuing. "I called to say that I'm sorry for everything, Mom. I didn't mean to hurt you."

"I know son." Tears were filling June's eyes. "It's just so good to hear from you. It's great to hear that you are doing well. We all miss you so much here."

"Are the twins handy? I'd like to say hello to them?"

"They sure are, son." June sat the receiver against her lap. "Susan. Mary. Your brother wants to say hello. Well you have a great Christmas with your Grandparents, Jim. God Bless you and thanks for calling."

June handed the telephone over to the twins. The conversation was strained but sincere. The room remained still quiet as the girls softly talked to their brother. Mary was the last to speak with him. "Bye Jim, thanks for calling. I'll give you Dad now."

Mary walked over to George and handed the phone to her father. "He wants to talk to you, Dad."

The emotions in the room were quickly reaching capacity with Christmas joy present in the form of warm tear drops. There wasn't a dry eye present in the room as George put the receiver to the side of his head. He managed a soft but clear, "Merry Christmas, Jim."

"Merry Christmas, Dad. I hear that you've got company. I won't keep you long. This is long distance and all." Jim hesitated. "Dad, I know this isn't going to come out right no matter how I say it."

"You don't have to say anything to me, son."

"Yes, I need to say this Dad. I just want to thank you. I'm not saying that everything is right but I'm getting along better. It's okay here. Grandma and Grandpa have been great to me; probably better than I deserve at times." Jim's voice began to break. "I've got along way to go but I just wanted to say thanks for what you did and for not giving up on me."

Tears flowed down George's face and he attempted to dry them with his shirt sleeve. His eyes focused on the family portrait that he had viewed earlier in the day and he singled out Jim's face. He studied it with great intensity.

"Are you still there, Dad?"

"Yes, Jim, I'll always be here for you in whatever capacity it might be. It's great to hear that you're getting along good. I miss you son."

There was another brief period of silence and then Jim quietly uttered, "Thanks again, Dad. Thanks for everything. Merry Christmas!"

George heard the click on the other end of the line and sadly acknowledged that their conversation was over. He quietly got up and walked over to the phone stand and gently set the receiver down. All eyes in the room were focused on him as they seemingly waited for him to speak. Even the girls waited in anticipation of what words of wisdom he would share with everyone. The room was utterly silent with not even a rustle of paper to be heard. His mind desperately grasped for suitable words to share with everyone but they eluded him. What could he say that they did not know already? They had received much more than just a phone call. The family had received a wonderful gift from Jim; a gift of hope that made the other gifts of the morning rather insignificant. He slowly walked back to his chair and sat down.

The peacefulness of the moment soon broke as June walked over and gave George a huge hug. "Merry Christmas, Hon! She smiled at him and the couple shared an enduring Christmas kiss. The gesture caught on like wild fire and soon everyone in the room began issuing warm hugs and embraces to each other. The Gift of Christmas spread over the room and it was good; so very good.

The End

Printed in the United States
140921LV00003B/8/P